Lucia Graves

The Memory House

Vineyard Press

Port Jefferson, NY

For my mother and my three daughters

ISBN: 1-930067-14-3
Paperback

The Vineyard Press, Ltd.
106 Vineyard Place
Port Jefferson, NY 11777

COVER: The triumphant dance of Miriam after the crossing of the Red Sea is described in Exodus *and is frequently represented in Haggadahs. This picture appears in the 14th century Spanish* Golden Haggadah, *now in the British Library.*

Eight lines from 'Androgué' *by Jorge Luis Borges are reprinted with permission of The Wyle Agency, Inc.*
Copyright (c) 1995 by Maria Kodama.

Permission for the use of two lines from a Juda-Ha-Levi 12th century poem, in The Jewish Poets of Spain *(translated by David Goldstein) has been granted by David Higham Associates.*

Photo of the author: Angelika del Negro

Beyond chance and death
they endure, and each has its own story,
but all this occurs in that fabled
fourth dimension, which is memory.

In memory and only in memory
are those patios and gardens now. The past
preserves them in a closed circle
which at one time embraces nightfall and dawn.

From 'Androgué,' Jorge Luis Borges
(translated by Lucia Graves)

I

THE EDICT

I had not seen my grandmother for several months when news came that she was very ill. As I hastened into the city I found it hard to believe what everyone was saying, that Madona Alba de Porta, my mother's mother, was at death's door. To me she was immortal.

My mother, Luna, who had been living with her since Grandfather died, began to cry when I arrived. 'She wants to see you,' she said between sobs. 'She doesn't want anyone else but you by her bedside. She says she's going to die very soon, perhaps tomorrow.'

I went upstairs trembling, fearful, while my mother, lost between grief and anger, called out to me: 'But how can she possibly know when she's going to die? Only the Lord knows the day and the time of our death.'

And yet the moment I saw my grandmother my own fears subsided, not only because she smiled when she saw me and did not appear to be in pain, but because every time I enter that room it gives me the same sense of wellbeing and calm, of protection and serenity. The beams across the ceiling are painted blue, the walls are white-washed, and it has a twin window that frames the view of Salonika and its port. By the window, on a small oak table, there is always a blue and yellow vase full of flowers. That day it held a bunch of jasmine.

'There you are at last, Alba Simha,' she said when I came in. 'Now sit next to me and listen to what I have to

say. I haven't much time left, but, please, don't cry. I cannot bear to see people cry. And don't contradict me the way your mother does. I'm over eighty years old and I've had a fruitful life, with more blessings than most. Listen well, Alba Simha. I need to tell my story, and there is nobody more fitting than you to hear it. Not only because you are my granddaughter and my namesake. Other mysterious affinities link us, and you are the only person I can trust to repeat my words, should you ever wish to do so, without bending the truth here and there to suit the opinion of others.'

Her voice seemed to me clearer and more melodious than ever, despite her illness. It was an ageless voice that took me back to the long afternoons spent by her side when I was a small girl, listening to the stories which she had brought with her from her Catalan homeland, stories about enchantments and adventures, about multicoloured rainfalls and flying horses, and about princes in love with damsels whose threatened lives only they could save.

I had never questioned my grandmother's orders. I adored her, and her eccentricities did not annoy me in the way they annoyed my mother; perhaps because the distance between two generations softens the harshness that can arise between mother and daughter. I gave her a kiss, sat down on a chair near her bed, and prepared to listen in silence as she began:

The first time I heard the town crier's bugle I should have guessed it was another royal decree, but I was hanging out the washing in the open loft and my mind was elsewhere. As I pulled out petticoats, shirts, sheets, handkerchiefs and kitchen towels from the bucket, wringing each article thoroughly and securing it with a peg on the line, I was remembering, one by one, every detail of the previous evening when my mother and I had dined at my cousin Isaac's and I had been formally introduced to Vidal Rubèn. It was a magical moment, as though spirit and matter had merged in me, and nothing else seemed very important, not even the arrival of the crier with a message from our king.

The loft formed a square tower beneath the roof rafters, with large open spaces between the columns and a wooden parapet all around it, and was not only a very good place for drying clothes, but a good place for daydreaming. From there I could look down on Girona, with its mesh of red-tiled roofs, and watch the waters of the Onyar, the Ter and the Güell sparkling in the sun; or let my eyes travel into the distance, sometimes to the north, where the Pyrenean foothills undulated like soft green ripples of air; and sometimes to the south, where a small cloud of dust meant that a horseman was approaching on the highway.

From the loft I could see the lower part of town. A bit higher up, within the walled precinct called La Força, which in Catalan means 'The Fortress,' was the *call*, the Jewish quarter, where I lived with my mother Regina. We lived in the house of my grandfather, Rabbi Ismael de Porta, who had passed away about a year earlier. My father had died when I was too young to remember him. Our house stood on the corner of St. Llorenç Street, a long, straight road that marked the limit of the *call*, so all the windows and doors on that side of the building were walled in with stone and mortar, in compliance with one of many royal decrees. People said that this one had come as a result of the bloody massacre of Jews that took place about a hundred years before my time. They also said that on several occasions the decree had been relaxed, then enforced again, but I personally had no recollection of ever seeing the sun shining through those windows. I felt separated from the world, and the loft always relieved my sense of isolation.

The truth is that even before his marriage to the intolerant Queen Isabel, our King Ferran, like his predecessors, had authorised the Girona magistrates to impose all kinds of restrictions on our small community, such as not allowing Christians to sell food inside the *call*, forbidding Jews to touch food in the public market, making us wear a long cloak with a red and yellow badge sewn on it, and not allowing Christians in our homes. According to the magistrates, all this sprang from a genuine concern for our wellbeing and a need to avoid a public disturbance, but I'm sure these regulations often masked personal envies and grudges. Still, we were used to the fact that the King granted permission for these restrictions every now and then, and we could understand it, because somehow he had to appease the protests of the bishops and the councillors of his kingdom, none of whom received any direct tributary compensations for our presence in their parishes or towns. We lived in Catalonia, but the Crown of Aragon was the name that encompassed all the lands in the union of Catalonia and Aragon, and our king bore the title of King of Aragon.

From a legal point of view we were royal property, the King's serfs, and he protected us with certain rights and privileges in exchange for a substantial contribution that went straight to the royal treasury. Moreover, just as here in Salonika, the country's good management greatly depended on Jewish skills. There were many Jewish counsellors and physicians in court, some of them *conversos*, converts to Christianity, but still Jewish at heart. So the attitude of each king to our people had always been rather ambiguous: on the one hand, he could not affect too much benevolence towards the 'enemies of the Catholic Church,' and yet it was in his interest that we should prosper and fill his pockets with gold, as well as provide his government with sound advice. Of course, over the years, quite a few *conversos* turned against us in order to ingratiate themselves with the Catholics, and although I'm no judge of history, I do believe that they were much to blame for the King's hateful game of taking away with one hand what he had given us with the other. It was less than a year since the Inquisition had concluded its stay in Girona, and all the New Christians of our town, most of whom had jumped out of the pan and into the fire, were still terrified of being persecuted on suspicion of secretly continuing to be Jews.

However, when the events I am about to describe began to take place, none of these issues worried me in the least, and it would be only right to add that although the windows remained walled in, most of the restrictive rules were either disregarded—I remember that we often 'mislaid' those hateful badges—or were obeyed with a half-smile. The fact is that all of us citizens of Girona, Old Christians, New Christians and Jews alike, were neighbourly, placid and hard-working people, whose main concern was the good management of our market-town, and nobody was in the mood for quarrels. We had been through quite enough during the civil war, said the older people, to go around looking for trouble in times of peace. To put it another way: the timeless balm that drifted down from the mountain forests weighed more heavily on the common air than any passing stench.

It was the third day of Iyyar of the year 5252, which was the last day of April of the year 1492 of the Christian era. A ground swell was gathering beneath the calm waters of our daily life and in all the different kingdoms of Spain things were happening whose consequences would be terrible for all its Jews. But this, though evident to me now, I did not fully comprehend at the time, or perhaps I did not want to understand it. When you are sixteen it is difficult to believe in the power of evil, all the more so when you feel the first glow of love inside you and your love is reciprocated, as was my case.

Despite the worried tones in which my elders sometimes spoke, and despite the sadness I had begun to notice in the rabbi's dark eyes, life seemed pleasant enough to me. And that morning, as I hung out the washing, I could only think of Vidal's words to me the night before, and how his strong hand had pressed mine as we sat side by side at dinner. I was dizzy with the newness of this love and felt completely happy as I looked down at the narrow street, at the people coming and going, donkeys pulling loaded carts, dogs running about, sniffing around for food. Everything followed its normal course in a carefree world. Even the cathedral, which I could see by turning my head to the right, looked less austere than usual, and beyond it, in Montjuïc, a hill to the north of the town where we had our cemetery, the pine trees seemed much greener on that bright spring morning.

I stood there for a while, feasting on the view, and it seemed to me that there could be no other place as beautiful as this in the whole world. Then I picked up the empty clothesbasket, and went down the spiral stairs to our kitchen where my mother was busy kneading dough. She looked up at me but said nothing and I wondered whether she too was thinking of Vidal and considering his suitability as her son-in-law. Two women alone in a house was a sad thing, she always said, and although necessity had trained me to handle the affairs of men, such as keeping the accounts of our bakery, or paying our contributions to the community, my mother's only thought since the death of my grandfather had been to marry me off to someone who could protect us both from 'the evil world' in those uncertain days. Her plump hands turned like the wheels of a water-mill over brown sticky dough, and as I watched her I fancied that I could read her thoughts: '*Naturally, I would have preferred someone whose family I knew well, but the plain truth is that there's not one marriageable man left among us. And yet, what do I know about this Vidal Rubèn? Only that he is newly arrived from Barcelona with his widowed mother, that most members of his family have abandoned our faith, and that he doesn't even live in the* call. *That doesn't say much in his favour. On the other hand, he seems a hard-working, healthy young man. Now that the lass has been formally introduced to him, I suppose I'll have to arrange with Isaac to meet his mother...*' But all she said was: 'Fetch me some water, Alba.'

I put the basket down in its corner and at that moment the crier's bugle sounded again, this time nearer the *call*, probably by the stone bridge. My mother went on kneading, but her movements became slower and I felt a flutter in my heart which I made an effort to disregard. We had all heard the rumours about the edict of expulsion, but it was generally believed that it would never be enforced in Catalonia. As I walked over to the well, at the far end of the kitchen, I remembered that I had heard Abraham the cobbler talking about it only a few days before, while I sat in his workshop waiting for him to finish mending my mother's shoes.

This tiny work-shop, with its low ceiling and its strong smell of leather, was the preferred meeting place for the men of the *call* when they had nothing better to do, because the cobbler always made good conversation and had a way of voicing the general views of the community to everyone's satisfaction. That day he was talking to old Moisès the silversmith, our next-door neighbour:

'Even taking into account that our King Ferran insisted on the Castilian Inquisition being imposed in Catalonia, disregarding the protests of the Catalan Government, I cannot believe he's signed the edict,' he was saying, lifting his head slowly, and leaving the needle halfway through a stitch in the leather. 'He owes too much to us Jews: his succession, his marriage to Isabel... And besides, whose money paid for the conquest of Granada, eh? Yes, I know, we might be talking about *conversos*, but they're still Jews, Hebrews through and through, there's no denying that.'

Moisès stroked his beard and nodded wisely in agreement, while Abraham pulled the needle through. 'And even if Isabel has forced Ferran to give in,' Abraham went on, 'Girona is a different matter altogether. You know that as well as I do, Moisès. He and his mother owe their very lives to the Girona Jewry. We all did what we could to help them when they took refuge here at the start of the war; what little we had we gave them willingly, and all the main expenses of the siege were covered by *conversos*, people like the Falcós and the Vidal Sampsós.'

'And a fine payment they received for their trouble,' answered Moisès. 'Years later those families had to run for their lives, they left the country with the Inquisition at their heels, and were burnt in effigy.'

'I agree,' insisted Abraham. 'But then, don't forget Ferran signed an extension of the rights and privileges granted to us by his father. And that does not expire for another seven years, my friend.'

'Look, Abraham,' answered Moisès shrugging his shoulders. 'I've lived longer than you and I know that a word pledged to a Jew is worth very little these days. So what I say is this: if we are told to go, well then, goodbye Girona. I'm too much of a Jew to change my ways. I'd

14

rather leave my land than my religion, though some young-sters may think otherwise. What do you say, Alba, eh?' he asked, suddenly turning to include me in the conversation. 'Would you come or would you stay?'

But before I had time to answer, Abraham, who liked to tease, put in: 'A pretty lass like Alba, with those dark locks and those full red lips? Regina the baker would be sure to bundle her into a cart with all her other chattels!'

The two men laughed and I ran out, red as a pome-granate.

I was thinking about all this as I unhooked the pail and sent it down the well. The chain slid through my hands and rattled round the pulley until I heard the swish of wa-ter when the pail brushed its surface. Then the dreaded tug, as the well seemed to swallow it into a bottomless abyss. I looked down into the dark damp hole, trying to catch a faint reflection of the water, but saw only a mass of black-ness. I wondered how many of my ancestors had also felt a tiny shudder when they fetched water from that well, as though it were haunted by a sombre ancient spirit. At that moment we heard the bugle again, this time only a few yards away, at the bottom of our street. It was a piercing, whining sound that filled the spacious kitchen and echoed in the well. I lifted the full pail on to the stone ledge and turned to face my mother. But she did not even look up. She simply went on kneading, insistently, as if trying to suppress her fear.

'Go and listen, child,' she said.

I filled a jug with water from the pail and left it next to the kneading trough. Then I walked up the three steps to the entrance hall, opened the front door, and looked out. Doors and windows were being opened in all the other houses, and the town crier's voice boomed up the alley-way. The words it carried began to scamper like a plague of pestilent rats into our quiet homes.

Today, April 30 of the year 1492, the Girona magistrates order the publication of the following decree, signed in Granada on March 31 of this same year of 1492:

... Don Fernando and Doña Isabel, by the grace of God King and Queen of Castile, León, Aragon, Sicily, Granada, Toledo, Valencia, Galicia, Majorca, Seville, Sardinia, Corsica, Murcia, Jaén, the Algarve, Algeciras, Gibraltar, the Canary Islands...

I remember that as I listened I had my eyes fixed on the round grey river stones that formed a pattern on the floor of our entrance hall, by the front door. It was the ten-point pattern of the Tree of God: each stone stood for a *sephirah*, a symbol of one of the divine manifestations of our Lord in His creation. I stood so still that I felt I was becoming a part of those stones, as if some invisible force were binding me to them. I wanted to scream, or simply run away from the terrifying words I was now hearing. But I could not move a single muscle.

... Whereby we order all Jews and Jewesses of any age who live or abide or be in any of the aforementioned kingdoms and seigneuries, whether they were born in them or have come to live in them after birth... to leave with their sons and daughters and all their Jewish servants and relatives, both old and young and of any age, before the end of this coming month of July, and that they dare not return to these lands, not even in passing or in any other way; and if they do not comply with this letter and act accordingly, they will incur the death penalty and the confiscation of all their goods for our royal treasury...

After what seemed like a long time, I was able to lift my eyes from the ground and see a patch of sunlight dancing high up on the wall opposite our house. The sunlight seemed to beckon me, so I cried 'I'll be right back, Mother!' and stepped out of the front door. Gathering up my gown, I ran up the narrow street, climbing the steps, two and three at a time, without seeing anything or anybody, thinking only of running away from the words. The edict was now warning Christians not to give us shelter in their homes or defend us in any way after the end of July, threatening them with confiscation of all their properties if they did.

When I reached the small square at the top of the *call*, I saw a group of women with their shopping baskets who were talking anxiously, as they waited for the town crier's arrival at this point in his rounds. But I had heard enough. I hurried down Ruca Street towards the cathedral, slipped out of La Força through the gate known as Sobreportes, and from there made my way to the next gate, called El Portal de Nostra Dona—the Door of Our Lady— which guarded the second set of walls on this side of the river Onyar. A stream of empty carts was making its way back to the country after the weekly market of Girona. The drivers whistled and yelled, keeping their mules in check to avoid collisions, utterly unaware, or uncaring about what was happening at that very moment in the *call*. As I walked past them under the archway I hugged the wall, feeling the heat of the stone—the dying heat of my land.

* * *

A few minutes later I was out in the hills. The air was fresh, the sun shone in a clear sky and the gorse was in full bloom, bright yellow. But nothing cheered me. Could this really be the same world in which I had felt so happy only a half-hour ago, while I was hanging out the washing on the roof terrace? I stopped for breath and sat down on a rock by the path. I tried to think, but could put no order in my mind. My head was aching and these words echoed through it without pause: '... That they dare not return to these lands ... not even in passing...' But, why? What right had they to throw us out? What would happen now? Where would we go? The fear which until that day I had dismissed in my natural need for happiness lay now unmasked: an unavoidable reality that made me tremble and filled me with confusion. The time had come; we would all have to leave. But what about Vidal? What would he do? The possibility of losing him filled me with horror far greater than the fear of exile. It was something that until that moment had not even crossed my mind, and now, the more I thought about it, the more real it seemed to me and the more it made me realise how deeply I loved him.

I watched the flight of a falcon slowly drawing circles in the air. What would Vidal do? I thought again. I knew that both his brothers had agreed to be baptised a few months before, and were now well introduced into the merchant class of Girona. That was bound to sway him. Sometimes it had even crossed my mind that he was only delaying his conversion to Christianity so that he could court me, as he had courted me the night before, at my cousin Isaac's. But I tried to brush that mean thought away. Vidal was not like his older brothers; he was not the calculating sort. I knew him well, despite the briefness of our relationship. I remembered Isaac's introduction: 'Vidal Rubèn, this is my cousin Alba Levanah de Porta, daughter of Regina, here present, and of my uncle Elies, on him be peace.' We began to talk in an animated way, as if we had known each other all our lives, which did not please my mother at all, for she kept giving me reproachful looks from the other side of the table.

In truth, Vidal and I had seen each other a few times before that night, although I had not told my mother about this. One of the times, when I was queuing up at the Jewish butcher's, he had stood behind me. 'My name is Vidal,' he said quickly, when I turned round to look at him. I did not answer, but I smiled before lowering my eyes, and when I finished my shopping I let him carry my basket until we reached the entrance to my street. As we walked along, he talked with great politeness, explaining that he had come from Barcelona not long before, and telling me how much he liked our town. I said very little, or perhaps even nothing at all, because I wanted to appear modest, but I felt a new joy growing inside me; a light, like the glow of dawn, that soon illuminated all my thoughts. After that day, whenever we met in the street we smiled at one another, so that when my mother announced to me: 'Isaac is going to introduce you to someone called Vidal Rubèn, and, who knows, there may be a wedding in the offing.' I found it hard to suppress my joy. None of the things Vidal said that night in Isaac's house surprised me: his frankness, the interest he showed for the world around him, the way in which he listened to others, the warmth he radiated. He seemed unconcerned about the future. Now, however, he would have to think of it. He would have to decide whether to stay or leave. So would I, so would all my family. Though I was little more than a child, suddenly the seriousness of the situation made me feel mature enough to think for myself. All these thoughts galloped through my mind like wild horses; they contradicted one another until they lost all sense or reason. In the sky, the falcon still circled slowly, ignorant of such human problems below.

II

TWIN SOULS

After a while I got up and followed a path through the pine trees to a place which the Christians called the Golden Ox, on the western slope of Montjuïc. There, on a piece of land that extended like an island between two torrents, was our graveyard. It was a solitary site, far from the town, and because it had rained heavily a few days before, a steady flow of water ran down the torrents and formed cascades and eddies here and there. The sound of the water seemed to muffle the echo of the words that still reverberated in my head, and I began to feel a little calmer.

I crossed the stone bridge over the wider torrent, opened the low entrance gate and began to make my way through the rows of tombstones. First I came to my father's grave, and I lingered there a few minutes, thinking about him and saying those words from the prayer to the dead that I have always liked so much: 'O Lord of compassion... shelter him forever more under the cover of thy wings; and let his soul be bound up in the bond of eternal life...' Although my father had died of the plague shortly after my birth, people still called me 'the weaver's daughter' because he had been a master in his trade and his dyes and patterns had never been surpassed. As I say, I never knew my father, but I knew all his patterns and designs because my mother had made a patchwork cloth with the samples that were left in his workshop when he died, and she had hung it up on the wall of our dining room. When I was a child I would stare for hours at those bits of woven fabric, joined together with very small stitching and surrounded by a frame of thick blue velvet. I would examine the lines and shapes of each piece of material, its stars or flowers, its feathers, spirals, waves or circles, and so many other strange figures I saw in them. It seemed to me that through those pictures I could touch my father's soul and get to know him, and if I ever saw a lady wearing a dress of some patterned silk he had designed, and which was now copied by all the Girona weavers, I would smile and consider that this was his way of greeting me.

Next to his grave were those of my two brothers, Israel and Ezra, neither of whom I had known either, for they had both died of the same illness that took my father away. I was brought up alone with my mother and my father's father—my grandfather Ismael, on him be peace. I now walked up to his grave, which was a little further away, by a low wall. His tombstone was larger than the rest, because he had been the rabbi of Girona for twenty years, until his death, not much more than a year before these events. The tombstone, which had recently been put in place, read:

> 'When my last hour came
> I was still bathed in light'
> In memory of Ismael de Porta,
> son of Yehuda. His light was scattered
> and he entered his heavenly abode
> in the month of Adar, of the year 5251.

I knelt down and closed my eyes, hoping to find some comfort by thinking of him. He had loved me like a father and I still felt his loss. He surely would have been able to advise me at that moment. The present rabbi was a good, simple-hearted man, intent on preserving the faith of the few Jewish families left in the *call*, but I could not go to him for enlightenment as I would have gone to Grandfather Ismael. So I let my thoughts wander, guided by the thread of his memory.

My mind went back to the first time I had been allowed into his library. I was very young, perhaps four or five years old, and when I saw all those coloured drawings, those quills, papers and ribbons, it seemed I had entered an enchanted cave. Later came my first reading lessons, sitting on his knee, his large hands guiding my little fingers patiently from word to word. It was not customary among the Jews of Catalonia for girls to be taught anything other than domestic skills—sewing, cooking, spinning and other such things—any more than it is here in Salonika, but our community had become so small, due to conversions, emigrations and untimely deaths, that when a girl showed a natural inclination for numbers and letters she was encouraged to learn. From the first day I entered my grandfather's study, with its smell of ink and parchment, I had been filled with curiosity for everything it contained. Straightaway, I wanted to know what the round brass instrument was, the one with discs and a moving ruler that hung from a hook on the wall. But he said: 'Don't be impatient. When you are seven I'll teach you how to read and write, and I'll explain how the astrolabe works.' He taught me much more than that; he taught me to love and revere each letter of our Hebrew alphabet as the most holy instrument that, he explained, had been shaped by the Lord and subsequently used by Him to create the universe. Although I was not aware of this at the time, Grandfather Ismael was unveiling to me, in a very simplified manner, the principles of the Kabbalah, the secret teachings through which one can reach a better knowledge of God.

When I was older, I sat with him by the hearth, reading texts copied from the holy books—from the Talmud or the Torah—or religious commentaries written by our famous ancestor Bonastruc de Porta, also known as Moisès ben Nahman, or Nahmanides, who had lived in our house more than two hundred years before us. Other times we recited poems of Ibn Gabirol, or verses from the Song of Songs, and my small voice would be lost in his, which was deep and resounding. I also remembered the clear nights spent gazing at the stars, when he would point out the names of the constellations and the positions of the planets. My grandfather Ismael used to say that however few of us remained, the golden days of Girona would always be with us, in these books, and in the dark stones of the *call*, for even the stones have memory. And one day he told me that one mind was enough to preserve all the treasures of the past. He spoke these words slowly and emphatically. We were taking a walk in the hills, gathering wild herbs we used as household remedies. In his long blue hooded cloak he looked taller than usual and the beads in his wine-coloured toque gleamed as they caught the afternoon light. I had stopped to pick some camomile flowers and when I handed them to him I noticed that his eyes were bright, as if with tears. He put his hands on my shoulders, and stooping slightly to draw closer said: 'One mind is enough to preserve all the treasures of the past, so long as it is not oppressed. Never forget it, Alba Levanah. Your mind is open and receptive; don't close it. Obey your elders, but never be a slave to anyone.'

I must not let anyone oppress my mind, I said to myself as I stood by his grave on the morning of the edict. I must not allow the priests from the cathedral to try to force their beliefs on me and stamp mine out. Clearly, the only way I could preserve my mind from enslavement was by going into exile, as my ancestor Bonastruc de Porta had done, expelled by a king who was forced to succumb to the pressures of the Church. The light of Spain—of Sepharad, as we called those western lands—was being extinguished. And yet, what would happen to all that now? To our old world, to our homes, our cemetery, where the long chain of generations had been buried? How could we leave it all? And Vidal, my beloved Vidal! Surely he would join the exodus; he would come with me. But would he? The thought of possibly having to leave without him filled me once again with horror. I stood up to go, and, as I did so, these lines of Ibn Gabirol came to my mind:

> *When dawn breaks I cry: 'Awaken, soul,*
> *and seek the face of my King and of my Beloved'*
> *I long to remember it,*
> *and am filled with such ardent desire that,*
> *like the partridge, I shall call him from my exile.*

* * *

I was walking down the hill with my eyes fixed on the ground, when a shadow fell across the path. I looked up and there was Vidal, leaning against a tree, looking at me. I ran to him and he held me tight. I could feel his heart beating. We're twin souls, I thought, meant to share life together.

'I saw you running down Ruca Street and I followed you,' he said. 'I wanted to speak to you before you returned to your house.'

'What are you going to do?'

He stroked my hair slowly, then put his hands on my shoulders and drew away from me a little so that he could see my face. I could sense what he was about to say. 'Listen to me, Alba: I have to no alternative but to stay. Some time ago my family decided that my mother and I, the only two members who were still in the Jewish faith, would accept baptism if things came to this. We cannot abandon Girona. We have too many interests at stake: our lands, the position of my brothers. It's not as easy as you think to throw everything overboard. If I left for religious motives, the Inquisition could start hovering over them because of me; they would have an excuse for accusing them of false conversions, of continuing to practice our religion in secret. They could confiscate all their belongings, all the properties they have obtained by working so hard during the past few years. Above all, I must think of my mother's health. She has to stay here. She's very frail and would never endure a long and uncertain journey. I can't just go and leave her behind. It would weigh too heavily on my conscience.'

I had no answer to that. What could I say? That if he renounced our faith voluntarily he would be considered a *meshummad* by the rest of the Jews, a person who has destroyed himself? I said nothing. My fears had been proved right and I began to see a weakness in him for which I could not even blame him. I could only stare at him, trembling from head to foot, knowing that, however much we talked, these two conflicting facts would never change: I loved him with all my heart, yet I could not stay.

Vidal read my thoughts.

'Alba, it's not that simple. My mother has not yet recovered from the loss of my father, although he died over a year ago. She says that she could not bear to lose me too, that it would kill her if our family were to disperse. And though I've always been a good Jew, I'm not devout enough to give up my whole life, my home and family for the sake of my religion. Come to reason Alba, try to see it my way.

25

You know I love you. I told you last night when you came with me to the door, and it's the truth. Nothing will change what I feel for you. Stay behind with me.'

'No Vidal, I can't... I couldn't embrace the Catholic faith. I couldn't do that. Besides, what about *my* mother? She won't let me be parted from her, and she won't want to stay behind, I'm quite sure of that.'

I was being torn in two and there was nothing I could do to prevent it. The more I looked at Vidal's eager face, and the more I felt his nearness, the more desperate I became. 'What hope is there for us?'

'Stay with me, become a Christian. You don't have to put your heart into the baptismal ritual. Then we could get married, and your mother would be unable to prevent you from staying behind.'

'No Vidal, I couldn't do that,' I repeated.

'But why not? Don't you see we belong to Catalonia? Don't you see this is our home, where all our ancestors are buried?'

I turned away. His words sounded sweet to my ears, but I knew in my heart that they were wrong. 'It's my ancestors I'm thinking of, buried here, on this hill. I cannot betray them. Think of all the suffering they have endured in the name of their religious beliefs: the persecutions, the slaughters, the burning down of houses...'

'So that is stronger than your love for me?'

'No Vidal, don't you see? They are two different forces. But I know in my heart that if I remained here I would never forgive myself, nor would I forgive you for having persuaded me. It would work like poison against us; it would kill me slowly. Vidal, please, come with me!'

He looked at me and gave a short and painful sigh. 'I can't,' he answered. 'I can't.'

I buried my head in his chest and he held me close.

Suddenly, all the anger and misery I felt was mitigated by the comfort of his proximity. It was as if everything and everyone in my life had ceased to exist, everyone that is, but Vidal, who with no restraint was unlacing the sleeves of my tunic; and the only thought left in my mind was how much I loved and needed him. All the holy words of the Torah evaporated, as did the constant warnings of my mother, who had always told me how important it was to protect my honour and preserve my chastity intact until my wedding night. At that moment nothing existed in the world but Vidal and me and the force of our desire. Without a word, we gave ourselves wholly to each other on the solitary mount of the Jews.

For a long time afterwards neither of us spoke. We were enveloped in silence and we sat holding each other on the stony ground. After a while I asked: 'What will happen to us now, Vidal?'

'We must each do what we think we should,' he answered. 'I suppose I won't be able to visit you, or meet you anywhere. But have faith. Nothing can draw us apart now, except temporarily. All this stupidity will end.'

'Perhaps the rabbi is right,' I said, without much conviction. 'He said that even in the event of an expulsion it might not be final. The King and Queen might reconsider their decision and allow us to return. We may be back for the olive harvest, or sooner, who knows?'

'Yes, that might be the case, and if not—'

'What then?'

'Then I will follow you, I will come and find you. I promise. Once I have been christened, nobody will interfere with my brothers' lives. It will just be a question of waiting a little, of letting a bit of time go by. I'll leave Girona as soon as my mother is strong enough to see me go.'

He meant 'when my mother dies,' but he dared not say those words out of respect. He's a good son, I thought. Although I knew that his promises of following me were vague, nothing could diminish the love I felt for him.

We walked back briskly, following the same route I had taken when I left the town, passing first through the Gate of Nostra Dona and then through Sobreportes, in the old walls of La Força. The streets were almost deserted, because it was lunchtime, and Girona seemed to have changed, the way places do when you are about to leave them.

Until the announcement of the edict, the weeks that had passed since I first saw Vidal had seemed to me part of a dream, in which everything around me had the colour, smell and touch of a rose petal. What I now saw was quite different, but equally unreal, for the buildings in the *call* seemed to have acquired a soul of their own, and looked like sad, defeated knights in armour. There was something new and ominous in the old familiar stones, in the ivy that clung desperately to them; and the houses had their doors closed, there was silence everywhere. On a sunny wall two lizards darted in and out of a mesh of leaves, two white and brown speckled creatures catching the warm sun of the month of Iyyar. We are like lizards, I thought, emerging from the crevices of our mutual feelings to share the warmth of our first union. Would it also be the last?

We made our way down the steep alleys, criss-crossed here and there by cobbled steps. The streets were so narrow that the tall dark houses almost touched at roof level. Each step we took was like a word of love spoken in silence, for the words lay hidden in our movements and the air was thick with mute memories and premonitions. The touch of his hand in mine made me unable to utter a single word. From the synagogue came the sound of voices sadly chanting and there our feet took us, for our minds were incapable of any decision. We sat down on a wooden bench near the main door. Tomorrow this quiet corner might be forbidden ground to him. Tomorrow. The future presented itself in my mind like a marshy field extending endlessly into the distance, empty of landmarks, without even a path to guide my way. 'How will I find the strength without you?' I said.

'I will be with you. My pain will be as great as yours. Don't forget that Alba.'

The sun shone in his eyes. They were the colour of amber. 'But I need you, Vidal,' I said. 'You're the man our Lord created to be with me. You say we'll meet again, but how can we be sure?'

We fell silent, hopelessly unable to change the sudden turn our lives had taken. Vidal looked down. Suddenly I felt a huge pity for him. He was about to renounce our faith. He would become a *meshummad*. He would destroy himself.

'I wouldn't mind dying,' I said, just to break the silence.

He raised his head to look at me, held both my hands in his and said very slowly and firmly: 'If you died, I could not bear it.'

A wave of love coursed through my body. Whatever happened, I would keep those words as a charm to guide me from then on, to bring him close to me in the darkness of the night.

III

A CATALAN GENTLEMAN

'At last, Alba!' cried my mother as soon as I opened our front door. 'We've looked for you everywhere. Where the devil were you? Answer me, you insolent girl, where were you, eh?'

'Don't scold her, Aunt Regina,' said Cousin Isaac.

'I went out to the cemetery,' I said, with my eyes downcast, thinking only of Vidal, and wishing above all things that I could run off to my room and be left alone with my thoughts.

My mother grunted, threw her apron over her face, and said no more. She was sitting at the kitchen table, in the middle of which was a long tray of freshly baked loaves. Next to her sat Cousin Isaac. Since the death of Grandfather Ismael, Isaac was the only adult male in the family, and as such my mother owed him obedience. What Isaac said was always done. But he never took advantage of his position, and I was very fond of him. Though almost twice my age, to me he was like an older brother who took the place of the two I had never known, and we were always glad for each other's company. He held his little son Josuè on his knee, bouncing him up and down to keep him quiet. Next to Isaac sat his wife Coloma, with her usual sombre expression, and I could see she had been crying. Cousin Coloma always looked like that: sad and tired. I don't remember ever seeing her laugh. And Rosa, their eldest daughter, sat on the floor by the open fire, stroking our cat.

'Papa says we're all going to leave,' she said. 'Will you let me take your cat, Alba? I'll put him in a basket and tie it up really tight, so he can't escape. And when we get to our new house I'll let him out again.'

'A new house indeed,' said Coloma. 'We'll never get a new house. We'll be dead long before we find anywhere to live. Isaac won't listen to me. He's as stubborn as a mule. We should stay, that's what I think, but he won't listen to me. Tell me Isaac, I keep saying, how can we leave with this child? That's what I'd like to know.'

'Don't insist, Coloma,' said Isaac. 'The Adonai will protect us, and all will be well. Here, Alba, come and sit with us.'

I sat down next to my mother and put my hand on her arm, for Isaac's words had filled me with tenderness. Josuè drummed on the table with a wooden spoon and laughed at his cleverness, and Rosa went on playing with the cat. From time to time my mother sighed. We were all quiet. I saw all my world concentrated in that room: the golden heap of bread, the white walls that glowed in the lamplight, the heavy oak doors, the stone well, the cabbages that filled the vegetable basket, the bunch of mint by the stove, the plates, the cups, the table on which so many meals had been prepared and served, year after year.

'I don't want to go!' I cried out suddenly. 'I don't want to leave this house. There can't be another one as beautiful as this anywhere else in the world!'

'We have no choice, Alba,' said Isaac. 'You will have to come with us.'

Decisions were being taken for me, because nobody knew I was no longer a child. Yet Isaac was right.

'Do you know what will happen now?' said Coloma. 'They'll lock us up in the *call* and they'll separate us from the New Christians, in case we try to drag some of them

31

back into our faith. You'll see, all the *conversos*, even the ones who live here in the *call*, will stop speaking to us. They'll turn their backs on us, as if we carry the plague, as if we are lepers. You'll see if they don't.'

'You are probably right, Coloma,' said Isaac. 'But in any case, it won't be through any fault of theirs. It will be the fear of the Inquisition. At this point they have much more to lose than us. We may lose our homes and our belongings, but the Inquisition cannot touch us so long as we remain Jews.'

'Won't I be able to play with Francina any more?' asked Rosa. 'She is a New Christian, she told me so one day.'

'Probably not, Rosa,' replied her father.

'It's not fair,' she answered. 'Because Francina has a big garden and I like going to her house.'

And Vidal won't speak to me either, I thought. He'll avoid me. Rosa is right: it's not fair.

The thought of departure filled us all with fear, despite Isaac's reassuring words. Where would the de Portas go? we wondered. Where could we start a new life? Would we take a ship to Africa or Italy? What if there was a pirate attack on our vessel? We had heard so many dreadful stories. Should we, instead, cross the mountains into France? The afternoon slipped by as we talked and speculated, and soon it was dinnertime and the candles were lit. Isaac, the man in the house, led the rituals and intoned the prayers, sheltering us with his male presence. Later, sitting round the table, we continued with our deliberations until it was quite dark, and the same must have taken place in most Jewish houses of the *call*. My mother heated some goat's milk for Coloma's children, who fell asleep by the glowing hearth.

* * *

A week later, when Rabbi Leví and the members of our council met to discuss the journey, it was decided that we should take advantage of our closeness to the lands of France. We would cross the Pyrenees into Roussillon, where we were likely to find home and work. This comforted me a great deal, for although by then I had heard of Vidal's baptism, the thought of being only a few days' journey away from him was enough to renew my hopes of a reunion.

My life had changed so suddenly and in so many ways that during the next few weeks I often fell into a daze and had to stop whatever I was doing and sit down. In moments like those my mind went round in circles. I felt like a small piece of driftwood caught in a whirlpool. My mother scolded me and told me to stop dreaming about the past and help her face the future. There was so much to do, and without a man about the house... She never missed an opportunity to lament the sudden end of Vidal's courtship. 'Vanished like a fly when winter sets in,' she would say spitefully. 'After all those flowery words and elegant manners of his that evening in Isaac's house—makes you wonder. Yes, I know, we hadn't spoken of marriage yet, but he knew very well that Isaac had invited him with marriage in mind. And now look: he's gone over to the other side and you'd think he'd never even set eyes on you. I thought he was a trustworthy Jew, but, of course, with so many *conversos* in his family I should have guessed this might happen.'

At other times she threw her hands up in despair and blamed it all on the general turmoil through which we were living. I could understand her bitterness, for her life had been marked by tragic events and this seemed like the culmination of them all, but I could not bring myself to feel any real sympathy for her material concerns when in my own mind I was struggling, alone, to put an end to my inner confusion. I felt remote from my mother, and was unable to open my heart and tell her about my encounter with Vidal on the day of the edict. Instead, I masked my feelings and tried to keep a cheerful face while we all busied ourselves with the difficult task of arranging to leave our home.

Coloma had been right. The *call* suddenly became a prison, in which we all suffocated, humiliated by the re-enforcement of discriminatory rules, frightened at the thought of the exile. The authorities closed the gates at night and did not allow us out on market days because they wanted to reduce contact between the *conversos* and us. When Vidal and I parted outside the synagogue, neither of us anticipated the severity and the cruelty with which the Inquisition would attempt to cleanse the Catholic Church of all impurities, as they put it; nor did we foresee that those who decided to convert as a result of the edict of expulsion would become their favourite target. Some *conversos*, like Francina's family, had never left their home in the *call*, and though they worked on the Sabbath and bought meat at the public market, instead of at our Jewish butcher's, we still considered them our brothers. But now the Inquisition seemed forever at their heels. A *convers* had only to lift his eyebrows at a Jew in the street and he ran the risk of being accused of relapsing. This was, in fact, the alleged reason for our expulsion:

> ...It appears that great harm has been done to Christians through the participation, conversation or communication that they have had in the past and still do have now with the Jews, who boast of attempting by all ways and means to draw the faithful away from Our Holy Catholic Faith towards their harmful beliefs and opinions.

The tension between *conversos*, Jews and Old Christians grew and thickened in Girona, until it was as immovable as our city walls. By order of the King, guards were posted night and day outside the *call* to avoid any possible disturbances. Thus, though Vidal lived only a hundred yards away, in a square at the bottom of St. Llorenç Street, I had to avoid him at all costs, for his own safety, now that both he and his mother had joined the Catholics and were being watched by the Inquisition. And what could be more difficult for a young girl who had just given herself to her lover?

Another consequence of the edict of expulsion was that all Jewish professional activities came to a halt, except, of course, those related to our own domestic needs, such as my mother's community baking. Men loitered in the streets, not knowing what to do with their time, looking bewildered and useless. For want of anything better to do, they would drift into Abraham's shop to hear the latest gossip or some new detail related to our journey to Roussillon. But whereas before Abraham had been the favourite cobbler of all Girona housewives, now his only clients were the few Jewish families left in the *call*, and we couldn't spend our money on shoe repairs.

In fact, money had lost its real value for us, because we were forbidden to take any silver or gold coins out of the kingdom. The same applied to jewels and all precious metal ornaments. What little we had left, after paying all the taxes imposed on us since the announcement of our expulsion, we spent gathering food for the journey. It soon proved hard to get, because we were not allowed into the Girona market, and we had to content ourselves with what supplies trickled into the *call* at extravagant prices. On market days the merchants set up a long table with their wares just outside the door of St. Llorenç Street. There we bid and haggled for hours, bartering our treasures for beans or flour. They took advantage of our predicament, of course, and the exchange always favoured them. I once handed over a pair of Toledo gold earrings for a pound of flour. But what could we do? I would have had to hand them over to the authorities in the end, and get nothing for them at all.

My mother was in a very bad way. She fretted and worried incessantly about the departure, and complained constantly: 'We don't need this. We can't leave that, it belonged to your great-grandfather, on him be peace. Let's take this jug, shall we? It might be useful.' Some of our neighbours even devised clever ways of hiding precious stones in food, or in hems or linings, but my mother decided against it, though it broke her heart to give up the family jewels that had been a part of her life, of her inheritance, of her dowry. 'Those scoundrels are robbing us,' she would say. But she had fear ingrained in her body and in her soul, and nothing could shake it off. One day she told me that as a small child, when she and her family were moving to Girona from her native village near Teruel, she had seen things 'that would make a rock tremble.' But she never told me what those things were, or where exactly she saw them; not even years later, when we had left all that behind. She carried her secret to the grave.

As for me, such was my state of confusion and distress that I did not really care one way or another. I just obeyed her instructions quietly, waiting anxiously for the night so that I could lie alone in my bed, with the door closed, listening to the distant barking of a dog or the singing of crickets. In moments like those I could not keep my mind off Vidal and wondered what he was doing, so close by and yet shut off from me. I heard no further news of him or of his family after the first baptism of Jews had been officially announced in the *call*, and how could I ask anyone who might know without putting him in danger with the Inquisition?

Unable to renounce his love, I cried myself to sleep more than once. I repeated his name over and over again, and traced his letters with my forefinger on my pillow. His name became my greatest consolation, my spiritual refuge. My body was feverish after its first awakening and I would press my hands firmly on my belly, wondering whether or not I had conceived Vidal's child, a child of grace. I felt no guilt or remorse for having lost my virginity to him. Then I began to understand the mysteries that surround the union of a man and a woman who feel something higher than mere physical desire for one another, and I tried to apply my grandfather's teachings to my agitated thoughts. Slowly it became clear to me that the male and female sides of each of our souls had found one another and achieved a perfect union. We really were twin souls. At the same time, the decision to leave with my people became stronger every day, like an unstoppable force. And when, as often happened, I retraced my meeting with Vidal on the mount of the Jews, remembering every word, every movement, every kiss, I knew that despite my resolve to leave and his to stay behind, we were bound to each other forever. Why then did we have to part? What was it that made me place my loyalty to my grandfather's memory and to my people above my loyalty to the man with whom I was so unquestionably in love?

One morning I awoke feeling the warm spring sun touching my cheek and I looked around my room at the small twin windows, the ceiling with its blue painted beams, the long low chest where I kept my Sabbath clothes, the wash-basin on the table under the windows. From St Llorenç Street came the voices of Christian children singing their latest skipping song:

The Jews of Girona
are running out of town
up across the mountains
up and then down

With nothing in their pockets
With nothing in their bags
They even left their hearts behind
In Sepharad!

Before we even knew about the expulsion we had
spring-cleaned the house, as we did every year for the Pass-
over, and the walls still sparkled with their recent coat of
whitewash. Vaguely I wondered who would live here after
we had gone, and hoped it would be someone capable of
recognising and respecting the imprint left by so many lives,
both lived and shared within these walls. But perhaps the
next tenant would be a priest with a pious aunt or sister for
his housekeeper who would sprinkle the rooms with holy
water and fill every corner with her hatred of our race. The
thought was so offensive that it made me jump out of bed
with anger, and I determined to find a way of avoiding
such a thing. None of the houses in the *call* had yet been
sold because Christians were afraid of putting anything
down on paper that could connect them with us. But there
was already talk of a decree being expressly published to
clarify the situation and dispel their fear, and, as Abraham
the cobbler put it, the *call* would soon be swarming with
red-faced priests and friars, who were already eyeing our
properties with greed, rubbing their fat hands at the prospect of acquiring a good house near the cathedral for almost nothing.

I was glad, in a way, that Grandfather Ismael had not

lived to see it. Then I remembered an old acquaintance of his, Senyor Bernat Muntaner. The Muntaners were an old and respected family of wealthy merchants, and Bernat, according to my grandfather, was a fine example of a Catalan gentleman. Robust in appearance, and of a spirited nature, he spent as much time cultivating his mind as he did cultivating his extensive lands, or travelling to Italy and France to attend directly to his interests there. Muntaner was also a devout Catholic, but his religious beliefs had never been an obstacle to his long and close friendship with Grandfather Ismael. On the contrary, I remembered how he seemed to derive great pleasure from discussing their differences, and how, at a deeper level, their mutual understanding cast aside such differences, for I would often sit in a corner of the study with my sewing and listen to them while they talked. These and other considerations made me resolve to go and pay Senyor Muntaner a visit.

I plaited my hair with care and put on my best tunic. It was red, cut loosely but gracefully, with pretty gold buttons on the tight cuffs which went half-way up to the elbow; it also had a velvet trimming in a darker shade of red, to mark the square neckline and the start of the skirt, about half a span above the waistline. My mother had given it to me on my sixteenth birthday. 'Here,' she said, 'you're no longer a child. You must dress like a marriageable lass now, without showing too much of your body, but allowing for plenty of guesswork.' And she had smiled at me with feminine complicity, something that was quite new to me. I had not worn that tunic since the night before the edict, the night I was taken to the formal meeting with Vidal.

Wrapped in my cloak, my head covered with the hood, I left the house, knowing my mother had gone to see Isaac and would take a while to return. I walked up the steps of our alleyway, which led to the top of the *call,* and left La

Força through the gate we called Portal Rufí. Once outside the walled Força I was in a part of town called La Vilanova. This quarter, like the one next to it, called L'Areny (which means The Sandbank because it occupies the sandy bank of the river Onyar), was set within the second ring of walls, built by our King Pere 'the Ceremonious' a century and a half earlier. I walked down a steep hill and soon came to L'Areny and to a street known as Carrer dels Ciutadans, or Citizens' Street, where all the most noble and ancient families had their homes. This was where the Muntaners lived. Their house was large and stately—or so I had heard, although I'd never seen it myself—with arches on the ground floor and beautiful gardens. White roses peeped over the high wall that enclosed the grounds, but there was no other sign of life. Nor did I meet anybody as I walked up to the door in the wall and pulled the bell-chain. From the street all one could see was the top floor of the house, with square towers at either end of the façade and three pairs of double windows set in handsome horseshoe arches. I heard a dog bark, then a woman's voice ordering it to be quiet.

'Coming, coming,' said the voice and her footsteps echoed in the courtyard.

It was one of the servants. Behind her I could see the gardens that I had heard so much about but never seen, with fountains and a profusion of flowers and greenery. The woman looked aghast when she saw the yellow and red badge sewn onto my cloak.

'I would please like to speak to Senyor Bernat Muntaner,' I said quickly.

'Senyor Muntaner is not here,' she said coldly, and began closing the door.

'Then pray, let me speak to his noble wife, Margarida.'

She closed the door and I heard her running across

the yard shouting 'Senyora, senyora' in a frightened voice, as if she had seen the very devil.

I waited, and thought I heard one of the top windows being opened. When I glanced up I could not see anybody, but I felt that unseen eyes were looking at me from behind closed shutters. Then I heard the rustling of a gown across the patio and presumed Senyora Margarida was approaching. When she opened the door and saw me, she was more welcoming, but equally nervous at the sight of my badge and cloak.

'I'm Alba, the weaver's daughter, senyora. I wondered whether I could speak to your husband?'

'My husband is away,' she said dryly. 'He's not here.'

'When will he be back?' I insisted.

At that moment her daughter Clara, a girl of my age, stepped out from behind the half-closed door.

'My father has gone to our country house to see how the crops are doing,' she said with her nose in the air. 'You can hardly miss it: it's the largest in the valley.'

Her mother pulled her aside and closed the door, looking both angry and embarrassed. Then I heard her scolding her daughter, and although I could not make out the exact words, they were easy to imagine. I had often seen Clara walking with her mother in the marketplace, or on her way out of church on Sundays, and she had always seemed to me a graceless, unfriendly girl. Now she had unwittingly done me a good turn. I knew where to find her father.

From Clara's house I made my way to the gate called El Portal de l'Àngel (the Angel's Gate) and then, leaving the eastern walls of town behind me, I crossed the wooden footbridge over the Onyar, always quieter than the stone bridge a little further north. The quarter I now entered, on the western side of the river, was known as El Mercadal, and was protected by the third set of walls, also built in the

41

days of King Pere. Choosing the quieter streets, I walked up-river for a while, noticing how different this part of town was from the side of the river in which I lived. There, the buildings were crammed together in a dense network of hilly streets and small squares, but here the terrain was flat, the houses were lower and newer, the streets were wider, and between the houses there were orchards and vegetable gardens. I was on unfamiliar ground, for I very seldom came here, and I felt uneasy. Soon I turned down a road that bordered the river Monar, a tributary of the Onyar, whose waters were used not only for irrigation but also to drive the mills that were built on its banks. Some of the people who saw me walking by turned their heads away, pretending they had not seen me, but others insulted me openly, and I had to bite my lips to stop myself from answering back.

I left the Mercadal quarter through the gate of Santa Clara, and passed the convent of the same name, which stood just outside the walls, a building encircled by high crenellated walls that made it look like a fortified castle. Then I followed a winding path through olive groves, at the end of which I could see a large country house, which I assumed was Bernat Muntaner's farm. A great feeling of calm came over me. After being bound to my house and to the *call* for days on end, it was wonderful to see such an expanse of land and sky, such a sea of silvery olive trees.

I was quite close to the farm when I heard the gallop of a horse approaching from behind, and I moved to one side.

'Sooo!' went the rider, and the horse stopped a few steps ahead of me.

With his fashionable pointed beard Muntaner's face looked longer than usual, his eyes more melancholy. But he smiled warmly. I had not seen him since Grandfather Ismael's funeral.

'Alba,' he cried, dismounting and walking up to me. 'What brings you here?'

'I've taken the liberty of coming to ask you for help,' I said.

Muntaner's horse snorted with pleasure and I went up to him and patted his head.

'Let's walk up to the house. And take your cape off, Alba, you must feel hot. You're safe without it here.'

An old peasant came out of the house to meet us and took the horse, bowing respectfully as he did so.

'Ask Maria to bring us some refreshments,' said Bernat Muntaner.

The peasant bowed again and hurried off to the house, with the horse trotting beside him.

When we reached the outer patio of the farmhouse, a paved semicircle surrounded by a stone bench, I turned around to look at the view, and an unexpected sight met my eye: old Girona, distant but clear, lying snug in its walled nest above the river Onyar, and the newer parts, with their second and third sets of walls, standing fearlessly on either side of the river. Muntaner came up to me.

'From a distance the city looks peaceful enough. But within those walls, with their well-guarded towers, Girona is a hotbed of intrigue and discord. Whenever I can get away, I come here. Here I always find peace.'

I followed Muntaner into the house and he took me into the dining room where the peasant's wife was placing a jug of lemonade and two cups on the long table. Then she left and we sat at one end of the table. From the window I could see Girona again.

'Let's see, Alba,' he said, as he poured lemonade into a cup for me. 'What can I do to help you?' I noticed a touch of pity in his voice.

It suddenly occurred to me that what I was about to do was, in fact, the responsibility of my mother or of my cousin Isaac, not mine. Perhaps they would not have agreed... But it was too late for regrets.

'Senyor Muntaner,' I began, 'when the sales take place, I want you to have our house. You have been inside it; it's solid and spacious, and you could find some use for it, I'm sure. I know my grandfather would have wished it so. Pay me what you like for it, in goods. Perhaps you could find me a horse and cart.'

He pursed his lips and nodded his head, but did not answer. So I added: 'Most of our neighbours are going to sell their homes to clergymen, but, if you will excuse my saying so, I would rather knock ours down or burn it than let those crows have it.'

He gave me a reassuring smile.

'You have your grandfather's pride,' he said. 'Yes, yours is one of the best houses in the *call*, not only on account of its sturdiness, but because of what it represents, and because its walls are imbued with the wisdom of your ancestors. I feel honoured by your proposition. A horse and cart, you say? That would pay for the cellars and the kitchen, but not for the upper rooms, the patio, the large dining hall, or the study...'

He paused, and stroked his beard thoughtfully. His good humour had lifted my spirits and I waited for him to speak again.

'The edict forbids you to take out money, but as far as I know, it does not mention bills of exchange. I can pay you that way. Tell me, Alba,' he added, 'what do you plan to do after reaching Perpignan?'

'The idea is to stay there as long as possible. After all, we speak the same language, so we won't be considered strangers, will we?'

'No, you won't be strangers in Roussillon. But I sometimes wonder how long the two Catalan counties on the other side of the Pyrenees will remain under the French Crown.'

I must have looked puzzled, because he went on to explain how the counties of Roussillon and Cerdagne, which for centuries had belonged to the Crown of Aragon, had been mortgaged to the French crown thirty years earlier by our King Joan II, in exchange for money and soldiers.

'The history of these two Catalan counties in France is linked to that of Girona,' he explained. 'In the summer of sixty two, King Joan needed French soldiers to help him fight the forces of the Catalan Government and free his wife and his son Ferran, who had taken refuge in La Força. It was the beginning of a civil war that lasted over ten years and divided the Catalans.'

I felt curious. I had never fully understood the causes of that war which was so often mentioned in Abraham's workshop. 'But, Senyor Bernat, what divided our people so deeply that it came to a war?' I asked.

'Our long civil war,' he began, 'resulted from two things: the differences between the government of Catalonia and its authoritarian King Joan, who had no respect for our country's constitution, and the abiding hatred between the land-owners of the north and their peasants, who demanded the abolition of their serfdom. The spark that ignited the war was a combination of both those things. You see,' he said, settling down in his chair, 'only two years earlier, King Joan had ordered the arrest of his first-born, Prince Carles of Viana, under the influence, it seems, of his second wife, Joana Enríquez, who wanted the Crown of Aragon for her own son, Ferran. In Barcelona there was a public outcry, Alba. The crowds were out in the streets, demanding the release of their legitimate king-to-be, and because the arrest violated the Catalan constitution, our Government was able to force the King to set Carles free. After the untimely death of Carles of Viana, poisoned, some say, by his stepmother Joana, the Government continued to restrain the abuses of the monarchy, which infuriated both the King and his wife. The crunch finally came when, with the King absent from Catalonia, the Queen tried to impose her authority on that of the Government by prohibiting the mobilisation of an army it had raised to stifle the peasants' revolt. The Queen's enemies declared that her prohibition was illegal and war began between the supporters of the monarchy and those who wished to defend our ancient laws and institutions.

'During those ten years of war three different kings were named to take the place of Joan II. Some of us would even have wanted to create a republic, such as they have in Venice, for example. We're a small country... But King Joan's power and influence were more effective than our ideals. A peace treaty was signed in 1472, and Prince Ferran, Joan II's son by Joana Enríquez, was officially recognised by the Catalans as the heir to the Crown of Aragon. As you know, Ferran, like his father, isn't a Catalan either, even though we consider him one of us. Only time will tell, but the way things look now, I believe that his union with Isabel of Castile will bring us no good. And to make matters worse, he hates your people as much, or perhaps even more than his wife does, because his mother, Joana Enríquez, was partly Jewish, or so they say, and he's obsessed with the idea of washing out every drop of his Jewish blood by his actions.'

'And yet I've heard that both he and his mother owe their lives to the Jews of Girona,' I said, remembering, once more, the conversation at the cobbler's.

46

'Ambition kills gratitude, Alba,' said Bernat Muntaner. 'Besides, Ferran was only a child when that siege took place, and children are more apt to remember the fear suffered during an adverse situation than its happy outcome.'

By the time I left Muntaner's house, I had a bill of exchange in my pocket, which I could present outside the kingdoms of Spain. He had also given me a sack of dried beans, which the farmer's son was to carry for me as far as the convent of Santa Clara. And he had promised to find me a good horse and cart for the journey.

'Nevertheless,' he said, as I was leaving, 'we should not altogether discard the possibility of this absurd law being revoked.'

'That's what Rabbi Leví says,' I answered. 'And some, like Benevist the furrier, the one who lives in Ruca Street, also believe it. He keeps saying: "It's only a question of time, a few months, perhaps; we'll come back to Girona, you'll see." But I don't think like him.'

'In any case,' concluded Muntaner, 'I want you to know that the house on the corner of St. Llorenç Street will always be the house of your ancestor Bonastruc de Porta, the wise Nahmanides, for generations and generations to come. And the house of my dear friend, a Jew and a Catalan, Rabbi Ismael de Porta.'

He pressed my hand as he spoke and looked earnestly at me, as if trying to recollect my grandfather's face.

* * *

I was hurrying back across the wooden foot-bridge carrying the sack of beans over my shoulder, when I stupidly tripped over a loose plank, caught my foot on my cloak and fell flat on my face. There were quite a few people on the riverbank at that moment. Some laughed openly when they saw me fall; others turned their heads to ignore me as I scrambled back on my feet. Then I heard a voice speaking softly behind me:

'Alba.'

I turned round and there was Vidal, leaning over the railing, pretending to look interested in the water below.

'Look the other way,' he ordered under his breath.

I bent down to collect the beans that had spilled with my fall.

'I was in Muntaner's house when you came by this morning, and I caught a glimpse of you from the office windows on the first floor. I've been waiting for you to return ever since. Are you still so determined to leave? Won't you change your mind?'

'No, Vidal,' was all I managed to say.

I wanted to get up and run to him, but checked myself. I felt as if everyone was looking now, threatening us with their gossip. Tears blurred my vision; I could hardly see the spilled beans. My whole body felt bruised and I tried to say something else, but somehow I couldn't think clearly, I couldn't find the appropriate words. Of course, I should have asked him how he would know where to find me when at last he was able to leave his mother. I should have made it clear to him that I would wait for him. Instead I said nothing. We both breathed in each other's silent proximity and my heart was beating fast. Through the planks I saw the river flowing by, and it seemed to me that it was taking all our love with it. When at last I finished gathering the precious beans and stood up again, I saw him walking slowly away, without even turning his head.

When I got home I was overcome by a sense of finality, although somewhere deep inside me I still cherished the vain hope of a sudden reversal of the edict, or of his following me into exile. Before my mother had a chance to scold me for my absence, I handed her the sack of beans and the letter of exchange. She read the letter and looked at me in amazement.

'Upon my word, child,' she said. 'Your father *would* have been proud of you.'

As soon as the dinner plates had been cleared away—mine untouched despite my mother's insistence that I should eat—I retired to my chamber and wept miserably. The following morning my head ached so much I could not rise, and my monthly sickness assured me that I was not with child.

IV

THE CHAIN OF LILIES

The next week I spent in a fever, and all I remember of those days is the creak of the wooden stairs every time my mother came up to my room, and the smell of vinegar from the wet rags she pressed against my forehead. And then, one morning, like someone emerging from a long dark tunnel, I awoke to a sunlit room with a bunch of mint leaves on the windowsill. I called my mother and she came hurrying up the steps, crying, 'Thanks be given to the Almighty, blessed be His Name! Alba my dear child, you are better, you are better!'

'What day is it Mother?'

'The first Friday in Sivan; or if you prefer it in Christian, the last day in the month of May,' she said, feeling my forehead with the back of her hand, for her palm was covered in dough. 'Yes, your fever has gone completely.'

Then off she went, down the stairs to her baking-trough, saying, 'This evening we shall both go to the synagogue to thank the Almighty for your recovery.'

I got out of bed, walked over to the window, and took a deep breath. Springtime would soon give way to summer. The air was warm and I wanted to live, whatever life had in store for me. Only a tiny spark of pain was still burning inside me, and I was not going to kindle it. What for? I'd rather wall in those useless feelings, like the windows on St. Llorenç Street.

I filled the basin with water from the brown jug that

stood next to it and bathed my hands and face until I felt the blood rushing back to my cheeks. Then I slowly dressed and combed my hair, putting a sprig of mint in it. Feeling rather weak, I went downstairs to the kitchen, drawn by the smell of freshly baked bread.

'And how is the apple of my eye?'

It was Cousin Isaac, who was filling a large linen bag with loaves from the oven tray.

I went over to him and let him put an arm around me. Through the wide open kitchen door I saw the first few roses in bloom on our patio. The pigeons cooed in the dovecote and our black and white cat lay stretched out in a pool of sun. My mother was busy cooking and baking for the Sabbath. It was as though nothing at all were amiss, as though the light mantle of eternity had formed a tent over our heads from which our troubled time was excluded.

'Why don't you come and deliver the bread with me?' said Isaac, 'a bit of sunshine will make my little cousin smile again.'

I looked at my mother.

'Oh, all right, Isaac,' she said. 'But your little cousin needs to have something more filling than sunshine in her stomach before she sets foot outside. Come, eat some bread and oil, Alba.'

So I sat down and obeyed my mother.

We always kept the olive oil in a glass jar on the table; the oil of Girona was dark green and thick, but when you held it up against the light its colour turned to gold. As I ate my slice of oiled bread I felt my strength coming back with every mouthful. Then I was ready.

I followed Isaac up the steps of our alleyway, and from there went all around the *call* with him delivering the loaves from house to house. I watched each of the faces as they came to the door, Astrugona, Bonadona, Margarida,

Ester, Aina, old Valentina... they all seemed to be under the same spell as I was, for they showed no trace of anxiety, as if everything was the way it had always been before the edict. Only Coloma, Isaac's wife, as usual, looked sour and miserable.

We went into their house, which was the last in our rounds, and for a while I played with my young cousins, Rosa and Josuè. Then I kissed them goodbye and went out again to enjoy the bright sunlight, carrying the empty bread bag folded over my arm. I began to amble along the well-known streets, thinking of nothing in particular, and after a few minutes, without intending to, I found myself outside the public bathhouse.

The bathhouse was just outside La Força, close to the fortified walls, and I had never been inside it, even though the finely carved wooden door had always intrigued me. Nor was it, strictly speaking, a public bathhouse, for it no longer belonged to the Girona Council, but to a wealthy family of the nobility. Nevertheless, I had heard my mother say that in happier times of coexistence with the Christians we had been allowed to use it for our rituals, because the baths in our synagogue were small, dark and uncomfortable. But all that was long before this story began, and my mother would have been horrified to see me standing there. And yet, suddenly, I felt an urge to go into that forbidden building. That day, as I said, there was an atmosphere of peace all about me, and I felt no fear whatsoever.

The door was ajar, and when I stepped in I was astonished by what I saw. The building was constructed in the style of Arab baths. It had vaulted ceilings and many Arab decorative patterns. The main hall, which also served as a dressing room, was spacious and elegant, with benches and chairs placed here and there, and luscious plants that doubtless thrived with the water vapours. But what impressed me above all was the white octagonal reservoir in the middle of the main room, shaped like a small temple, from which stemmed eight slim columns of white marble; its capitals, decorated with leaves and flowers, supported a central dome open to the outside at its crown. I called out, but no answer came. I was alone. All was quiet save for the faint hissing sound of the steam coming from the hot water. Silence had become petrified in the white marble of the columns.

I locked the main door and undressed, then I wandered from room to room, feeling the warmth of the floor under my feet and breathing in the scented air, until I entered the hottest chamber. I submerged myself in the hot pool, letting the water wash my body, wetting my hair with a wide seashell that stood on the side of the pool, next to the sponges and the bottles of pine essence. Afterwards, I slowly returned to the dressing room and stretched out on one of the cushioned benches. I felt at peace with myself, purified and renewed in body and soul. At that moment I was not thinking about Vidal, or about anything thing else that might have caused me distress. In fact, I was beyond ordinary thought, and as I lay there in this way I observed the shaft of light that poured down from the dome above the reservoir and became trapped, as it were, between the white columns; and I noticed how the light changed in intensity as clouds were being pushed across the sky by the spring breeze. It was then that I began to comprehend, for the first time, what my grandfather used to tell me about there being an invisible ladder that unites our earthly world with the higher spheres of the Divine Being: for just as the movements in the shaft of light that I beheld in front of me were giving my mind an image of the clouds in the sky outside, which my corporeal eye could not see, making me rise in my imagination to invisible spheres, so certain human beings could learn to climb into the celestial world of the divine emanations. He was referring, of course, to those initiated in the teachings of the Kabbalah, who, by meditating on visible images, such as the letters associated with the ten *sephiroth* of the Tree of God, or those of the great unspeakable name YHVH, can actually feel the divine force that is in our Hebrew alphabet and in our world, and are then able to ascend mentally up a ladder of light, whereby they hope to reach the heavens and view the unseen mysteries of the Creator. Later, as I dressed and my body resumed its movements, so my mind also came down from its dream-like state, and I knew that, once again, I had received a sign from my grandfather Ismael, though I could not yet understand its meaning.

* * *

That afternoon, as arranged, my mother and I went to the synagogue to thank the Almighty for my recovery. But when we reached the top of our street and turned right, we were overwhelmed by the sight of a whole crowd of strangers who also seemed to be making their way towards the synagogue. Did we not know, asked a neighbour, that there was going to be a very important meeting, after prayers, which all Jews from the neighbouring villages had been urged to attend? 'Cousin Isaac never remembers to tell me anything!' my mother said.

We were told that people had come from Besalú, Banyoles, Vilamarí, Ullastret, Olot, Figueres and all other nearby villages and hamlets that still had a few Jewish families living in the faith. And many of the wives had left their work and had come along with their husbands, to make sure they attended the meeting.

I had never seen the synagogue so full. We women

always sat in the back rows, with the men occupying the rows in front of us, and we were separated during prayers by a movable screen, made of wood and damask cloth. That evening, when the screen was removed for the assembly to begin, all I could see was a mass of heads, though I craned my neck to catch a glimpse of the Chief Rabbi of Catalonia and of the rest of the rabbis, *hazzanim* and representatives of the neighbouring towns and villages who were supposed to be sitting on either side of him. But once the meeting began they each in turn went up the wooden steps of the *bimah* to make their address, and then I was able to see them clearly, with their colourful long gowns and beautiful head-dresses, and hear their resonant and melodious voices as they exhorted us to remain true to the Law, and not to listen to the Christians who were tempting us to convert in order to be able to stay on in our homes. They spoke of the small value of earthly goods. One of them praised the Jewish women of Catalonia, many of whom were responsible for making sure their husbands and sons did not abandon the faith. We were reminded of the flight from Egypt and told that we must take this new exodus with the same spirit as our ancestors, trusting in the design of the Almighty.

It could not be a coincidence, said another, but divine intention, that barely two days after the time limit for our departure would be the Ninth of Av, Tish'a Be'Av, when both destructions of the Temple of Jerusalem took place, the second some six centuries after the first. By the ninth day of Av, he said, we would be safely in foreign lands, but hereafter this date would also mark, for us, the destruction of Sepharad.

As I sat there in the crowded hall, the present rushed back at me with all the force of its implications. But I was ready to listen and accept my fate with something more than mere resignation or a submissive sense of duty.

At the end of the meeting I stayed on to straighten the rows of chairs, a task that I had been performing in the name of my family for some years. People were slowly making their way out to breathe in the fresh evening air, some with their cape only half on, or folded over their arms, as if the words they had heard had made them lose all fear of their oppressors. But I was not in any hurry to leave, nor did I feel like speaking to anyone. My mother had gone out without me, and I could hear her by the main door in animated conversation with our neighbours. After a while she peeped round the door and said: 'Alba, come when you've finished with the chairs; I'm going home to get dinner ready.'

When I thought I could hear no more voices in the street I opened the door and stepped outside. Night was beginning to fall, warm and clear.

I was startled by the sound of someone coughing behind me. For a brief moment I thought it was Vidal who had somehow managed to come into the *call* unobserved. But it was only our rabbi, Daniel Leví.

'Follow me, Alba,' he said. 'Astruc, the rabbi of Besalú wants to speak to you. And please don't ask any questions yet. Your mother knows you're with me.'

His words sounded oddly familiar, like the words in a dream that one knows before they are spoken. So I nodded and followed him in silence, while he looked anxiously around him, as if afraid of being followed or spied upon. It was pitch dark by now and as we hastened noiselessly through the labyrinth of the *call*, I began to wonder why Astruc, the young rabbi from Besalú, whom I vaguely remembered as one of the students under my grandfather's tutelage, would want to speak to me. Perhaps he wanted me to take charge of the small children during the journey to Perpignan. In the meeting he had shown great concern for their welfare. His red hair and beard blazed over a pale, almost milk-white skin, suggesting a mixture of physical vigour and composure which had pleased me as I sat in the synagogue listening to him talk, competing in ideas and rhetoric with the other spiritual leaders who took their place in the *bimah*.

When at last we reached the house where Rabbi Astruc was lodging, he himself opened the door for us. He was wearing a long surcoat and held a candle in one hand. The candlelight cast a long thin shadow behind him.

'So you're Alba, the weaver's daughter, and Ismael de Porta's granddaughter.'

His voice was gentle, and a smile lit up his face; I felt at ease in his presence. He made us come in and from the entrance hall led us into another room, where we all sat down.

'I remember you as a child,' he began, 'when I came to see your grandfather for my Talmudic studies. That must have been at least seven years ago.' From the way he looked at me, with respect and care, I knew this was not going to be a straightforward request. What did he want?

'The rabbis of the province of Girona have elected me as their spokesman for this most delicate matter,' he continued. 'And as I know how hard it must have been for you to decide to come into exile with us, when in your heart you felt otherwise inclined, I feel encouraged to speak to you. Will you swear to secrecy before I continue?'

I turned for reassurance to our own rabbi, but he had retreated to a dark corner of the room, where he sat with his eyes downcast, his hands folded over his lap. I wondered who had told him about Vidal. A grim thought came to my mind: this would be my first step towards exile, the first in a march that was going to take me away from Girona and from Vidal. I felt the cold fear of the unknown, but did not hesitate.

'Yes, you have my word,' I heard myself saying.

We were sitting opposite one another at a bare unvarnished pinewood table, on which he had placed the candlestick he was holding when he opened the door. The soft light picked up the grain of the table top: rivers and paths ran between us, and near his freckled hand a knot in the wood took on the appearance of a black cloaked figure with a large bubble coming out of its mouth.

Rabbi Astruc talked about the deep significance of our imminent exile in terms of the history of our people. He spoke to me not as a child, or as a woman, but as his equal, and I must admit that his trust in my ability to understand him pleased me immensely. We could save our bodies and souls by leaving Spain, he said, and would find new homes, God permitting, in a country where we would be treated with more respect. Yes, it was going to be painful to have to leave our homes and so many cherished family goods. It was going to be distressing to have to part with the tombs of our ancestors, but with the help of the Lord we would soon get over our pain and distress and begin a new life for His glory.

'You have to understand, Alba,' he went on, 'that just as Torquemada, the Inquisitor-general, is intent on confiscating as much as he can from the New Christians, which is why he wants as many insincere conversions as possible before the 31st of July, so the King and Queen, our masters, want us to leave in great numbers, that they may take possession of our riches. They're already demanding new taxes; and as soon as we leave, all the goods we have not sold will end up in the royal treasury, which is empty after all these years of war against the Arabs in the South. There are those who believe that this is the main reason for our expulsion, and I share that belief. I think that their desire to protect their religion and to "clean their lands of the weeds of sin," as they say, is only an excuse to satisfy their greed and that of their followers; and all those unspeakable slanders that reach us from time to time, about the killings of innocent children by Jews, are spread with the sole intention of creating animosity against our people. What's more, I'm afraid we will have to satisfy that greed not only with taxes and our personal belongings, but with those precious ritual objects that our ancestors managed to preserve throughout the violent attacks on our communities one hundred years ago, all the valuables of our synagogues. These are things we can never sell because of their religious nature, and we will not be allowed to take them with us, either. Silver boxes, breastplates, jewelled ornaments, coffers, all kinds of treasures.'

Here Rabbi Astruc suddenly became lost in thought; his eyes looked misty, his mouth was half open. In his dark corner, Rabbi Leví cleared his throat. A long time seemed to pass, the three of us trapped in an awkward silence.

'Yes?' I asked finally, as quietly as possible.

'Ah, yes, yes, they're so covetous, Alba, you know,' he said at last, blinking and shaking his head, like someone waking up after a nap; 'but all this is inevitable and we must accept it as part of the Lord's design for His chosen people.'

He sighed, looked down at the table, then up again at me. I could sense that he had kept something to himself. But now he was coming to the 'most delicate matter' he had mentioned earlier. When he spoke again, his tone was earnest and confidential.

'But even more important than these treasures,' he said, 'are some texts that express the highest thoughts of the Girona mystics, the men who studied the Kabbalah.

We can't afford to lose them. The synagogue scrolls and the registry lists will probably be allowed through the frontier, where there will be a good number of *conversos* whose job it will be to translate for the guards. But if we took any of the religious treaties with us they would be immediately seized, confiscated and probably burnt. They think of our books as a source of evil.'

'But surely, Rabbi Astruc,' I dared to say, 'the works of the great masters have all been copied and taken out of Sepharad many generations ago. I once heard Senyor Muntaner telling my grandfather that he had seen a number of such books written in Girona, in the home of a Jewish banker in Italy.'

'That is true,' he answered. 'But not all the books have been copied, not all the books can be found in Italy. Let me explain: Since the edict of expulsion was proclaimed, I have been honoured with the task of cataloguing all the documents of the Girona synagogue. In doing so, I came across a sheet of parchment, hidden in the false bottom of a drawer. This piece of parchment, written in obvious haste, mentioned a book by a Girona master, which had never been copied, nor its contents divulged, and revealed its hiding place. I found the book in the synagogue, under a trap door that had been cleverly disguised by the tiles on the floor. It was a book of religious meditations, which contains the thoughts peculiar to the Girona School of Kabbalah. A gem, a real gem.'

Rabbi Astruc paused and looked at his hands. When he spoke again he did it slowly, as if that would make it easier for me to understand.

'Now,' he said, 'there is only one safe way of carrying the word of our Lord out of Sepharad, and that is in one's mind. This irreplaceable book, of which only the original manuscript exists, must now be memorised, and I need someone capable of such a task. I myself cannot do it. In the weeks remaining before our departure I have to devote my time and attention to collecting and classifying all the civil documents scattered about the small communities around Girona. Nor do I think I would be able to, even if I had the time.'

'But the school no longer exists. There are no kabbalistic scholars left in the *call*. My grandfather was the last one,' I said.

'You were brought up on his knee and have absorbed his knowledge. You can read and write in both Hebrew and Catalan and you are familiar with Aramaic too. I know you are the right person,' he replied.

'I'm only a woman, rabbi,' I answered quickly. 'I've never gone deep enough into the study of the holy books, and it would be impossible for me to learn a whole book by rote without understanding its meaning.'

He was looking at me with such hope, such intensity, that even as I spoke my words grew weak and lost all conviction.

'Your grandfather,' he insisted, 'always spoke of you with pride. He once said that although your name meant 'dawn' you were like a clear pool in which the new moon casts its reflection, and that if you had been a man you would no doubt have devoted your life to reaching a higher understanding of God. Tonight, just after the synagogue meeting, I caught the reflection of the moon in the little fountain at the end of this street, and there have been other omens, dreams and warnings, all of which lead to you, Alba.'

'My Hebrew name is Levanah,' I said, 'but I have never used it.'

'Levanah: *the white one*, or *moonlight*. Ah, that explains everything. The Lord is with us, revealing His mysterious ways.'

He went on to say that I was the only living descendant in the line of the great Nahmanides and that, in the circumstances, he believed that my grandfather's words must be taken as a clear indication that I was the only person in the Girona Jewry capable of memorising the book in question.

I held my breath.

'I'm asking you to undertake the responsibility of carrying the text in your mind and delivering it to the rabbi of the Perpignan community.'

As he spoke, he walked across the room, took a box out of a cupboard, and brought out a vellum-bound book tied with white ribbons. Then he came back to his seat, untied the ribbons, and with great care placed the book in front of me, on the table. I opened it. The first page had no letters but only a pattern that I recognised at once as one of my father's cloth designs. My heart missed a beat.

'You seem to recognise this.'

'It looks like one of my father's patterns.'

'Your father was not a teacher, but he was well instructed in the secret traditions of Girona, or so your grandfather told me, and he must have been acquainted with its symbolism.'

I stared at the familiar design, which I had always taken for a simple decorative element. I suddenly understood that those three large lilies, one placed over the other in a vertical row, so that only the top one showed its full shape, clearly symbolised the ten points of the Tree of God, the ten *sephiroth* on the sacred tree. This time I felt more than a warm closeness for my unknown father. I felt committed to his memory. The knowledge that he too had been instructed in the Kabbalah made me all the more determined to accept the mission, whatever the risks. I turned the page. The next one was the title page.

'*The Chain of Lilies*,' I read out. 'Dictated in a dream by an angel and thereupon written down in the *call* of Girona, in the year 5005 since the Creation of the Universe.'

Then it all came back to me.

'I remember the title well, Rabbi Astruc,' I explained. 'Grandfather Ismael told me about this book, which he in turn had heard about from his own father. But my great-grandfather did not know where it was either; all he knew was that a member of the synagogue had hidden it during a pogrom, and that this man had died, beaten to death by a frenzied mob, without having revealed its hiding place. He would have been so happy to know you had found it! But who is the author?' I asked.

'Here it says plainly that the author is an angel,' answered Rabbi Astruc. 'The person who received the inspiration in a dream did not think it fit to claim any authorship. Personally, I believe he must have been a disciple of Ezra ben Selomó. I noticed similarities of concept and expression with Ben Selomó's famous commentary on the Song of Songs.'

Then these words from the Song of Solomon came uncalled to my mind:

My beloved is gone down into His garden, to the beds of spices, to feed in the gardens, and to gather lilies.

'Teach me how to memorise,' I said.

* * *

Rabbi Astruc was a patient teacher, and I was an eager pupil. There were only eight weeks left until our departure from Girona, and my mind was kept so busy that I

63

had no more time for melancholy moments. I began to memorise the book. It was a treatise on the different realms of the universe, from what is invisible to the human eye, to what is visible, showing how they are all interlinked by the ever-flowing rays of the Divine Light, so that nothing, not even a drop of water, and nobody, not even the most unworthy human being, can be isolated from the divine artifact of creation, the great cosmos. It was the first time I had ever read a text of this nature, and suddenly all the concepts my grandfather had taught me over the years also became linked in my mind and were filled with light. God is invisible and incomprehensible, said the book, He is the Divine Infinite, or En-Sof, as the kabbalists say. But through His emanations, En-Sof is transformed into the Divine Being. It manifests itself and creates the universe through the power of the word; and that is why all the words of our Hebrew language are a part of God, and all the words of the Torah are a mirror of His wisdom and form the great concealed name of God, the name which the mystics search with such intensity. Creation is no more than the external development of those powers that are active and alive within God himself. In this way, the universe reflects God's own essence and glory and maintains its harmony through the balance of grace and severity, the feminine and the masculine, and other opposites. These opposites are in turn reflections of God's divine attributes, the *sephiroth*, symbolised in the ten points of the sacred Tree of God, the ten river stones on the floor of our entrance hall. Every single thing in the world exists only because some of the power of the ten *sephiroth* exists in it, for the Tree of God spreads its branches throughout the whole of creation.

The book was divided into two parts, and each part into four chapters. To begin with I was unable to grasp the full significance of the words. Indeed, some parts of the text I could not comprehend at all at the beginning, and some words and concepts, such as 'spiritual oneness' or 'primordial wisdom,' refused to lodge in my mind unless I clothed them in a more material attire. This I soon learned to do, for it is one of the artifices most commonly used for memorising.

Learning a long text by heart is not, in itself, a difficult task, but it requires a great deal of practice and concentration. In order to remember such a vast number of words, I had first to choose a building that I knew well and found pleasing to the eye and the soul, since the method works better when there is a warm flow of affection sustaining it. The building is then considered the complete shape of the work to be memorised. The divisions of the building correspond to the different parts of the text, so that every door and window, every chamber, every wall, every column or step, is assigned to one particular paragraph, and within that paragraph a further number of interrelated images give the key to every sentence. Rabbi Astruc suggested the synagogue, but to me it seemed more natural to chose my own home for the exercise. He agreed and together we decided how best to divide up the house. He even went around the different rooms with me, helping me find associations of words and place.

And so it was that the house of my ancestors became incorporated in my mind and took on a new significance. It began to speak to me from every corner. The wooden railings, the open loft, the doors, the stairs, the flagstones, the chairs and tables, the well and the dovecote, the patio and the flowers, were all words I could touch and see. If I stood in the centre of the main hall, all those fine thoughts, expressed harmoniously in well chosen words, filled the inner space with sweet music coming from below and above, from east and west, from north and south. And if I stepped into the street and closed the front door, I could take my home with me wherever I went, packed, as it were, into a nutshell.

V

EXILE

The weeks that followed my meeting with the rabbi of Besalú passed swiftly, like the winds that sweep across the valley of Girona in wintertime. When not memorising the little kabbalistic book, repeating every word again and again until they were all well lodged in my memory, I worked about the house, preparing for the departure. Almost without my noticing, the day we had all feared so much was upon us.

My mother and I rose when it was still dark and lit some of the large oil lamps that hung from the ceilings. From my bedroom window I could see the glow of other lamps in the house across the street and two cats chasing one another on the rooftops. A dog barked, disturbed, no doubt, by such early signs of life. I stripped my bed, and as I was folding the sheets to pack into the trunk I remembered that I had left my red tunic hanging on the washing-line upstairs, with a few other garments I prized, so I went up to the open loft to fetch them.

The town was bathed in moonlight, and to the north I saw the silhouette of the mountains we would soon be crossing. I did not want to think about Vidal, but still his image came to my mind, and I wondered whether he was awake and thinking of me, or fast asleep in his bed. Again the dog barked, and I thought I heard a human voice trying to silence it. I leaned over the parapet but St. Llorenç Street was sunk in shadow and I was unable to distinguish anything from up there. Suddenly, as I turned to go downstairs, I heard a muffled thump and saw that something had fallen on the tiles. I bent down to pick it up: it was a long slim object, wrapped in cloth. Again I looked over the parapet but could neither see nor hear anything. The barking had stopped and I rushed down to my room to unwrap the parcel. It contained a small box made of dark wood that gleamed softly in the lamplight, with 'ALBA' carved on it in Hebrew letters and some decorative motifs round the edges. I knew immediately that it came from Vidal, and I also knew that he had made it himself, because once he had told me that when he lived in Barcelona he worked for a time as a wood engraver.

I opened the box eagerly, hoping to find a letter or some message in it, but it was empty; then I rushed upstairs again, and again leaned over the railing. The sky was lighter now, and I could just make out the shape of the street and the doorways. But the place looked deserted. I felt helpless standing there, not being able to call out his name, not knowing whether he was hiding in one of the dark doorways and could see me looking for him. In the meantime, my mother was calling me impatiently to go and help her, so I had to tear myself away from the loft and go downstairs. There I set to work again, packing, tidying, fetching and carrying, with a heavy heart.

Down in the kitchen the furnace was still warm from the baking of the previous day. My mother and I had worked without a moment's rest, making large quantities of bread for all the community, exposed to the heat of the furnace on a day that was already baked by the sun. Half way through the morning I had tried to humour my mother. 'Mother,' I said, 'at least on the eve of this new flight into the wilderness, the Almighty, blessed be His Name, has given us time and plenty of heat with which to leaven our bread!' But far from amusing her, my words seemed to have provided her with a new understanding of our predicament and I think she fancied herself as a biblical figure in this story of our Exodus, for she stopped her usual complaints and began to sing psalms and pray aloud as she carried on with her work, well into the night.

As I was saying, in the early hours of the day we left Girona, the oven was still warm. My mother threw some fresh wood on the glowing embers and put in a last tray of buns and honey cakes to eat during the journey. Then we both went on with our tasks, not pausing once, for without a man about the house to help us, as my mother reminded me again and again, we could not waste a single moment. Up and down the stairs we ran, tying up bundles, filling baskets with food and pitchers with water, looking around the rooms a hundred times to make sure we were not forgetting anything. Finally, at sunrise, I scattered some breadcrumbs for the two pigeons left in the dovecote (we had eaten or bartered the rest, but I had persuaded my mother to leave a pair behind for Senyor Muntaner), and then I stroked our large black and white cat who lay unconcerned in his favourite corner of the patio. It was time to go.

Soon Isaac arrived to help us carry the heaviest trunks and bags down to the bottom of the alley, the meeting point for departure, where our horse and cart, gifts from Bernat Muntaner, were stationed. When there were only a few small things left to take down, he began to load the cart, talking about this and that to my mother and to the other neighbours who were gathering there, and I walked up the old steps for the last time. I went into the house. By the front door stood the few remaining bundles, waiting to be taken away. The silence of the empty rooms wrapped itself all around me. I leaned against a wall, closed my eyes, and in the silence I felt the presence of my grandfather Ismael. And it seemed to me that I could hear his voice saying: 'Go without fear, Alba.'

I had trouble turning the key because my hand was shaking so much. Though now every corner of our home was stored securely in my memory, never again would I perceive it through my senses; for despite what Senyor Muntaner had said, I knew that I would never return. Besides, the thought of having come so close to seeing Vidal again only a few hours previously and of knowing that he still felt the same love for me, made leaving even more difficult than I had foreseen. I tried to think of other things. I turned my head to see my people gathered at the bottom of the alleyway, but what I saw seemed strangely unrelated to me: human figures, cart, horse, bundles and trunks, were all images that had frozen into a miniature, a vignette in the story of the Girona Jews, like the pictures I used to look at as a child in my grandfather's illustrated *haggadah*, with its minute details of the flight from Egypt and its brilliant colours. As I stood there, time only counted backwards, as it were, covering my past and that of my forefathers; and this was the last page of the book. I, Alba Levanah de Porta, was only an instrument, with no will of my own, a key-holder, a door-closer, a history-ender.

A child's voice and a small hand tugging at my sleeve brought me back to my senses. 'Come on, Alba, come on! Hurry up, Alba!'

Cousin Rosa had been sent up to see why I was taking so long. I put the key into the deep pocket of my skirt. I felt Vidal's box, and realising what it was intended for, I opened it and put the key inside. As a last farewell gesture I lifted Rosa up and we both touched the *mezuzah*, placed in its niche in the door lintel, and together we said the words from the Deuteronomy written on that small piece of sheepskin, with which my family reaffirmed its adhesion to the law of Moses: 'Shema, *Israel! Hear, O Israel: the Lord our God is one Lord. And thou shalt love the Lord thy God with all thine heart, and with all thy soul, and with all thy might...*' Then we walked down the steps, two at a time, and climbed into the cart.

When all the travellers had gathered together at the meeting point and the rabbi of Girona had announced the start of the journey, we all turned our heads at the same time, as if by common consent, to take one last look. Our sighs and lamentations reverberated on the walls of St. Llorenç Street, until they seemed to penetrate the stones. I felt a spasm of longing, and would have liked to rush back up the alleyway and touch the door of our house just once more. But Rabbi Leví cried out in his shrill voice: 'No more tears! Sepharad will stay with us wherever we go. May the Adonai bless you all! We shall go into exile singing a cheerful song. Come on, Rosa,' he said, pointing at my cousin, 'play the tambourine, you're good at that.'

Poor rabbi, his voice lacked the authority of a natural leader, but he was doing his best, I suppose. Reluctantly, with dull, hoarse voices, we began to sing:

And he gathered them out of the lands, from the east, and from the west, from the north and from the south.
And he led them forth by the right way, that they might go to a city of habitation.

We were leaving the city of the rivers, the city of light and of the Kabbalah. Every step drew us further away from the *call*, but I could still feel the shelter of those tall dark walls, of the ivy that clung to them as my heart clung to the memories of a life that was now concluding. There were fifty-four of us leaving. Only about a dozen of our people had decided to stay and accept conversion, like Vidal. We must have made a pretty sight as we guided our mules and donkeys with their bulging saddlebags, or drove, as I did, a cart that screeched and shook under the weight of its cargo: small pieces of furniture, crockery, linen, sacks of food, looms, mattresses, baking trays and troughs. And covering it all, my father's patchwork wall-hanging. Despite the heat, we had to wear those ugly hooded capes which distinguished us from other citizens, with the red and yellow badge sewn on the front, and little children clung to their parents' skirts or smocks as if they feared they might change their minds and leave them behind, as they had done with so many things that morning.

As we advanced through the streets of our home town, first crossing the Cathedral Square, then passing through the gate of Sobreportes into the quarter of Sant Pere, I felt grief giving way to a mute anger. I drove our cart with growing fury, mistress of those sharp bends and uneven cobbles that had been smoothed by our own tread over the centuries. The screech of wheels rose above our sullen chanting, and I remembered how I had run around those streets and squares as a child. Farewell Girona, I thought; farewell childhood, farewell Vidal. Where was Vidal? Locked in his house after his daring visit to the *call*? Waiting outside the town to catch a last glimpse of me? Or would he be praying with other New Christians in the cathedral? The delegates of the Inquisition were keeping a close eye on all *conversos*. My anger and indignation grew when I thought how those monarchs had interfered with our lives and ruined the happiness Vidal and I could have shared, but at the same time I had a quiet feeling of satisfaction. If our King and his Queen thought they could take all our riches away they were mistaken, for my mind held one of the greatest treasures of the *call,* and it was leaving Girona with me, outwitting their vigilance. The original text had been returned to its hiding place, under the synagogue tiles, where it had already lain unharmed for a century, and where nobody, I was quite sure, would ever find it again. I whipped my horse and hurried on towards the northern gates of the second walls, looking defiantly at the rows of people who stood silently in the streets to watch us leave, at the woman who scolded her child for waving and calling out, 'Goodbye Abraham!' to his playmate. I was glad, in a way, that the time of waiting was over.

* * *

A week later I awoke, about an hour before dawn, and saw the line of the Pyrenean foothills marking the southern horizon. It was the eighth day of Av, the first day of August of 1492 in the Christian calendar. The previous evening, after what had seemed like an endless journey, we had passed through a border station near Cervera, where the Pyrenees lose height due to their closeness to the sea, and camped a few miles further north, on the bare hills of the coast of Roussillon.

I sat up and stretched my limbs, trying to ease the stiffness in my muscles. The campsite looked more like a battlefield, with human bodies scattered about like wounded soldiers. There were robes, jerkins and blankets strewn on the stony ground, and bundles of all sorts piled up here and there. During our march we had been joined by other groups of Jews and by the time we reached the frontier there must have been over a hundred of us. But we had arrived here in such a state of exhaustion, due to the heat and the difficulty of the mountain tracks, that we had not set up camp in an orderly fashion. Rising above this chaos was the sound of heavy breathing, of bodies stirring in their sleep, the whimpering of restless children, the incoherent mumbling of anxious dreams. I fixed my eyes on the mountains in front of me, and then, as I had found myself doing time and time again during the journey, fumbled for the key-box in my pocket, and slowly moved my forefinger over the letters and the designs that decorated the lid.

The day we left I had not seen Vidal in the streets of Girona, or outside the town, though more than once I wondered whether I could make out his shape in the distance; and then I began to imagine he might spring out from behind a tree at any moment to bid me farewell and tell me when and where he hoped to join me in exile. Mile after mile I resisted giving up all hope of seeing him, until at last that hope was lost, like the houses and the trees that were slowly disappearing into the distance. Now all I had of his was this box, and I had started to look for some message in the design carved round my name. The outer rim of the pattern was formed by a row of five-pointed stars—I counted thirty-two—and then came nine crescent moons. What did they mean? My Hebrew name meant 'moonlight.' Was this only a way of saying he loved me threefold three times, that his love had no end? Or was he asking me to wait for him for at least nine lunations? It might also refer to the three kabbalistic triads, like the three lilies on the cover of the book... What of the stars? Kabbalists spoke of the thirty-two paths to wisdom, the sum of the ten *sephiroth* and of the twenty-two letters of the Hebrew alphabet, since each letter, charged with symbolic, numerical and cosmic significance, is a key to the divine speculation in search of the name of God. Was Vidal at all familiar with such things? Was he telling me, through those symbols, that he was still faithful to the Law of Moses, that he was not a *meshummad*?

Touching the carved wood and letting my mind wander among such considerations gave me great comfort, and I offered a prayer of thanks to the Lord that the officials at the border had not seized my love token. They could easily have done so, for they had been ruthless, confiscating objects that we were by law allowed to take out of the country, things like clothes, crockery, and rugs, and causing much distress, especially among the older people. But I had been lucky. Not only had my trunk, the letter of exchange and my key-box all passed safely through in the crammed cart, but my white mare, a gift from Bernat Muntaner, which had been the object of covetous looks in all the villages through which we passed, had not been taken from me either. As for the books: just as Rabbi Astruc had anticipated, they had been systematically requisitioned. I had brought with me a few volumes from my grandfather's library, but was not allowed to take any of them through, and we were only permitted to keep the scrolls, documents and registries from the synagogue, which a *convers* identified one by one for the soldiers.

Though I had slept well, the weariness of the journey flooded over me again and I closed my eyes. Images from the long march filed past my mind. The highway, coming out of Girona, wide and dusty; rocks, stones, trees, forests, an occasional farm, a stream where the animals had stopped to drink and we had filled our water skins, the first bright glimpse of the sea; and then castles, monasteries, fortresses on the tops of craggy hills, bushes and dry grass, and the roads becoming narrow and stony as they lead uphill, with the dark mountains looming in the distance. Finally, the dazed faces as we stepped on foreign land, and the tears of relief because at last we would be able to rest without fear.

And here I was now, on the other side of the hills that had once formed the bulwarks of my universe, guided by the mysterious ancestral power of which I had first been aware in the graveyard on the day of the edict. Another image came to my mind: the moment when Rabbi Leví stopped the march outside the town walls, on the road that skirted the hill of Montjuïc, to pray and chant below our cemetery and bid a last farewell to our ancestors. The older women wailed loudly, and I no longer knew who I was weeping for, whether for Vidal, or my dead relatives, or just for myself. And yet, as we proceeded on the journey, I began to notice a dominant mood amid all the pain for what I was leaving behind in Girona, a feeling that, until then, had been dormant in me: the recognition of my own Jewishness. That is how I can best describe it, something significantly stronger and clearer than any devout feeling I may have had before, stronger even than the awareness of my personal link with Girona's mysticism. Despite the rejection shown to me by the Christians during the past weeks, I had not really given much thought to the consequence of that rejection and to our growing isolation from the rest of the Catalans. It was only now, at the sight of other groups like ours who had joined our party as we trudged on towards the border, that I came to consider not what made us unlike the Christians but what made us like each other. The sight of these families, with their characteristic clothes and chattels, the songs we now sang at night in the campsites, the food we ate, the stories we told, the Hebrew words with which we filled our Catalan language, were all things that had never meant much to me when I lived in Girona, when our lives had been woven into the common fabric of the town. But now, all those customary acts were precisely what held us together and gave us renewed courage with which to continue our journey into an uncertain future. And when, on the previous evening, we had reached the border station, I had found myself admiring the ingenious ways in which some of us had successfully hidden gold and silver.

One woman from Figueres had actually swallowed a handful of gold coins, deceiving the officials who searched us in a most abusive manner.

My mother was still sleeping soundly beside me, her ample body covered by the patchwork cloth from which she would not be parted for an instant. I stood up, smoothed my gown, and walked down the hill to where the horses had been tied for the night. Ours was in fact the only horse among the small crowd of mules and donkeys. Her name was *Falaguera*, which means 'Pleasing,' and she was a very beautiful, docile and resilient mare. I gave her fodder and water and made much of her, to show that I appreciated the great efforts she was making. During the last, uphill lap, she had carried not only our belongings, but also the weight of my mother and two heavily pregnant women, while I had guided the cart on foot. And today's march, with steep hills to descend, would be even more strenuous for her. However, Rabbi Leví assured us that we would be in Perpignan in a few days' time. Then *Falaguera* would be allowed to rest.

I thought I was the only person awake in the camp, but I was wrong. When I looked up I saw Rabbi Astruc standing a short distance away, his eyes fixed on the vast grey sea. His sleeveless surcoat, which he always wore over his shirt or smock, flapped like a sail in the sea breeze.

I walked over to him. He did not seem surprised to see me and his face bore an expression I had never noticed in him before. He looked excited, elated, triumphant.

'The treasures are safe,' he said. 'May the good Lord be praised!'

'What treasures, Astruc?' I asked.

He looked at me as if he hadn't really noticed my presence before, as if he'd been talking to himself. He took a while to answer.

'What treasures, you say? The book Alba, the words in the book that are in your head.' And then he added: 'But come over here. Sit down and look before you. Have you ever seen the sun rising from the sea?'

I shook my head.

'It is one of the Lord's most beautiful gifts,' he said, his voice dropping to a whisper, his eyes half closed, 'and today it bears a special significance since it marks the beginning of our exile from Sepharad.'

With these words he was implying that he saw our banishment as the first step towards the final return to the Promised Land; he had once told me that he believed the birth of the Messiah was imminent.

I sat next to him but said nothing, hoping my silence would dissuade him from his tiresome habit of interpreting everything he saw as a sign from Heaven. You stumbled on a stone: there was a reason for that stumbling. It was a warning that you must watch your step, learn to keep away from Evil. You lost something and spent hours looking for it. Ah, said Astruc, your patience was being put to the test. Whether it was the wind blowing, or the rain falling, a bird singing, someone sickening, or someone else being cured, everything, simply everything, bore a deep significance for Astruc. Sometimes I wished he would at least keep his opinions to himself and let life follow its course in silence.

I had grown accustomed to his company after two months of regular visits to our home, and had observed him long enough to sketch a portrait of him which was, by and large, a pleasing one, despite what I have just told you. He would come to the house, usually in the evenings, when his work with the community archives was done, and after greeting my mother, we would climb the stairs to my grandfather's study, the room that held so many abiding memories for me. There we would sit, he at the table, me at the other end of the room, while he made me recite at random parts of the text I was memorising. He had asked me to drop the title 'Rabbi' from his name when I addressed him, to make our exchanges less formal.

'Good, good,' he would say, stooping over the lectern, his eyes fixed on the text. 'You're working well, dear girl.' I would have been unable to memorise the book without his persistence and encouragement; besides, his kindness and concern for other people's troubles were truly exemplary. He was, through and through, a man of integrity, a good person. And yet, when he sat in Grandfather Ismael's chair, I could not help comparing the two men: Astruc, for all his knowledge of spiritual matters, for all his generosity of heart, lacked the poise that had been so natural in my grandfather. At times he seemed to be completely at odds with the world around him, so immersed in the Holy Writings that he lost touch with the material world. Was it a just question of age? Would Astruc, with time, also acquire that earthy affability that characterises truly wise men?

My mother, who was still sour about Vidal's disappearance, had discarded Astruc as a possible suitor, a prospect that would not even have crossed my mind but for her. 'His head is always in the clouds,' she said, 'and that's not the sort of husband a nice Jewish girl wants in times like these, when everything is topsy-turvy.' Nor had Astruc shown any interest in me as a woman of flesh and blood during those long spring evenings, when the perfume of the roses came floating in through the open window.

Now, sitting there, near the edge of the cliff, I saw the last lingering stars vanish and a pale blue light gently push the night away. Slowly, the colours of dawn began to fill the eastern sky, becoming increasingly warm and fiery. Then, suddenly, a bright speck emerged from behind the horizon and as the sun rose it made a path of light over the calm surface of the sea. I felt a shiver down my spine and goose pimples on my skin, and I clutched my knees tightly to steady myself: it was as though the colours now dancing on the sea were also shining within me. Was this the Shekhinah I beheld, the radiant presence of God on earth, His female aspect? In the pattern of the sacred Tree of God, the Shekhinah is represented by the lowest point and is therefore the ultimate receiver of all the attributes that emanate from the Crown, the uppermost point of the tree.

The Shekhinah is the Bride of God, His female aspect, who was banished from His side when Adam sinned. For Adam, seeing that the Shekhinah held within her the sap of all the other branches of the Tree of God, mistook her for the whole of the Godhead, and adored her separately, paying no attention to the Divinity as a whole. By doing so he shattered the unity of God's action and His perfect harmony between male and female, between judgement and mercy. The reunion of God and His Bride will signify redemption, the restoration of the perfect and infinite harmony that existed in the beginning of times. And then the chain of lilies will be linked forever, forming a complete circle, with no beginning and no end.

Those words from *The Chain of Lilies* made me think once more of Vidal, and the circle we had formed in our perfect union. My beloved Vidal, I said to myself, will you always be as close to me as you are now? The unspoken words skimmed the water's surface and sank like so many smooth pebbles thrown into the sea by children at play.

This sudden closeness to Vidal and the ecstatic feeling of being before a divine presence seemed far more real to me, far more meaningful, than the ordinary world around me. The beauty of that sunrise would soon have been forgotten without the feelings that came with it; and yet the two things were inseparable. Although my exile had only just begun, I suddenly understood that I had undertaken not one but two journeys, the physical and the spiritual, without knowing where either of them would take me.

Quite lost in thought, I had not noticed that Astruc was not looking at the sunrise but at me, and with searching penetration. The discovery made me feel uncomfortable, as if he had been prying into my thoughts, and I turned my head to face the camp.

'There is such a lot to do before we set off again,' I said, rising abruptly.

VI

A WEDDING

The town of Perpignan, capital of Roussillon, looked reassuring as we approached it from the south, tired of all the walking, of the dust that got in our eyes, of the pebbles that made our feet ache. Above the turrets of the walled castle, which looked pink in the early morning sun, the French royal flags fluttered like arms waving to greet us. Indeed, we had all livened up when Benjamin, the son of Moisès the silversmith, who was always well ahead of the rest of the group, had shouted from a bend in the road: 'Look, it's Perpignan: I can see it from here!' The pace of the procession had increased noticeably at the sound of those words, and faces had begun to look less weary with the anticipation of an end to our journey. It was a very thin hope, however. We were promised accommodation by the head of the Perpignan Jewry, but then rumours began to spread from group to group that the *call* of Perpignan was not a shadow of what it had been before the French took over.

Abraham, the talkative cobbler, had fallen silent during the first part of the journey. Deprived of his bench and table, his piles of leather and his small workshop, he felt like a fish out of water when it came to discussing his views in public. But as the journey proceeded, his old friends began to gather round him again in the evenings, recreating the former atmosphere of the shop, while Abraham, sitting on a rock or a bundle, busied his hands mending harnesses and shoes until nightfall. In that imaginary work-shop rumours were collected and given shape, hope was raised and quashed again, views were applauded or rejected. It was there that the first comments were heard about the impoverishment of the *call* of Perpignan and the neglect with which King Charles VIII of France treated all Jews in Roussillon.

It became less and less clear to Abraham and his com-panions what we were all going to do when we got there, or what sort of a welcome we would get from the delegates of the French Crown. On the other hand, said the optimists, in view of the extraordinary abundance of grapes that filled the vineyards, there was bound to be an immediate demand for labour.

That morning, with Perpignan already visible in the distance, we made a halt in a small oak thicket that showed signs of having sheltered other travellers. Someone pointed out that another party of exiles was probably ahead of us, perhaps Jews from Lleida and Saragossa, who would have crossed the mountains further west, at the Puigcerdà pass. 'The first to arrive in Perpignan will have an easier time,' said Abraham.

We left the horses tied to the trees on the edge of the wood and walked in, under the thick shady branches, until we came to a clearing where we found the remains of a cooking-fire. Flies were swarming around some leftovers—bits of fruit peel and a few crusts of bread—and my mother, who was very fastidious when it came to flies, quickly cov-ered the rubbish with earth. Suddenly, she threw her arms up and shouted: 'The buns, the buns and the honey cakes!'

'What are you talking about, Mother?' I asked.

'I forgot them! I left them in the oven!'

She looked so upset that I should have restrained my laughter, but I could not. It began as a giggle, but grew in intensity, until everyone else was laughing with me. In the end, even my mother joined in the merriment.

'Let's hope our honest Jewish cat got them before the bailiffs did the rounds of the *call*!' she said.

'Or even your honest Jewish mice!' said our next-door neighbour.

Just a little beyond the clearing, between two boulders, we discovered a spring with a small but steady flow of cool water. As we had not come across any fresh water since we had left the Pyrenees, shouts of 'Water! Running water!' were soon heard throughout the forest and it was not long before a queue of women had formed in front of it, all carrying their empty skins and jugs. It made me think of the book: *And God's wisdom is an everlasting fountain, flowing without pause around His creation; and those who are thirsty of Him can quench their thirst.*

Meanwhile a delegation of four members of the last council of Girona—Rabbi Leví, León Avinay, Salomó Serra and Salomó Samuel—as well as Astruc, who acted as their secretary, was setting off for Perpignan to talk to the authorities. I left the water queue and followed them to the edge of the wood. They climbed into a cart, and Astruc sat on the driver's seat, rolled up his sleeves and wrapped the reins round his hands. Then they set off down the gentle slope leaving a cloud of yellow dust behind them. And all the while I thought: Please God that we may settle here, so close to Sepharad and to Girona. Please God that I may be able to wait here for Vidal, who is sure to come for me as soon as he is able to. Then I returned to the spring and took a long drink of water to quench my thirst.

From the spring I made my way to a place between two large trees where my family had gathered, and as I passed from group to group I felt more than ever that I belonged to this enlarged community of exiled Catalan

Jews, and that their future would be also be my future. Old men and women, worn out by the exertion and the heat, sat under the trees, resting their heads against the trunks and fanning themselves with straw hats. Children ran about, some played 'horses' with a stick between their legs. Mothers prepared food and took an interest in one another's recipes. After an initial shyness, we were beginning to mingle in the campsites, sharing accounts of our past lives and often discovering family connections. Those my age had taken longer than the rest to make friends, but we all knew each other by name: Estelina, Sol, Aina, Ester; Aaró, Salomó, Daniel, Jacob. They were all pleasant enough, though none of the young men could compare in any way to Vidal, being mostly peasants from isolated hamlets who spoke coarsely and had never been associated with town people. But these were no times for comparisons, and I scolded myself for thinking that way: Do you think yourself superior just because you can read and write, and because you have, on occasion, worn silk dresses? And do you think Vidal is better than these Jewish lads, when he has abandoned his religion?

* * *

The delegation returned in the late afternoon, and those of us who had been waiting by the highway crowded round them immediately, eager for news. So many questions were being asked at once that Rabbi Leví, who was still sitting in the cart, stood up, raised his hand and demanded silence. 'Calm down, brothers. Let us have an orderly assembly in the clearing of the wood,' he said.

We made our way towards the clearing, and those who had not yet joined us left whatever they were doing, until we were all sitting in a wide circle around Rabbi Leví and the rest of the delegation, to hear of the outcome of their visit to Perpignan. We were first addressed by Salomó Samuel, the eldest of the group. But though he spoke slowly and clearly, those at the back of the circle began to call out: 'Louder, please!' at which he turned to Astruc and said: 'You tell them Astruc, you're good at speaking in public.'

So Astruc took over. He told us in plain words what they had seen in Perpignan. There were a few empty houses within the *call*, most of them very run down. A great deal of work would have to be done on them. A party from Lleida, Osca and other inland towns had arrived a few days ahead of us and had settled in the less dilapidated buildings; however, Rabbi Samuel Adret had kept his word to us, and it seemed that nobody would be left homeless. There were also some houses to rent, at varying prices. To avoid resentments and bad feelings, he said, the delegation had drawn up a list of all the families and assessed their needs and means, and it had already been decided where each of us would live. We would be told when we reached the town. He added that he hoped common sense would prevail over pettiness and that we would each accept our lot until more permanent arrangements could be made. The assembly ended with Rabbi Leví standing up and proclaiming: 'Let us give thanks to the Adonai for our wellbeing, that we have found a place to rest for as long as it may please Him.'

Now people were ambling back to their places in the camp, some raising their voices and saying they were being treated like a flock of stupid sheep, forgetting that an hour earlier they had not even known for certain whether they would be allowed in the town. My mother was engaged in conversation with Rabbi Leví on the subject of baking facilities in the *call*, wanting to know whether she would be able to continue baking for the community, and I went up to Astruc, who was standing a little apart, carefully rolling up a scroll with a list of names. Occasionally he would jerk his head back to free his wispy red beard, which kept getting caught in the paper. He turned around when he heard me call his name.

'Did you tell the rabbi in Perpignan about me?' I asked. 'When will I be able to start dictating?'

'Not yet, Alba, not yet. You will have to retain all you have learnt a while longer.'

'I don't know whether I'll be able to remember it for much longer. Perhaps, if we could get hold of ink and parchment —'

'If you tried to transcribe the words you have memorised, your imaginary house would collapse. It is a well-known fact that what has been memorised must be dictated, so that one's memory can flow uninterruptedly. You'll have to wait.'

'But how long, Astruc? Can't we find a scribe here?'

'Tomorrow we will begin to establish ourselves in Perpignan. But soon we may have to pack our bags again. We did not want to discourage everyone, but the rabbi was very clear; he said the rumours were that King Ferran was plotting something, and that we might have to leave the county soon, either by order of the King of France or by order of Ferran himself, if he catches up with us. As for the book, he said that this was not the place to release such valuable information, for there are periodic confiscations of Jewish goods. And once you have dictated the text you run the risk of not being able to remember it again in all its details. He advises you to travel to Venice, since of all the Jewries this side of the Mediterranean, that is at present the most established one, the safest too. The journey from here would take a fortnight or three weeks, travelling by ship from Marseilles to Genoa and then crossing overland on horseback.'

Before I had time to reply, my mother, who had been standing within earshot, butted in: 'You don't imagine I am going to allow my daughter to travel all that way, through the Lord knows how many deadly perils, just to go and dictate a book. Haven't we enough trouble without all this? I am quite shocked at what you are proposing. My daughter is a respectable girl, the only treasure I possess, and you suggest she goes off to some distant land, leaving her poor mother in this God-forsaken town of Perpignan.'

'Madona Regina,' answered Astruc, looking at my mother with sudden intensity, 'your sense of responsibility towards your unmarried daughter is admirable, and allow me tell you that I share it with you. But she would be back within a month or six weeks at the most. And since Alba has no father or brother to accompany her, she could go with me, I could protect her.'

'She shall not go anywhere at all, my learned friend,' retorted my mother. 'Unless—'

'Unless I marry her first, is that what you were about to say, Madona Regina?'

There was a deathly silence. Rabbi Leví did not know which way to look. I was going to laugh, then realised that Astruc had not meant this as a joke. He was looking at me in the same way as he had looked at me on that previous morning, when we sat on the cliff watching the sunrise.

'Unless she first got married and her husband could go with her,' my mother said, 'but I was not thinking of anyone in particular. There are plenty of marriageable young men among us now. It would then be all right for Alba to travel, if that was God's will.'

My mother was looking at me too, her words slowing down as she ended her sentence, waiting for me to say or do something. But all I could think was that she had gone raving mad.

'Well?' she said looking at me straight in the face. 'Well, girl, have you lost your tongue?' Then she waved her hand energetically at Astruc and Rabbi Leví to indicate that she wanted them to leave us alone, and they obeyed at once.

'Alba, dear daughter,' she said, 'these are strange times when strange things happen which I can do nothing to control.' Though she appeared calm, I could see that she was agitated. My mother was often like that, trying to look stronger than she really was. Somehow, that made me respect her all the more. 'But one thing is certain: marry you I must, and the sooner the better. Only last night I was talking to Cousin Isaac about that young man from Olot who works as a smith with his father. A smith can make a living anywhere, and this family have managed to bring all their tools with them. He would make a good match, in the circumstances.'

'A young man from Olot?' My voice sounded like an echo, as if it had not come out of my mouth, and the words were senseless.

'But what will Astruc do?' she went on. 'He might be very learned, he might be very good at drawing up lists and raking up lost papers, but how can a registrar and a legal advisor find work outside his own community? How can a man who always has his nose in a scroll of parchment make a good enough living? And yet,' she went on, changing the tone of her voice, and lifting her eyes to Heaven above, 'I somehow feel that perhaps the Almighty, blessed be His Name, wishes this union. After all, Astruc is an older man and a worldlier one. He was married once, you know, but his wife died before giving him any children. He would definitely be a more appropriate protector for you in foreign lands.'

'But Mother—'

'So Isaac and I will make the necessary arrangements,' she continued, seemingly unperturbed. 'We'll speak to Astruc tonight and see what assets he has brought with him.'

'But Mother! Vidal! He said he would come and fetch me.'

'Don't talk to me about Vidal!' she interrupted, suddenly angry. 'Forget him. Your story with Vidal is in the past, Alba, as past as Girona and as past as everything that was left behind in that town. I'm talking to you about Rabbi Astruc, a good man if ever there was one. I am your mother and your owe me obedience.'

And she went on to speak about my dowry, about Muntaner's bill of exchange and a thousand other particulars concerning the marriage contract. I felt my world falling apart, but could not think of anything else I could say to prevent it.

When she had finished speaking she looked at me again and repeated: 'So? Have you nothing to say? You know Astruc well. Are you not happy about this marriage?'

In my mind I was back on the wooden bridge over the river Onyar, with Vidal only a few steps from me, as I watched the water taking our love away with it. Now it was also taking away our hope. There was nothing left but to give in to the current. 'If it pleases you and it pleases the Lord, blessed be He,' I said, almost inaudibly.

'Good. That's settled then,' said my mother, raising her voice and signalling to Astruc, who was discreetly talking to Rabbi Leví a short distance away. He walked back to us.

'Astruc,' said my mother, in the same firm tone she had used with me. 'I'll speak to you later, but I think you and Alba had better have a word with one another now.'

And with that she turned and walked away, calling

out Isaac's name. Rabbi Leví also scuttled off.

Astruc came closer. But before he had started on a long persuasive discourse I said: 'I'll marry you, Astruc, if that's what you think is best.'

'Yes, I do,' he answered in a half whisper. He took my hand in his, pressing it lightly. Then he looked at me and smiled. Behind him, in the clearing of the oak thicket, I could see a group of women cooking a pot of beans, wiping the sweat off their foreheads with bared arms. Two men were mending a cartwheel. Others were rearranging packages and bundles. Life maintained its steadfast course, building invisible walls and roofs around our precarious community.

I waited for a while, but the expected discourse did not follow, and for once I saw he could find no fitting words for the situation. Then, suddenly realising that he was still holding my hand in his, he let go awkwardly, turned on his heels and walked back with hesitant steps towards the camp, aware that I was following him with my eyes.

There goes my betrothed, I said to myself. My mother is right. The world has turned upside down.

That night I hardly slept, and when I did doze off I dreamed that Vidal burst in during the wedding ceremony and killed Astruc with a sword.

* * *

The following morning, Astruc set off towards Perpignan with the first group of homeless Jews, among them the two women who were on the point of giving birth. He was to stay there to help make accommodation arrangements and instruct each family as they arrived. We had been advised to enter the town in small groups, so as not to call excessive attention to our arrival, and my mother and I spent two more days in the camp. During that time there was little to do and I took to sitting on a smooth grey rock just outside the oak thicket and looking out towards the distant sea, going over and over the words that were stored in my memory house, so as not to forget them. It was, moreover, the only way I could remain calm. Only once, when I was resting from my mental exercise, did I try to envisage daily life as Astruc's wife, and to kindle the almost brotherly affection I felt for him, and the respect I owed him as my tutor, into something warmer and brighter. I tried to imagine him in domestic situations; I even pictured Astruc and myself, with three or four children, all with their father's red curly hair, sitting around the dinner table. But I found no joy in those imaginary settings.

When my mother and I finally arrived in Perpignan with the last group of exiles, Astruc was waiting for us by the town gates, his gaze absent, lost among the people coming and going, and when he saw us a timid smile touched his lips. We made our way up with our loaded cart towards the *call*, which was just below the royal palace; the midday sun was beating down on our heads. I sensed a deep hostility in the locals who stood by to watch us, for although they said nothing, they seemed to be thinking: You're not wanted here, foreigners. This land is ours, this air is ours, and we are not going to give you anything!

The house allotted to my mother and me, which we shared with the family of my cousin Isaac, was within the *call*. I think it was probably one of the worst houses, with only two habitable rooms, and a well with putrid water that had to be cleaned of dead rats and cockroaches. The roof was missing half its tiles, and almost all the beams were loose and hollowed by woodworm. Astruc stayed with us for a good while to help with the most urgent repairs, but he didn't make any reference to our betrothal or treat

92

me any differently than usual, and it was not until we had stopped working and were sitting in the only clean corner of the house, that the subject of the wedding was brought up.

'Have you made any arrangements yet, Astruc?' asked Isaac.

'That's just what I was about to ask you,' said my mother, before he had time to reply. 'The sooner you leave on this voyage, the sooner I'll have you both back here with us. Besides, the girl can't keep all those words in her head much longer, I'm sure. She'll get ill if she goes on like this.'

'I've already spoken to the rabbi of Perpignan,' replied Astruc, looking first at my mother and at Isaac, and then, for what seemed like an endless moment, at me. 'He says we can get married any time, so I thought we could have the ceremony a week from today, for the new moon.'

'That sounds all right to me,' said my mother, and turning towards me she arched her eyebrows, gave me a meaningful look, and asked: 'Is it all right with you?'

At first I did not understand, then I realised that she was asking me about my monthly cycles. Strange though it may seem, until then I had not even thought about the more intimate aspects of my marriage to Astruc.

'Oh! Yes, yes,' I blurted out.

There was a long, awkward silence. Nobody knew what to say. We were like boats floating aimlessly about on a night sea. Sitting on the floor with her two children Coloma looked at me with her melancholy eyes and her expression of perpetual dissatisfaction. Suddenly, Astruc stood up, made some vague gesture and left.

* * *

93

The next seven nights we slept crammed into the two musty rooms. The heat persisted, bugs multiplied. The days were spent cleaning up the house, and we saw very little of our travel companions. We had all dispersed into different parts of the *call*, and some families had even gone to nearby villages; the sense of unity that had given us so much strength during the march was now lost. When we did meet any of our old neighbours or camp friends, it was only to hear about some calamity. 'Our house is a complete ruin...' 'Bonadona has fallen ill with worry.' 'Raquel's baby was born dead.' And since none of us had any ready money, we had to borrow from merchants or moneylenders in order to pay the rents and cover our daily needs. Dejection soon took hold of us.

The wedding took place a week after our arrival in Perpignan, city of false hopes, in the small synagogue of the Jewish quarter. The night before the ceremony, my mother had cried and pulled her hair in despair, remembering her own marriage. Sighing repeatedly as she spoke, she told me how she had been accompanied by numerous relatives who loaded her with gifts (most of which, she recalled bitterly, she had been obliged to sell or leave behind in Girona). She told me how the marriage feasts lasted three or four days, with song and dance and good food. 'And now my only daughter is to marry when we have lost everything we ever had!' she wailed.

But to be fair to her, once she had given vent to her sorrow she did her best to liven things up a bit. In the morning she fussed over me and took me to the *mikveh* for the ritual baths ordered by the Law. Later, when we returned to the house, she helped me put on my red tunic, which had no gold buttons now, for they had been removed in Girona and left behind, and she placed a coronet of white flowers on my head, which she had somehow managed to make for me amid all that misery and chaos. She even invited two or three of my girlfriends, whose families lived nearby, to come and celebrate my nuptials 'by the book', and made a plate of sweetmeats for them. Rosa and Coloma joined the chorus when the girls started singing that pretty song, the one that begins: *Under the shade of an orange tree sit the bride and her groom*, Coloma in her low voice, full of dark sentiment, Rosa with a voice like a goldfinch; but I listened absently, almost unaware that it was me they were singing about, that I was the bride in the song, sitting under an orange tree in blossom. In truth I cannot say how I felt or what thoughts went through my mind, because everything about that day still seems to me like a strange dream in which I was only a rag doll, with no will of my own.

In the afternoon my mother took me to the synagogue, where I was to marry Astruc ben Salomó, of the town of Besalú, Girona, of thirty-two years of age, son of Esdras ben Salomó and of Blanca Hebrea. Rabbi Leví and Abraham the cobbler acted as witnesses. Also present were Isaac, Coloma and their two children. We were married in a walled garden behind the synagogue by Samuel Adret, rabbi of the town of Perpignan, with the same rites as I had always seen in Girona weddings: Astruc and I stood under the *huppah*, and the rabbi blessed the cup of wine before offering it to us to drink, as a symbol that we were to share everything in our lives. At the betrothal ceremony, Astruc had put his hand in the breast pocket of his surcoat and pulled out a gold ring, which he slipped onto my finger; he must have bought it in Perpignan, the Lord only knows with what money. It was a special ceremonial ring, crowned by a miniature house, so finely wrought that one could see all the details of its construction: its roof tiles, its columns and arches, its tiny doors and windows, all in perfect proportion. And when he said the words: 'Behold you are consecrated unto me with this ring, according to the Law of Moses and Israel,' I felt all the divine force of that sentence, as if the words were coming from afar, an ancestral echo. I looked at Astruc anxiously, hoping to be able to please him, realising that the house he had placed on my hand represented not only the home that he wished for us, in which we would live and have children, but the memory house in which I kept the words of *The Chain of Lilies*.

After the wedding blessings we all went outside. The rabbis and Abraham the cobbler congratulated us, and all the members of my family embraced me tenderly, one after the other: my mother, Isaac, Coloma, Rosa. Little Josuè, in his mother's arms, waved goodbye to me with his hand, as it was the only gesture he knew.

'She's not gone yet!' cried my mother, and we all laughed.

We stood there in the street for a while, not quite sure what to do next. Under normal circumstances a banquet would have been arranged in the bride's house. But we had no table, or chairs, or tablecloths, nothing, in fact, worthy of the occasion.

'I've been thinking,' began my mother 'that since we have no adequate house for the banquet, we could walk out of town and find a pretty spot for a little celebration. I've brought some bread and a bottle of wine. As for tonight, Madona Dolça, the rabbi's wife, has generously offered a comfortable bedroom for the bride and groom.'

But the rabbi's wife, a small plump woman with a bright smile, had just come out of her house next to the synagogue to offer us her congratulations, and had overheard my mother. 'But, no! You must come to our house right now. I will set the table and get some chairs out in no time.'

So we all followed her into the house and she guided us to the dining room, which was pleasantly cool, and well furnished. It had various oil lamps hanging from the ceiling and a tall cupboard with fine designs carved into the wood, in which Madona Dolça kept her crockery and her table linen. When the table was ready my mother brought out a loaf of bread she had baked that morning, while I was still asleep. It was shaped like a nosegay with a bright blue ribbon tied round it, so pretty it seemed a shame to eat it. She had also made some honey cakes (which she had not forgotten in the oven this time) and had brought a bottle of sweet wine. Madona Dolça came and went, with her smiling face framed by a white toque; she served us a delicious fish soup, thick with vegetables and sliced bread, and her husband produced a few bottles of clear white wine. We had not eaten so well for a long time, and with the good food our spirits rose and our conversation grew more lively. Halfway through the dinner Madona Dolça announced that they were going to let us use their own bedroom that night. I protested, but she would not listen to me. 'This is your special night,' she said patting my hand. 'And may the Lord bless you both with true happiness and many healthy children.'

'And may you live to see it,' I answered.

Through a small window opposite my place at the table I could see the sky change colour in the sunset, and soon the first stars shone on a pale background, with that delicate and timid glimmer that can only be seen on the first days of the new moon. Soon after, when I was saying goodbye to Isaac and my mother at the door, the slim moon was already visible. Rabbi Samuel, who had also seen the curved thread of light, walked out into the front courtyard, and raising his hands to Heaven recited the familiar words: 'Blessed art thou, O Lord our God, King of the universe, by whose word the heavens were created...who bade the moon renew itself, a crown of glory unto those that have been upborne by him from the womb, who in the time to come will themselves be renewed like it, to honour their Creator for his glorious kingdom's sake. Blessed art thou, O Lord, who renewest the months.' Never had the blessing of the new moon held such uncertainty for me, or for any of us.

It was not long before I was lying in the large soft bed, waiting for Astruc to come into the room. I had drunk more wine than I was used to, and my head was spinning, but I summoned all the strength in my being in order appear calm and contented and banish the image of Vidal, once and for all, from my mind.

Astruc came in and looked away when he saw my naked arms and loose hair spread over the pillow. He came nearer the bed, but instead of coming closer still and embracing me, he covered my arms with the sheet and sat on a stool by my side. Then, taking a deep breath, he said:

'I was in earnest, Alba, when I said I would marry you to protect you on this journey. You have pleased me, and you have pleased the Adonai, by undertaking the arduous task I set you. But I am not going to lie with you until we have a home in which to settle. After a long discussion with our host, the rabbi of Perpignan, concerning my duties as a spouse before the eyes of the Lord, I have concluded that this marriage is exceptional, for it would not normally have taken place until we had found somewhere to establish ourselves and have children. I do not think the Lord will think it sinful if I do not lie with you while we are travelling. Besides, I know you were about to marry Vidal Rubèn before the edict of expulsion took him away from you, and although some time has passed since then, and I have come to know your soul, your mind, and your temperament, I have never had occasion to court you as a lover, not even in these ten days since we were betrothed, being too concerned with other matters, as you well know. I hope, my dear wife, that with the help of the Almighty, blessed be His Name, you will learn to love me. And now, rest well, for we have a long day ahead of us tomorrow.'

I looked at him in surprise, touched by his gentle manners, relieved at the thought that, for the time being at least, I did not need to know him carnally. The room seemed to fill with peace and I murmured: 'You are a good man, Astruc.' Then I quickly fell asleep.

VII

ON THE ROAD TO VENICE

That night I dreamed that I was standing on the stone bridge in Girona. It looked different, as familiar things often do in dreams. On either side of it rose two tall golden pillars, each one surmounted by a crown of precious stones that sparkled in the light of the setting sun. I was watching Vidal walk away from me, and from the way his back shook, I knew he was crying. I called out his name, and the sound of my voice made the water move so that the reflection of the precious stones glittered and their colours mingled, forming multicoloured designs like those on my father's wall-hanging. Vidal was heedless of my call, so I tried to run after him, but my sandals seemed fixed to the cobble-stones of the bridge and I could not move. Suddenly, a magnificent ship came into view, with blue silk sails and a dragon's head on the prow. It glided down the river but when it reached the bridge it stopped, for its masts hit the railings, banging against them insistently with a hard metallic sound. Then I saw that there was no one on the ship; it was adrift, with nobody to man it. I cried after Vidal again: 'Vidal, come with me on board this ship! If we remove the masts it will easily pass under the bridge and will take us to the sea. Then we'll find a land where we can live together.' At that, Vidal turned his head, but it was no longer Vidal, it was Astruc, who came smiling towards me.

I awoke with a start and when I looked about me it took me a while to remember where I was. Sunlight streamed through the cracks in the wooden shutters, bleaching a bunch of white daisies on a corner table and the white ribbons that were tied to the dark fluted bedposts. I was alone. The empty space on the double bed showed that Astruc had slept on it, but without getting under the sheets. On a chair were my clothes for the journey: petticoat, bodice, grey skirt, cape and a white married woman's toque. On the floor, my shoes, and a bag in which I had packed my red tunic and a few other personal items. Then I realised that I could still hear the banging sound I had heard in my dream. It came from outside. I got out of bed, walked over to the window to see what it was and rested my head on one of the shutters, opening its twin just enough to look down into the courtyard without being seen. There, in the patio, was Astruc, helping the smith shoe our horses.

His shirtsleeves were rolled up high, showing a milk-white freckly skin and bulging muscles. I wondered how he had developed such strong arms and it occurred to me that I knew very little about this unusual man who was now my husband. I did know, because it was mentioned in the marriage contract, that he had married his first wife, Gabriela Leví in his native town of Besalú in the year 5245 of our calendar, and that she had died childless two years later. I wondered vaguely what Gabriela had died of, and then, less vaguely, how deeply he had felt her loss. Through half-closed eyes and half-closed windows my gaze stole over him in an effort to capture some of the thoughts and feelings that I felt sure he kept locked in himself. But the absence of love on my part made it impossible for me to penetrate his soul.

At that moment I saw my mother coming up the steep alley towards the rabbi's house. She was carrying a heavy basket and walked with some difficulty. She looked unkempt and haggard, with wisps of greying hair sticking out from under her dark veil. I realised that she was losing her strength and had aged suddenly with our exile. She did not smile when she passed Astruc but they seemed to exchange polite greetings.

A few minutes later, when I went down to the kitchen, she was standing with her back to the door, looking out of the window; the basket she had been carrying was at her feet. Astruc and the smith were still there, shoeing the two horses: Astruc's mule, and *Falaguera*, my white mare.

'Good morning, Mother,' I said.

She turned and looked at me with a sorrowful expression. 'Do you really have to go?' she asked.

'Would I have married him if I didn't think I had to go?' I answered dryly, trying to suppress the anger that her question provoked in me.

We were both silent for a while. Then she lifted the basket onto the table and removed the white linen napkin that covered it. 'Here are some provisions for the journey,' she said. 'Buns, meats and apples.'

'But, with what money? You must have had to borrow it...'

'Very early this morning I sold my embroidered silk dress at the market place. Yes, I know, we have the bill of exchange; but Isaac told me not to take it to any notary in Perpignan until we know how long we'll be staying here. It's registered in Naples and transactions are very slow between the two countries. Nothing but paperwork, authorisations, journeys from one place to another. They take forever!'

'Your beautiful tunic made of silk from Father's loom.'

'And what else could I do, Alba? What were you going to live on during the journey? Had you thought about that?'

102

She paused and her eyes grew vague and distant. 'Besides,' she added, as if she were only speaking to herself, 'what need have I for that silk dress now? It only brought back memories of Girona, of all that. I have the wall-hanging. I'll never sell that. They'd have to wrench it from me.'

She gave me a melancholy look that reminded me of autumn evenings, of songs sung low to a sleepy child. Then, raising a hand, she straightened and rearranged the white linen veil that for the first time covered my head and shoulders.

'Look at you, Alba, you're a married woman,' she sighed. 'Now remember, you must be meek and obedient in your husband's presence. I know you well, and I know how proud and headstrong you can be. You are now his servant in the eyes of the Lord, blessed be He.'

'I will keep my pride to myself, Mother,' I answered. 'Have I not already accepted everything that has come my way without complaining?'

'You have accepted too much, if you ask me,' she answered. 'Astruc and Rabbi Leví had no right to require a young girl like you to memorise all those holy words. I'm sure it will weaken your mind. And now there's the danger of this journey to Venice.' And raising her hands to Heaven, she added: 'Oh Lord, Creator of the universe, protect my Alba.'

'If that is His wish, He will, Mother.'

'While you are away I will try to set up a large oven and work as a baker again. Every day I will pray for your safety.'

At that moment Astruc walked into the kitchen.

'The horses are ready,' he announced.

We bade our farewells in the house, not wishing to draw the neighbours' attention to our departure, and thanked Rabbi Samuel and his wife for their hospitality. Then we began our journey to Venice, leading our horses first down the alleyway, then through the dark archway that led to a wider road, and finally down that steep hill all the way to the eastern gates of the city. There were not many people about at that time of the morning; only a few women with brooms and pails sprinkling water on the bit of street outside their front doors, to refresh the atmosphere and help keep the dust from rising.

Once we were out of Perpignan and on our way to Narbonne, we mounted our horses and I turned my head a few times, until the town with its red walls looked as small as a pin box.

The country on the eastern side of Perpignan was also covered with vineyards and fruit trees, but gradually, as we headed towards the hills, the earth became wilder, until it turned yellow and dry, with large patches of white rock; nothing of any use grew there, only thick bushes all leaning towards the same side due to the persistent force of the wind. The weather was still very hot, and when the horses had finished climbing the rocky path to the top of the first hill, I saw with dismay that a new stretch of road extended before us, long and deserted, with no houses or hamlets to break the monotony. I was not used to riding on horseback and all my bones were aching.

Around noon we came across a group of travellers who had dismounted to drink fresh water at a roadside spring, under the shade of a pine tree.

'Let's stop for a while, Astruc,' I said, 'I'm parched.'

'I have plenty of water left in the cask,' he answered, bowing his head gravely to the travellers, who looked at us and probably wondered, as I did, why we were not stopping.

When we had passed them by and were out of earshot I complained:

'How do you think I'm going to last with no water and no rest, Astruc? Why couldn't we stop?'

Astruc gave me an angry look. 'But I'm supposed to protect you! Didn't you see how they looked at you? Didn't you see what might have happened to you? You're too innocent Alba, too innocent! Didn't you see the lust in their eyes, the violence of their intentions?'

I was so taken aback I did not even answer. The three young men we had passed at the spring had looked at us with great curiosity, it was true; after all, we must have looked foreign to them. But lust or violence? No, I thought, it's Astruc himself who feels a violent desire for me, without even knowing it. His reaction has nothing to do with his zeal for protecting the kabbalistic text in my head.

Despite the heat and the discomfort, our journey was cheered by the sight of the shimmering sea on the right, forming inlets and lagoons among the low bare hills, and before sunset we had reached Narbonne, a town of white stone and graceful courtyards, about which I had heard so much from Grandfather Ismael. The Jewry of Narbonne had old ties with Girona: three centuries earlier, this had been the home of Isaac the Blind, the first pure kabbalist, the inspirer and master of many of the Girona kabbalists. And it was here that Astruc and I were going to find the first link in the human chain that would lead us, we hoped, to the city of Venice.

This was a man called Simon, a jeweller, and a cousin of Dolça, the wife of the rabbi of Perpignan. We found his shop easily enough, on the main street of the Jewish quarter, and as soon as I stepped into that panelled room with its shiny bronze scales presiding over the counter, I felt its serene atmosphere enveloping me.

Simon made his appearance from behind a curtain, holding a small metal rod with two magnifying glasses attached to it, one for each eye, I presumed, and in a deep rich voice inquired politely what we wanted. He wore a simple smock of dark red cloth and the pleats under his belt fell with precision and grace. His beard was short and well kept, his features bold, and his dark eyes irradiated a warm intellect. He was delighted, he said, with news of his cousin Dolça, and it would be easy for him to help us. It so happened that the following day a group of merchants was heading for the port of Marseilles, from where they were taking a ship to Genoa. He would ask if we could travel with them. They would not refuse, he said, because they owed him more than one favour, and their company would guarantee our safety on the high road and a good passage by sea. Once in Genoa we were to seek out a man called Salomone Canetti, the rabbi in charge of the main synagogue there, who would be able to arrange for the journey by land to Venice. Meanwhile, if we had nowhere else to go, we were welcome to spend the night in a small outhouse behind the shop. There he kept a straw mattress on which he sometimes rested during the day, when business was slack.

'The Lord be praised for your kindness,' answered Astruc.

'Where would we be, brother, in times like these, if we did not help one another?' replied Simon.

And I thought: things are going too smoothly. How long will our luck last?

Early next morning, we said goodbye to our host and began the second stage of our journey. The merchants in question were three Christian brothers, with booming voices and coarse manners. Their wares, which they carried in a small cart pulled by a mule and in the saddle-bags of their horses, consisted of fine pottery and small bottles of perfumed oils, rose-water and the like. They also carried embroidered cloths and damasks, as well as rolls of a very fine gauze which, Astruc informed me, came from the north of France.

Being the only woman in the group I rode in silence close to Astruc, and I slipped gratefully into the role of young, shy wife, the shadow of my husband. Over the jingle-jangle of the metal cart-frame and the steady trot of the horses came the sound of the merchants' shouts and laughter. And as we moved along, passing fields and farmhouses, vegetable patches and cattle, passing men and women at their toil, watching the shadows of the trees slowly elongate in the afternoon sun, I thought only of travelling forward, almost forgetting the aim of my journey, surrendering to fate, as a child surrenders to sleep when his mother gently rocks him. I felt at one with the visible world which was also moving blindly into tomorrow, following the unfathomable will of the Creator, and I understood how every single thing is linked to something else, and that other thing to yet another, so that the world forms a fabric of firmly woven strands, producing infinite combinations of patterns and colours, like the silks and damasks of my father's loom.

It was almost dark when the outline of a walled hamlet came into view.

'We're stopping here!' yelled the cart driver.

'Where are we?' asked Astruc.

'Close to the city of Béziers,' answered another merchant. 'But this inn is better than any you'd find in the town. I'm afraid the innkeeper has a dislike for Jews. But then that's your affair, not mine!'

As we approached the hamlet a ragged youth slowly opened the wooden gates, smiling idiotically and bobbing his head up and down until the last horse had gone through into the enclosure. Then he took the tired beasts to the trough, at the other end of the long cobbled patio.

The inn was a large house with a wide front staircase of six or eight steps, which lent the place a certain elegance, and on either side of the main building, filling the patio's rectangle, were the outhouses, stables, barns and chicken runs. The three merchants bounded up the stairs to the entrance and burst in without knocking. We were left standing in the patio, our bags on the ground.

'I'll go in for some fresh water,' said Astruc. 'You wait for me by the front door.'

We went up the stairs and I waited outside. Astruc left the door ajar, and I caught a glimpse of the large dining hall, with its two long tables and rows of wine barrels on either side. There was great rejoicing and patting of backs as the merchants greeted their friends, and two young women in very tight bodices hurried to and fro, setting jugs of wine and plates full of olives and bread on the tables. I saw Astruc standing patiently by the kitchen door, waiting for the water. No one seemed to be paying any attention to him, until at last, after what felt like an endless wait, I saw him asking the innkeeper again. The innkeeper, a very fat woman who was clearly enjoying the merchants' latest tales, stopped laughing and looked him up and down with obvious disdain, shaking her head. But one of the merchants must have put in a good word for Astruc, because she then grabbed a jug of water from the table and handed it brusquely to him, as if to say: 'Take this and shut up!' I still do not understand what happened next, or how Astruc could have been so clumsy, but somehow the jug of water fell and broke. The innkeeper raised her arms and waved them about in a threatening manner, shouting: 'Get out you dirty Jew! You're not wanted in your country and you're not wanted here either, you water poisoners. You bring ill luck wherever you go! Out! Out, I say!'

Astruc did not even flinch. He strode proudly out of the tavern, then took me by the arm, and said: 'Only a small matter, Alba. We still have some water in our carafe, though it could be a good deal fresher.'

We slept on our cloaks out in the open. I did not mind. On the contrary, I enjoyed lying under the heavenly vault, observing the intense glow of the stars. I felt the peace of the universe penetrating my soul, soothing it with its harmony. Its unerring balance became mine, and I felt the wakeful and the dormant, the male and the female and all the other opposites of which the world is composed, entering me. It was like a blessing, a serenity that came from the night sky, the same sky that I had observed as a child in Girona with Grandfather Ismael, when he would take me up to the balcony outside his study and show me the signs of the zodiac and the situation of the planets. The same sky that Vidal might be scanning at that very moment, the same sky that would continue to glimmer mysteriously to the end of time. And yet such awe-inspiring beauty was only a very distant echo of the beauty of the Creator, which is beyond human understanding, as are all of His holy attributes. For this much I had learnt from the kabbalistic book I had memorised: that God created the universe through the emanations of His being into four spheres or worlds, like the four letters of His unspeakable name, and that our world of matter stood at the lowest rank.

That night the world of matter, which at times, I admit, seems coarse and unworthy of being called 'the Creator's garment,' looked magnificent, and I thanked the Lord for giving me sight with which to behold it. As the book said: *No one can count the stars but the Creator, for His power is infinite. And therefore it is written: 'He counteth the number of the stars; he giveth them all names.'*

As I lay there, looking up at the myriad of stars, and

thinking of the vastness of the universe, I felt a flash of understanding, similar to the one I had glimpsed in the bathhouse. That day, lying on a comfortable bench, breathing in the scented vapours of the hot water, I had grasped the idea of the ascension towards a more perfect knowledge of God. Now, lying at night on the hard surface of the earth, I had the certainty that a ray of divine light was descending towards my soul, reassuring me that what I was doing was pleasing to the Lord. Perhaps, I thought, Astruc was right when he said there was some holy purpose to this new exodus. My husband believed and maintained that our expulsion had come about because the excessive wickedness of mankind had broken the balance of the cosmos, and that we, the Jews from Sepharad, had been chosen to restore order through piety and righteousness. And our first act of piety, he said, was to carry the lantern of the Girona mystics across rivers and seas, and to wherever was required, for the glory of the Lord. Perhaps that was why I felt such peace within me despite the turbulent events that had recently taken place all around me and why, lying there next to my sleeping husband, I was as unperturbed as the starlit sky above.

VIII

EVIL OMENS

The port of Marseilles was like an anthill. I had never seen so much activity, not even on high market days in Girona, and the air was heavy with the smell of tar and fish. Astruc and I weaved our way through heaps of crates, planks, ropes and sackcloth, and between groups of arguing traders. We were deafened by the incessant yelling of sailors who repeated orders from prow to stern and from deck to mast, and the thick-throated cries of fishmongers selling their fish. Dockers, clad in dark blue smocks, loaded or unloaded, their faces straining under the heavy weights, and, all along the sea-front, vessels of every kind were moored: small fishing boats, tall merchant vessels with fortified forecastles, large and small galleys, and sailing ships. I knew very little about boats, which until then I had only seen in pictures, but Astruc was telling me the names of each one as we passed it, and of the ones that were anchored in the middle of the bay, and was explaining their differences.

'And look over there,' said Astruc, pointing his finger into the distance. 'Do you see that round vessel with three masts? That's a caravel. They're sturdy ships, but also very light, and well equipped for making long journeys. I remember that just before we left Girona a Jew from Valencia came to see me. He was looking for some papers related to his wife, and talking about this and that, he told me that someone called Cristòfor Colom, a Portuguese navigator—or did he say Italian?—was about to set off with three of these caravels on an expedition to the Indies across the western seas. So just imagine how far that ship can go...'

The truth is that Astruc was not in the habit of talking about such worldly matters as ships, nor about men who set off on expeditions, but he was trying to keep my mind off the pain I was feeling after having to part with *Falaguera*. I would have wanted to leave her stabled in Marseilles until our return, following the example of the merchants with whom we had travelled from Narbonne. But Astruc did not trust the stable owner enough and decided to sell him both our horses then and there. I protested, I pleaded with him, I even cried, forgetting the promise I had made to my mother of not contradicting my husband. But it was to no avail. Astruc had been inflexible: we needed the money, he said later by way of explanation and besides, we sold the two animals for a good price. All this sounded very sensible, yet no logical reasoning could convince me, and while I gazed at those unfriendly ships I could not help remembering the sad, knowing look in *Falaguera*'s eyes when I had patted her back and put my face against her muzzle to say goodbye.

We were walking along the docks now. Astruc was still talking.

'We're heading for that three-masted ship,' he said, 'the one with a forecastle and another castle in the stern. There's a sailor climbing up its mainmast now, see? and he's unfurling the sails. The merchants have told me that the weather is good for sailing and that we'll set off this very morning. If the winds are favourable, it should get us to Genoa in four days. Oh, do cheer up,' he said in sudden desperation, seeing that he was not succeeding in distracting me.

We were now close enough to the vessel to appreciate its graceful deep curve from prow to stern and the pretty mock turrets on the castles. I forced a smile and tried to think with pleasure of the voyage ahead. The Narbonne merchants had shown us a map of Italy during the journey (a large square parchment in coloured inks) and I had learned the names of the towns we would go through on our way to Venice: Tortona, Piacenza, Cremona, Mantua, Rovigo. Each of these towns was marked with a miniature representation of its main church or its walled citadel. The picture of Venice, a city-island surrounded by neat hexagonal walls, reminded me of a wooden box inlaid with mother-of-pearl in which my mother used to keep her jewels when I was small. Like that little treasure casket, whose key was always kept on a string under my mother's skirts, it held a strange fascination for me, as if the promise of its contents were lighting it up from within. What I liked least about the map were the vast expanses of sea, depicted by the cartographers with tall blue waves, curved like feathers, and fish with enormous mouths. And as I looked at the boats preparing for departure, I remembered, once again, the frightening accounts of pirate attacks and shipwrecks so often recounted by Abraham the cobbler.

When we reached our boat it was still too early to board. The merchants who had guided us to Marseilles were supervising the loading of their wares, shouting and swearing at the dockers. Other passengers stood around waiting. Astruc and I sat on a nearby pile of rope and he put his arm around my shoulders. I heaved a deep sigh. 'I'm very tired, Astruc,' I said, and closed my eyes.

The words that filled the air were mostly spoken in the local Provençal, to which I had already grown accustomed, but I also distinguished sentences spoken in other languages. I imagined they must be Genoese and other Italian tongues, unknown to me. I was almost dozing off when

I heard two men conversing in Girona Catalan.

'Not a bad deal, eh?' one was saying.

'Italians have a good eye, Jaume,' answered the other. 'They know a good velvet when they see it.'

I opened my eyes. The two men, whom I knew well, were sons of *conversos* from Girona. One of them lived near a small square we called Plaça de les Cols— Cabbage Square. The other in the Mercadal quarter. The father of this second one had a textile mill and had been a good friend of my father. They were standing only a few steps away from me, with a group of people who seemed to be waiting to board the ship that was moored alongside ours. I sat upright, arranged the pleats of my skirt and smoothed my headdress. Astruc, who had taken his little book of psalms out of his bag, did not even look up. At that moment, the one called Jaume turned his head and saw me. But when I opened my mouth to speak, feeling sure he was about to greet me, he turned away again and whispered something in his friend's ear, after which they both moved hurriedly to the front of the group, out of sight. Though I felt hurt by their behaviour, I did not take this as a sign of contempt towards me, but as an expression of the terror felt by *conversos* at the thought of the Inquisition. It astounded me to think that even so far from home they were afraid of being seen speaking to me, and I wondered whether their fear would keep them also from telling neighbours and friends that they had seen me sitting next to a man, and wearing a married woman's veil. I started to cry again at the thought that Vidal might hear of my marriage and be saddened by it. Astruc raised his head and looked at me.

'Are you never going to stop crying about that mare?' he asked. Then he buried his face in his psalm-book again.

* * *

114

Two hours later we were rounding the eastern point of the port, Astruc and I sitting under the forecastle, the Narbonne merchants on the quarterdeck, talking to the captain. Two sailors, high up on the mainmast, had hauled up her sails and made them fast before leaving port. They waved madly at first, like a bird flapping its wings when it is trying to escape from a trap, and then filled out with the steady push of a south-westerly wind. With all the sails unfurled, the ship soon reached a speed that seemed prodigious to me and filled me with terror. It was, of course, my very first sea journey, and I was frightened by the blackness of the waters and by the choppy waves that licked the sides of the vessel. I felt sick in my stomach from the constant rocking motion and the strong smell of tar. But as we advanced due east, keeping close to the shore for fear of pirate attacks, I was able to see how abrupt the coast of France was, and I thanked the Lord that we were not making our way on foot, or on horseback, through that dangerous and unfriendly-looking land.

The wind blew favourably during the first two days and the ship made easy progress, but on the third day, at dawn, the sky clouded over. It began to rain and the sea grew rough. Soon the wind seemed to come from all four corners of the earth at once. The rain stopped and the sun appeared, but that did nothing to appease the waves that were now as high as two men standing one on top of the other. I was petrified and could think of nothing else but accounts of shipwrecks. I remembered the story of Rabba bar Bar-Hana that Grandfather Ismael used to tell me, which began with these words: 'One very windy day two sailors were sailing in the open sea when suddenly a giant wave lifted them up to such heights that they were able to see the base of a small star, which was the size of a mustard-field; and had it lifted them even higher they would have been burnt by the brightness of the star.'

My stomach turned with every upward and downward movement. Wrapped tightly in my cloak, I rested my head on Astruc's shoulder and sat as still as I could, while the waves grew higher by the moment. I began to fear the worst. What if I was suddenly swept away by a wave? Gone would be not only Alba, but also the precious contents of her mind. I imagined the return of Astruc to Perpignan and the expression of utter dismay on the face of Rabbi Leví, while Astruc tried in vain to remember some of the passages only I knew by rote. My mother would weep disconsolately, her black shawl thrown over her head, but would soon resign herself, as usual, to the Creator's will. And what would Vidal do if the news of my death reached Girona? I remembered, once again, the words he said on the day of the edict: 'If you died, I could not bear it.' At that very moment an enormous wave, much higher than the others, swung the vessel violently to one side and left us all drenched. I screamed: 'We're sinking!'

'If you fall into the water I'll save you,' said Astruc, putting an arm around my shoulder. 'Don't be afraid, I can swim. You'll reach Venice safely, I promise. The precious text will be delivered for the glory of our Lord and of His people.'

'If I am allowed an opinion,' I answered indignantly, raising my voice to make sure he could hear me above the roar of the waves, 'I hope to live for many years after I have dictated the text to the Venetian scribe.'

'You will, you will,' said my husband, breaking into a sudden smile, taking my words for a hopeful anticipation of a long married life with him. I was touched by his ingenuousness, for he had not noticed the sarcasm in my words. Then, just as suddenly, his smile vanished and he looked at me fixedly and with kindness, while with a trembling hand he mopped my forehead and cheeks with a dry cloth, and quoted the words from Solomon's Proverbs:

Who can find a virtuous woman?
For her price is far above rubies.
The heart of her husband doth safely trust in her
So that he shall have no need of spoil.
She will do him good and not evil
All the days of her life...
She is like the merchants' ships;
She bringeth her food from afar.

I now see that moment as marking the beginning of his courtship, because from then on, and during the long journey from Genoa to Venice, he did everything he could to please me and took every possible opportunity to woo me with longing looks, pressing my hand between his, and pampering me with small gifts: now an apple, now a fig, now a new straw hat. And I accepted it all in good faith, knowing that one had to ride the waves, even if they were not taking you anywhere near where you had first intended.

That, indeed, is what was happening to our ship, for we were driven many leagues off our course, having slipped towards the south side of the Italian gulf, and it took us a good three hours and tremendous effort from the sailors, who kept changing the position of the sails, trying to catch the wind and challenge the force of the currents, until at last the port of Genoa came into view.

The merchants swore they would never trust that captain again. He should have foreseen the force of the impending storm, they said. It had been utter madness to venture out while the weather was so unreliable.

'The weather in mid-August is always very treacherous,' answered the captain, with a confident smile. He seemed quite unruffled by his passengers' anger.

'All the more reason to play safe,' retorted one of the merchants. 'What if we had lost all our merchandise, eh?'

'What if I had lost my ship, and we had all lost our lives?' protested the captain.

We had entered the port, flanked on either side by watchtowers of imposing height, and were making for the main quay, on the left-hand side. On the right, the town of Genoa spread from the very waterfront as far as back as the eye could see. Above it, the sky was streaked with clouds, copper-coloured and purple, through which the setting sun shone on rain-drenched rooftops. Seagulls came to meet our ship in great numbers, and a small group of people standing at the quayside were cheering and gesticulating enthusiastically as we approached. I felt like Jonah being cast safely onto dry land at last.

We had disembarked and were about to make our way towards the town, when all of a sudden one of the port officials stood squarely in front of Astruc and me, his arms outstretched, and looked at us with impudence.

'Your papers,' he said.

Astruc started rummaging in his bag, but I knew he had no travel papers.

'Nobody comes through without a permit,' he said. 'No one who looks like a homeless Jew. Look, behind you, there are your Spanish brothers! Those have no permits.' And with his arms still outstretched he kicked Astruc so sharply in the shin that he almost lost his balance.

We turned our heads. In a corner of the quayside, which during our approach had been hidden by the bulk of a merchant galley, was a large crowd of people—fifty, or seventy, perhaps—whom we recognised immediately as Sephardic Jews. Some were sitting on crates or bundles, or on rolled-up mattresses, others were standing about; a few had strayed from the group and stood by the water's edge, staring out to sea. They all looked bewildered and weak, and yet they waited with dignity and resignation, with the patience of Job. Half a dozen guards, armed with sticks, stood around them.

'You're not allowed to settle in our town, see?' he went on. 'Those over there arrived from Seville three days ago, and they're still waiting for an authorisation. Doesn't seem likely they'll get it either,' he added, laughing. 'Go on, go and wait over there with them!'

I had to bite my tongue to keep myself from answering back.

We were saved by the timely crash of one of the merchants' boxes. The rope snapped as it was being lowered from the ship on a pulley. In the pandemonium that followed Astruc and I were able to escape unobserved and take shelter under the dark archways that edged the buildings along the sea front. We hid behind some empty crates.

'Perhaps it would be better to wait here until nightfall before we venture into Genoa in search of Rabbi Salomone's house,' whispered Astruc. 'If those poor souls cannot find a way of entering the town, neither shall we.'

'The Lord is with us, Astruc,' I answered. 'We were saved from the storm, we were saved from the official's fury. Let's go now.'

'Let's go now, let's go now!' came a voice echoing my words in a harsh Italian accent.

'What was that, Astruc?' I cried in horror.

'Ha! Ha! Ha!' came a cackling laughter from somewhere behind us. 'Let's go now, ha, ha, ha!'

We both turned our heads towards the sinister voice and the laughter changed into a piercing wail: 'Ayee! Ayee! Ayee!' There, next to a pile of fishing nets, sat what looked like a bundle of black rags that shook uncontrollably. All of a sudden the rags were drawn apart like a curtain and the horrible face of an old hag appeared: a toothless drooling mouth, enormous pale tongue hanging loose, eyes lost behind cataracts and swollen eyelids, an inordinately large nose covered in warts, and a disgustingly hairy chin, from which she kept wiping a constant flow of saliva, now with the right hand, now with the left. I had never seen anything so repulsive.

Astruc looked in our food bag for something to give the old woman, though I was tugging impatiently at his sleeve and trying to dissuade him. He scolded me for my uncharitable feelings and went on rummaging until at last he brought out a piece of fig-bread, left the bag on the ground and made his way between the piles of nets that surrounded her. When she saw him coming she smacked her lips noisily, her tongue moving in and out, like a snake's tongue; then she grabbed the slice of fig-bread and stuffed it into her mouth. Astruc stood over her, holding her hand in his while she battled without teeth with the lump of food and finally managed to swallow it. Then that woman did something extraordinary: she closed her eyes and began to hum, and the hum rose in pitch until it was as shrill as the voice of a screaming child. It mesmerised us both, forcing itself over our minds in such a way that we froze like statues. I could not tell you how long we stood like that, but at last she stopped chanting and opened her eyes, which, I now realised, were large, even beautiful. With Astruc's hand still in hers, she fixed her eyes on his and spoke slowly and clearly, so that we had no trouble in understanding her Italian:

'Oh son, my travelling son! Radiant is your mind and your soul, and full of goodness. I see your past life before my eyes, and all the sorrow that wrenched your soul in two when you were younger. I see also that you carry, all alone, an important secret for your people.' Her speech became slower still, though without losing its shrillness. 'Oh, wandering Jew,' she wailed, 'your wanderings will soon come to an end.'

As soon as the voice stopped, I came back to my senses and called Astruc again.

'Astruc, let's go now, please,' I said.

Astruc turned to me, his features distorted. Two large tears rolled down his cheeks. He stumbled back over the nets towards me and I whispered: 'Why, Astruc, what's the matter? Surely you didn't pay attention to the old witch's words?'

But he gave no answer. All of a sudden he put his arms around me, pressing his body against mine, and began feverishly kissing my face all over until at last, when his lips met mine, he drew apart.

'Alba,' he said, looking straight at me. 'I am so fortunate to have you. Yes, you're right. Let's get out of here as quickly as we can.' He seemed like a child who has woken up from a nightmare.

We picked up our bags and walked off towards the town, which was beginning to sparkle as the houses lit their lanterns. After a while Astruc smiled at me and said: 'She had the foulest breath I have ever smelled!'

'And the face of the ugliest demon in Gehinnom!' I laughed, relieved that he had overcome his shock.

Simon the jeweller had given us instructions on how to get to the synagogue, but once we entered the maze of backstreets that formed the heart of the city of Genoa, we lost our bearings. All the streets looked the same, narrow and full of rubbish, with dark clothes hanging from the balconies and a smell of fried fish drifting by over the general stench; but there was not a human being in sight to whom we could ask the way. After going round in circles for a while, we came to a little square with a church and two very tall pine trees, and there, at last, we saw a few men sitting on a stone seat, in their short working tunics, enjoying the cool evening air. They eyed us suspiciously at first and stopped their talk, but when Astruc went up to them and courteously asked for the way to the synagogue, they all began shouting and gesticulating at once, though we did not understand a word they were saying. At last one of them called out 'Domenica!' and a little girl, who could not have been more than six or seven, came running out of a house in the square.

Domenica guided us through the labyrinth and a few minutes later we were standing outside a low shabby building that looked like a disused warehouse. She pulled at my sleeve and said: '*La sinagoga, bella signora,*' then turned and ran off like a gazelle on her bare feet. I called after her: '*Grazie*, Domenica!' and she raised an arm as if to say farewell, but did not look back.

Astruc knocked on the door. In the sliver of pale grey sky that was visible between the rooftops the white moon waited patiently for the night. With the patience of Job. There was a strange silence and I shuddered, the old hag's words still echoing in my ears. Then we heard a door open somewhere within, and a deep voice called out: 'Who comes at this late hour?'

'It is Rabbi Astruc from Besalú, a town near Girona, and I am here with my wife. We bring a letter from Simon the Jeweller of Narbonne for Salomone Canetti, rabbi of the Genoa community.'

The front door was opened and the rabbi appeared. He was a small, frail-looking old man with a long white beard. I was expecting someone large and robust after hearing his booming voice.

'I'm Salomone Canetti, but I'm afraid I cannot help you in any way. I cannot obtain authorisations for any of our Sephardic brothers,' he said.

'We don't need an authorisation,' answered Astruc, 'only some help in arranging a land trip to Venice. This is my wife, Alba de Porta,' he added.

'Did you say de Porta?' asked the rabbi.

'Indeed. My wife is a descendant of Bonastruc de Porta.'

'A descendant of the great Nahmanides!' he said, taking both my hands in his. 'What a blessing, what an honour for our synagogue!'

We stepped inside, into an unpaved patio, full of puddles from the recent downpour. There were boxes of red and white geraniums lining the walls of the small building that now appeared before us, which I supposed must be the synagogue. The rabbi led us down a narrow side-passage between the main building and the low wall enclosing the premises, until we reached his living quarters, at the back of the synagogue. The rooms were poorly furnished and small, but Salomone Canetti treated us with such hospitality that we would not have been more comfortable or better fed in a palace. We sat down to share his dinner of bread and garlic soup, followed by cheese with fresh figs, and while we ate, he told us that he lived alone, for his wife had recently died and his two daughters had both married that very year, the Lord be thanked, and gone to live in Mantua.

'I live in constant fear of an attack,' he explained. 'Genoa is a violent city, like most busy harbours; worse, I am told, than Naples. The poor and the sick flock here from neighbouring towns and villages, asking for help which they don't get, and when the town sleeps and all is silent, robbers and criminals of all kinds lurk in the shadows. And now, with the order of expulsion from the kingdoms of Spain, there is also an influx of exiled Jews. There are already close to seventy Sephardim waiting in the port, and every day I hear of new arrivals. I cannot understand how you were allowed into the city.'

'The Lord helped us.'

'I don't know what will become of them. I am doing all I can to help, but the times are bad for us. I feel very disheartened.'

'I thought the community in Genoa was a large and prosperous one,' said Astruc.

'On the contrary, it's dwindling fast. Until last year, the two most important bankers in Genoa were Jews. They handled all the commercial transactions in the port. But things were getting very difficult for them, and they were forced to leave and try their luck in Venice, where there is daily trade with the Turks and where money, not the Church, is the ruling power. We are not persecuted to the same degree as you have been in Spain, but the situation doesn't favour us either. We, too, have been accused from time to time of killing Christian children and of other barbarous deeds, just like you, and have had to wear discriminatory signs on our clothes. These are things which, unfortunately, happen to a greater or lesser degree in all the kingdoms of Christendom, except that in Italy the political situation is forever changing because it has no ancient ruling dynasties, and anyone here can become duke or king, depending on his wit and the passion with which he searches for power. So one day everything is fine, and the next day we must run for our lives. One day they want our advice on financial matters, and the next the monks set up a *monte di pietà* and tell all Christians they will burn in hell if they borrow money from a Jew. Only in Venice, Florence and other city-states can Jews survive with some measure of dignity.

He paused to eat a slice of fig on cheese. Then he wiped his mouth with a white napkin and looked at us, smiling. 'But you Sephardim,' he said, 'give us new hope with your deep religious certitude, and I do believe that the Lord Almighty, blessed be His Name, has brought you here to lift our spirits and light the way for the return to the Holy Land and the coming of the Messiah.'

The coming of the Messiah was one of Astruc's favourite subjects and I knew it would lead to a lengthy discussion. I begged to be excused and retired to bed, which consisted of a large wool mattress the rabbi had unrolled for us in the main room, behind an old linen curtain. Through the curtain I could dimly make out the figures of the two seated men in the soft candlelight and hear their earnest voices. They spoke in Hebrew, and every now and then they expressed something in their vernacular, understanding each other well because of the similarities between the two languages.

'There have been so many signs, so many predictions concerning this year of 5252 since the creation,' Astruc was saying. 'The eclipse of the sun seven years ago was only the first of many omens... Two days after the date of our final expulsion from the Crown of Aragon was the day of the destruction of both Temples, the Ninth of Av. I'm sure we are getting close to the year of the Redemption. Do you share my view that the catastrophe that has befallen us is a way of selecting those who wish to stay in the faith, so that the Divine light may shine with greater strength in their souls on Judgement Day?'

'Who can interpret the designs of the Creator?' answered the Italian rabbi. 'But any common affliction can act as a strengthening bond between those who are suffering from it, of that there is no doubt.'

I was comfortable, but, even though I felt exhausted,

it took me a long time to fall asleep. A procession of disturbing images marched relentlessly through my mind: the Girona merchants in Marseilles, the storm at sea, the crowd of homeless Sephardim in Genoa harbour, the terrifying face of the hag, and the pain she had awoken in Astruc. Evil omens, I thought; and, yet, as Rabbi Salomone so rightly says, who can interpret the designs of the Creator? I wondered why Astruc had been so affected by the old woman's words. She had obviously read into his past. But what was the secret he carried? And what was the grief that had torn his soul apart when he was younger? Was this a reference to his first wife Gabriela? I did not feel close enough to him to ask such a question. Best leave the past alone, I said to myself. But what of the future? Were we really going to end our wanderings soon? Would I be at last dictating the text that I held in my mind? On that more pleasant thought I finally fell into a deep sleep from which I did not wake until long past the ninth hour when Astruc, sitting on the side of the mattress, gently roused me. 'We will be leaving presently,' he said.

IX

THE WATERS OF THE CANAL

It was going to be a long dictation, six hours at least, and I was glad to be sitting in such a comfortable armchair, with a glass of water to keep my throat from getting dry. Seven weeks had passed since the day in Girona when I had finished memorising the text and given it back to Astruc to hide again under the synagogue tiles, and in all that time *The Chain of Lilies* had been running constantly through my mind, a chain of words and thoughts that at moments seemed to shed light on my own life.

The scribe sat opposite me, in a chair with a high back surmounted by a small canopy. While he settled at his desk, a wide table that was well provided with inkstands, scrapers, quills and parchment, he carefully folded up his shirtsleeves. He was a young man, with sandy hair cut above the ears and a shaven face. His smile softened the intensity of his gaze. He wore green breeches, a blue doublet with its pleats gathered by a metal belt, and pointed black shoes, all of which was very fashionable in Venice at the time. A brightly-coloured carpet was spread on the floor between us and the wall behind him was covered with bookshelves.

My chair, with arms and a curved back, and a few cushions for extra comfort, was placed by the window. It was a wide window, divided by a single column of grey stone, from which I had a view of one of the many palaces that lined the small canal, with its reflection shimmering in the water. The city of Venice had not yet awoken and the air had the stillness of sleep. My eyes rested at once on that intangible watery image whose gentle movement lulled my senses, like the soft music of viols and lutes, and allowed me to scan with my inner eye the wide landscape of my memory. Instinctively, I slipped my hand into the deep pocket of my tunic and felt the shape of Vidal's key-box, my fingers running over the familiar arrangement of moons and stars surrounding my name. Then I prised open the box and took out the key.

The front door of my old home opened and I stepped in, over the ten grey river stones, smoothed and rounded by the force of water, that formed the pattern of the Tree of God in the entrance hall. When I was very young, Grandfather Ismael had taught me the name and meaning of every stone, that is, of each of the ten *sephiroth* or attributes of God, which are linked to one another like the branches of a tree. The first *sephirah* was called Kether, the Crown, or the Primordial Point, in which all other *sephiroth* are contained; number two was Hokhmah, or Wisdom; number three Binah, or Understanding; the fourth *sephirah* was Hesed, meaning Mercy or Love, and also called Magnificence; the fifth was Geburah, or Strength, also known as Justice; number six was Tiphereth, Beauty; number seven Netzah, meaning Victory or Firmness; the eighth was Hod, Splendour; nine was Yesod, the Foundation; ten was Malkhuth, the Kingdom, or the Shekhinah, the Bride of God.

As I stepped over those stones, I began to recall the text, moving like a ghost from room to room as I recited, opening cupboards and coffers, going down the stairs to the kitchen with its baskets of pears and figs, the water pitchers lined up against the wall, the sacks of flour, the kneading troughs, the pots and pans; then, walking out into the yard I saw the pigeons pecking greedily at scattered bread crumbs and our black and white cat lying in the sun among the pots of geraniums and daisies. Passage after passage brought my far-away home back to me in all its smallest details and with such vividness that I was filled with a longing to smell and touch and listen; a longing to listen to the steps of someone coming down the alleyway, to see my true love walk into the house and hear his voice telling me again that he loved me, despite the distance, despite our separation, despite my marriage to Astruc. Tears began to fall down my cheeks, though I tried hard to stop them, as all the sadness accumulated over the past three months was at last able to flow.

The scribe put down his quill and looked at me. By then I could not control my weeping. 'Signora, are you not well?' he asked. He looked confused. His job was to copy texts or to take down dictation, not to nurse the sick. 'You were saying: *These are the brightest stars in the heavens, and every star in heaven corresponds to a flower on earth.*'

That sentence belonged to the open loft, and there I was again, hanging out the washing the morning of the edict of expulsion. Vidal must have been watching my house at that moment, waiting for me in the street below, aware of the news that was about to change our lives. Of course, I thought, he was waiting for me, and when I went out he followed me to the cemetery.

'... *to a flower on earth*, signora.'

'...*to a flower on earth, or a stone that has been rounded and smoothed by flowing water.*' Vidal and I embracing on the grassy hillside, near the flowing torrents. His arms like vines entwining me.

He must have been standing on the corner of St. Llorenç Street, spying on my house, waiting to catch a glimpse of me, inflamed like me by the passion that had been kindled in our hearts the night before. Only the night before. How clearly it all came back: the way he had looked at me across the table in Isaac's house, the way his words seemed to me pregnant with secret meanings. And later, when he was taking his leave, and Cousin Isaac had said to me 'Cousin, show our friend Vidal to the door,' and we were suddenly alone in the entrance hall, the way he had stood with his back to the street, as if he wanted to stop the world from moving forward, and had run his fingers through my hair, and then, very quietly, had said: 'I love you so much, Alba.' The recollection was too vivid to be a simple act of memory. I could hear myself whispering back: 'I love you too, Vidal,' words I had never said before to a man, but which had come easily to my lips, as if they had drifted in on the weightless night air. He had drawn so close to me I felt his cheek touching mine. Behind me I could hear my mother and Coloma washing the dishes at the kitchen sink and Isaac telling his children a story, but in a faraway manner, as if all that family life were completely unrelated to me. The hall in which we stood became a temple for our love, and I knew—we both knew—that something sublime was occurring, that we were now joined forever by unseen bonds. Outside, the night was splendid, starry and luminous. When Vidal kissed me, softly, I felt the warm moisture of his mouth. 'I will see you tomorrow, my love,' he had whispered at last. 'Where, when?' I had asked him, awaking suddenly from that ecstasy and afraid that my mother would not allow me to meet him, or that his work would stop him from coming, or that some other obstacle might come between us. A premonition perhaps, something in the air of the *call*. At that moment my mother called me and Vidal covered his head with the hood of his cape and was gone without an answer.

'Signora, are you not going to continue?' insisted the scribe.

I forced myself to leave Isaac's house and go back to my own home. Once more I went down the spiral staircase into the kitchen, approached the well, remembered the objects placed on the small table next to it, the flowers in the vase, the mortar and pestle. Then I looked through the window and saw the tall almond tree in the courtyard heavy with blossom. I began to recite again:

> *So a female soul that has found its male counterpart and joined it blissfully, bears the glow of the Shekhinah in her union with God. And in that joy lies the hidden mystery of the force of creation, whereby the tree of life is filled with new sap, pushing the moon forward in her cycles, causing rain to fall on the earth, so that the tender green shoots of the lilies can break through the soil. For as Solomon sang: 'My beloved is mine, and I am His: He feedeth among the lilies.' Lilies have six petals, and each petal represents one of the days of creation.*

It was no longer my own voice I heard in my head, but the voice of Vidal reciting those words from the book, as though he knew them too and was present in me. The text acquired a male tone, which added a new quality to its meaning.

'*Likewise the precious stones that are hidden in dark caverns or buried beneath the ground are distant reflections of the Heavenly Light...,*' I continued, calm again, urged on, or so it seemed to me, by Vidal's own energy. And so my voice carried on reciting as the sun streamed into the ample room and gondolas began to glide past the window.

A few hours later, when the last word of the text had been written down, I heaved a sigh of relief. My task was over, my heavy burden had been removed. Never again would I be required to produce those words to perfection, though, in fact, I could still recite them all now, after so many years, without a single mistake. They remained with me, helping me in moments of trouble, of which there were still many to come. With my eyes still fixed on the canal waters I watched the door of the house in the *call* close and the reflection of the Venetian palace take its place again in the liquid mirror.

The scribe smiled at me approvingly, and I stood up and went over to look at his work. It was, indeed, a work of great skill. The letters were neat and were written in an attractive round hand. It had no smudges, nor had anything been crossed out and rewritten despite my initial hesitations. I congratulated him.

'You speak Hebrew in a clear way, with an accent that is similar to our Italian intonation,' he explained, as he put away his quill pens and his scraper and covered his inkwell with its glass top. 'And you knew your text well. I too congratulate you.'

At that moment there was a knock on the door and Astruc came in, looking happy, even radiant. He had been waiting outside, as I had asked him to do, for I feared his presence might have distracted me and undermined my powers of concentration.

'You have finished, Alba!' he cried.

He walked over to the table and a look of immense relief and joy came over his face when he saw the completed work. Then, rolling his eyes, he chanted: 'Thanks be given to the Lord, blessed be His Name, for the deliverance of the text by Levanah, descendant of the great Nahmanides of Girona!'

The scribe looked at Astruc, then at me, and courteously lowered his eyes, aware of the devotion behind

Astruc's words. Then he went over to the windowsill to pick up his cloak and cap. Astruc asked: 'When will you add the illuminations?'

'Tomorrow morning, signore. What do you think would be appropriate?'

'I could make you a sketch of the pattern which was on the original cover and you could copy it,' I said hastily. In my mind I smiled at my father and said to him: See, Father? You have travelled with me to Venice. 'And within the text,' I added, 'you could depict stars and flowers, trees and planets, birds and fish, to symbolise the constant flow of the divine light from earth to heaven and from heaven to earth.' I turned to Astruc again. He looked concerned. 'Don't you agree, Astruc?' I asked.

'Slowly, slowly, Alba,' he answered with a smile. 'There is no need for so much adornment.' Then he turned to the scribe. 'But there is one particular illustration I would like added in the margin.'

'Signore?'

'A seven-branched *menorah*. I want you to draw it in the margin next to the fourth paragraph of the third chapter in part two. You won't forget, will you? It's easy: 4,3,2.'

'I will make a note of it right away,' said the scribe, returning to his table, dipping the quill once more in the inkstand and writing down what Astruc had said.

'And one more thing,' said Astruc. 'You must add this sentence at the end of the book: 'The Chain of Lilies *was memorised and dictated by Alba de Porta, of the town of Girona, using the house of her ancestors as her memory house.*'

I looked at Astruc, wondering why he had made such unusual requests. But by now I was used to his sudden outbursts of fervour and to his erudition. Later I would try to work out which paragraph he was referring to for the *menorah* picture, and I was pleased that my name would be written down in the book. Now all I wanted to do was rest my mind.

His day's work done, the scribe walked over to the mirror that hung on the wall by the door. With meticulous care, he first put on his cape, of the same bright blue material as his jerkin, and tied it round his neck. Then he took his cap, which matched the green of his breeches, patted it briskly to puff it up, and placed it on his head, making sure the curls of his fair hair were arranged neatly all around it. I had never seen a man spend so long in front of a mirror. But in Venice nothing surprised me any more and, besides, I had never seen such a clear mirror in all my life. We had one in our Girona home, but the image it reflected moved about, making one look broad on one side and narrow on another, whereas this Venetian mirror, set in a gold frame, reflected the person so faithfully one could even detect the smallest irregularities of one's skin. Pleased with his appearance, the scribe turned to me, kissed my hand, bowed respectfully to Astruc and left the room saying, 'Signore, signora, come in the morning if you wish to supervise my work. And I expect I will see you at Signora Anna's banquet tonight.'

And with that he was gone.

* * *

But let me tell you about how we arrived in Venice, and how that city charmed me, and who this Signora Anna was.

On the previous day, after a long journey from Genoa through the lands of Lombardy, we had arrived in Mestre, the town of the Veneto which is closest to the island of Venice. I have heard that nowadays the Venetian Jews live in the city itself, in a quarter named the Ghetto, but when Astruc and I arrived there in the year 1492 of the Christian era, no members of the Hebrew community were allowed by law in the town except as travellers, even though they had lived there on and off for generations, and they could not spend more than a fortnight on the island at a time. So although there were many Jews in the streets of Venice, moneylenders and all manner of traders, and although many Jewish scholars and physicians were welcomed into the palaces, they were only there in passing, as it were, and their homes were mostly in Mestre. There were some exceptions, of course: where there is a rule there is always a way of twisting it to one's advantage. One exception was Anna d'Arco, who was married to a Jew from Corfu.

Mestre was a drab place, with no outstanding buildings or landmarks. It had the anonymity of a waiting-hall, but the people in that waiting-hall seemed happy with their lot. The first thing I noticed when we entered the town was that people walked with their heads up and a contented expression, talking in a lively manner, and that shopkeepers exhibited a great variety of wares and products. Even the Jews, who were obliged to wear a yellow beret, seemed unconcerned by this discrimination, and mingled with the other inhabitants in a natural way. The citizens of Mestre were, moreover, open and helpful to travellers, being used to the traffic of tradesmen through their town, on their way to Venice, or to the other surrounding cities, so it did not take us long to find the house of Rabbi Giuseppe Caravita, whose name had been suggested to us by Salomone Canetti, the rabbi of Genoa.

Salomone Canetti had known Giuseppe Caravita in his youth, when they both lived in Rome, and the last time he had heard from him, a few months before these events, he was in good health, and as concerned as ever with the communal library of Mestre of which he was the keeper.

'He understands books, he loves books, he lives for the preservation of his books,' Rabbi Salomone had told us. 'Giuseppe Caravita is just the person you are seeking. Besides, he knows the best printers in Venice, and I'm sure that once the book has been copied down he will make sure it gets printed. I know that there is a printer in Venice who has Hebrew characters. This printing invention is remarkable, almost a miracle.'

'Without wishing to offend you, rabbi, I don't think our book is fit for general circulation,' Astruc had answered. 'Printed books run the risk of falling into the hands of people who are not qualified to read them. In my opinion it is an ill-fated invention.'

When we reached the librarian's house we knocked on the door and a girl of about ten opened it. The morning sun bathed her in light. She was very pretty, with dark curls falling over her shoulders.

'Whom shall I announce?' she asked.

'Tell Rabbi Giuseppe Caravita that two travellers from Sepharad are here,' replied Astruc.

She did not seem to understand Astruc's broken Italian, so she repeated the question in Hebrew. Astruc smiled at her and repeated his answer in Hebrew too, adding: 'Tell him we bring news from Rabbi Salomone of Genoa.'

She let us into the hall with such graceful manners and such composure you would have thought she was a noblewoman of the highest rank. 'Please wait here. I will fetch my grandfather,' she said.

There was a look in that child's eye that I have never forgotten. It was a look of fearlessness, which in those days was rare in a Jewish child. Even during the quietest times of my own childhood we had always been told to be guarded and cautious, especially with strangers. What I saw in those eyes was not rashness, but the deep happiness that comes from a stable existence, and I prayed to the Lord that it should be a sign of an equally profound change for the better in the destiny of the Sephardim.

When Giuseppe Caravita appeared, he greeted us with the same courtesy as his granddaughter. Though we knew he was a contemporary of the rabbi of Genoa, he looked much younger, and I thought about the effect that oppression and anxiety can have on the body. He took us both into a small study on the ground floor and there Astruc told him about our journey and our mission, just as he had done in Perpignan, Narbonne and Genoa. I watched the rabbi's face as he listened, enthralled, to Astruc's tale. When he had finished, he stretched out his hands towards us.

'The Lord has guided you to the right place, brothers,' he said. 'I myself have a great interest in the writings of the kabbalists, and in Venice, where the social order invites men to discuss such matters, the Kabbalah has generated so much curiosity among some scholars that it has become the common ground between our religion and Christianity. I can say, without exaggerating, that despite the difficulties we Jews always suffer in Christian lands— and we have had our fair share here, I can assure you—, we are better appreciated in Venice than in any other town of Italy.'

He then turned to me and added: 'I will arrange for a scribe to come along tomorrow, and you will at last be able to dictate the text. It will be a great honour for the community to have such a unique book in the library. Once it has been taken down I will also see to it that copies are made.'

'I do not think it is a book for general circulation, owing to its very special nature,' Astruc put in. Thank goodness Rabbi Giuseppe has not mentioned the printing press, I thought.

'Of course, of course,' answered the Italian rabbi, 'but we must at least ensure that the book never again risks extinction. And one day, when the decree of expulsion is revoked, the original manuscript will be recovered and given a dignified place among other treasures of our people. But come, brothers,' he added, getting up, 'you've had a long journey. A rest will do you good.'

We went out into the main hall, a large room whose only source of daylight was a window at the top of a staircase. Giuseppe Caravita called his granddaughter. 'Antonina,' he said, 'please take our guests to the spare room upstairs and make sure there is plenty of fresh water in the jug. And when your mother comes back from the market, let her know there will be two extra guests for the midday meal.' Turning to us, he explained:

'I live with my daughter and her family: her husband and three children. My son-in-law is a moneylender and does his business in Venice.'

We followed Antonina up the stairs and were shown to the bedroom, a small but well-furnished room with a large window. When we were left alone, we took off our dusty travel-clothes and went over to the washstand to refresh ourselves. My naked forearm brushed against Astruc's and he turned to look at me with a mixture of surprise and desire. Only for an instant. Then he put on some clean clothes, sat on a chair by the bed, took his psalm-book out of the bag and began to read.

Dressed in my red tunic—very crumpled, but clean, at least—I lay down on the bed to rest, for all my muscles were aching after the last part of the journey, which had been overnight in the back of a merchant's cart. It was a relief just to lie still. The window looked out on a sea of tiled rooftops and beyond that were the waters of another sea, the Adriatic.

'The Lord is protecting us, Astruc,' I said drowsily.

He did not answer, so I assumed he was concentrating on his reading. But a sudden thump made me turn my head towards him. He had dropped his book. He looked very pale and was breathing with difficulty.

'Astruc, are you unwell?' I asked. 'Astruc,' I repeated, 'what is it?'

I ran over to the washstand, dipped a corner of a towel in the water and began to cool his forehead and wrists with it, as I had sometimes seen my mother do. I fanned him with his psalm-book. I patted him on the cheeks. I opened the windows wide. When I couldn't think of anything else to do and was about to call out for help, Astruc seemed to recover. A few moments later his breathing became normal again, but he still looked very pale. I bent down to see his face better and, looking at his freckled skin, his weary eyes, his sunken cheeks, I wished with all my heart that I could feel more tenderness for him, more love for him than I did, after all we had been through together.

'What is it? Speak, Astruc!' I urged him.

'I'm all right, Alba. It is nothing at all,' he said. 'I am not as young as you and the journey has tired me, that's all.'

At that moment there was a rap on the door and we were called down for lunch. I suggested to Astruc that he should stay in the bedroom, but he insisted on coming with me. And the truth is that throughout the meal he ate well and was lively in his conversation. My fears subsided.

In the hall we were greeted by Giuseppe's daughter, Raphaella, her three children (Antonina and two younger brothers) and Menahem, her husband. Behind them stood another woman.

'This is our friend Anna d'Arco,' said Giuseppe Caravita. 'She is almost one of the family.'

I liked Anna instantly, for her gaiety, her intelligence, her frankness. We went into the dining room and sat at a round table, spread with a damask cloth which in Girona we would have reserved for the Rosh Ha-Shanah or the Pesah. She told me she was married to a banker, who was away in Istanbul at the time, and that she herself devoted her life to her husband's library, which was one of the best in Venice. She was, as I was soon to discover, one of the most admired women in Venice, not only for her great beauty, her fair hair and fine taste in clothes, but also because she was so well instructed that she could hold conversations on learned subjects with the most prominent men of letters of the time.

'I would like to hear about Girona,' she said. 'Isn't that where Bonastruc de Porta, the great Nahmanides, lived and wrote?'

'Alba is a descendant of the eminent kabbalist,' put in Rabbi Giuseppe, and he went on to explain my mission. 'Tomorrow I will call the synagogue copyist and he will take down the precious text, that it may be preserved for posterity.'

'What? Your old Simon?' laughed Anna. 'But Giuseppe, you know he is almost deaf and his hands shake so one can hardly read his writing. Besides, he is a bad-tempered old man. Alba needs someone who will help, not hinder her enormous mental effort. And where do you propose to have her dictate it?'

'In my study. Are you going to object to that too? I have a good desk and two good chairs, and all the necessary items for a dictation.'

'And a view of dirty backyards, full of screaming children. No, Giuseppe. With all due respect, and not wishing to offend you, this is not the best place for the task that awaits Alba. Let her come along to my palace tonight,' she said. 'I will arrange for my husband's private scribe to come and take down the text.'

She turned to me. Her pale blue eyes looked straight into mine.

'You and your husband can stay with me in Venice tonight and tomorrow morning, when you are well rested, you can dictate the text in our library.'

And so, as fate would have it, Astruc and I found ourselves walking out of Mestre with Anna that very afternoon. A carriage was waiting by the town gates and we were driven swiftly down the road that followed the winding river to the small port of San Giuliano. Through the tall reeds that bordered the river I could distinguish the masts of ships, and then, as we went round the last bend in the road, a vast expanse of sea appeared before us, with the island of Venice just visible in the distance. We then boarded a ferry that made the journey to the city-island, and as we crossed the still waters of the lagoon it seemed to me that the city was smiling at me, beckoning me with the glitter of its glass and tiles and the chiming of its bells. The sun was setting behind us, tinting the water and the buildings with a soft orange hue as we entered the Canareggio and then made our way up the Canal Grande, which serves as the high street of Venice. Never had I seen such splendour nor such beauty made by man. This canal is so wide, that galleys and all kinds of vessels pass through it, in both directions. The houses are very large and tall, made of stone and brickwork; some (the oldest ones, as Anna d'Arco explained) have their whole façade painted blue, green, rose-coloured or yellow; others are covered in white marble which the merchants bring over from Istria, and are inlayed with porphyry and serpentine.

Through this avenue of colours we came to St. Mark's Square, where we alighted, and Anna told the guards who watch over the arrival of travellers that we were her guests. The guards knew her well, and saluted us with respect. After crossing the large square, leaving behind us the Doge's palace and St. Mark's basilica, with its domes like enormous grey clouds, we made our way into the city, walking down alleys, under arches, and across wooden and stone footbridges. The black gondolas slid down the canals like swans, and I enjoyed watching the skilful gondoliers, who push their boats forward with a single oar. Some corners reminded me a little of Girona, though many of the grander buildings were far more ostentatious than the noble houses of my Catalan town. At last, emerging from a dark alleyway we came into a spacious square presided over by a three-storey redbrick house with a gallery of white arches running along the first floor, where torches had already been lit for the evening. Anna said: 'We have arrived. Come, let me show you to your rooms.'

X

THE ANGEL OF DEATH

The following morning, in my mind I travelled to Girona and wandered through my lost home, moving from room to room, remembering and reliving my past. Now the house of the *call* drifted away, and with it, the memory of Vidal. But I knew that *The Chain of Lilies* would empower me to bring both memories back whenever I wished to evoke them. The thought troubled me, however, for at that moment I only wanted to look ahead.

The scribe took his leave with a nod and left the room briskly. I too went over to the mirror and looked at myself, but what I saw did not please me. Sorrow and tiredness had left their traces on me; my eyes looked more serious, my face, framed by the white veil that had belonged to my mother, had lost the radiance of early youth. I was wearing my red tunic, the best garment I owned, but it was creased and discoloured, and next to the beautifully dressed Italian ladies with their rich velvet and silk robes, their jewels and elaborate hair fashions, I looked more like a pauper than a visitor in the house of Anna d'Arco. Astruc stood behind me. He took me by the shoulders and smiled at my reflection.

'Thank you, Alba,' he said. 'You have served the Lord well.' There were tears in his eyes.

I turned round and he held me close.

'I love you,' he said. 'The good Lord put you on my path.'

I could feel his body closing in on mine, thighs pressing against thighs, with the same feverish impulse that had taken hold of him in the port of Genoa. To my bewilderment, my body responded now to his and I parted his mouth with mine, and kissed him with passion. I said something like: 'Master... now you must teach me how to love you like a husband.'

'I'll start by offering you a home,' he said in a whisper, kissing my neck, breathing fast. His whole body shook.

'A home, Astruc? Where?'

'In Mestre.'

'What are you saying, Astruc?' I whispered back, lost somewhere between carnal desire and mental exhaustion.

Astruc suddenly disengaged himself, smoothed down his surcoat and tried to compose his appearance, running his hands through his hair, stroking his beard, overcome by his natural shyness. His eyes looked here and there nervously, averting me. He walked over to the scribe's desk and stared at the completed text.

'I didn't want to distract you with any news last night,' he said after a while, clearing his throat and looking at me again, 'but the rabbi in Mestre asked me to stay and teach the Talmud at the synagogue. The wages are not very high, but enough to meet our needs, and to pay the rent of a small house. Tell me, does that please you Alba?'

After so much journeying, so many changes and so much uncertainty, the thought of a home where I could settle was a very happy prospect. All the more so when the house was in Mestre, the doorway to Venice, close to Rabbi Giuseppe's family and to Anna d'Arco. Once we had settled there, my mother could come over to live with us, and maybe Isaac with his family. Besides, I felt flattered by Astruc's wish to please me. I knew that his action was sincere, that it stemmed directly from the centre of his soul,

144

and now I was sure that he loved me for being who I was, not for what I had done to serve the Lord. Something began to stir in my heart, as well as in my body. I wanted to be wooed by him and live in the present that I was breathing and feeling, not in the intangible regions of memory. This new home would give me a chance to find the inner peace I longed for, to begin a new life far from my beloved Girona.

I walked over to the table and put my hand on his cheek.

'My beautiful, good and honest wife,' said Astruc. 'Do I deserve such a bounty?'

'When can I see the house? When shall we move in?'

'Tomorrow morning if you wish. Tonight we must stay in Venice for the banquet. You know how much I dislike all this show of wealth, all the ostentation that seems to prevail in every corner of this city, but I feel we should attend out of courtesy. Anna has treated us very well. Tomorrow we shall return to Mestre.'

* * *

That afternoon, while Astruc busied himself reading in the library, I spent two or three hours in Anna's rooms. We bathed together in her round bath, with hot water and perfumed soap; we dried ourselves with soft towels and scented our skin with oils shipped to Venice from faraway lands of the East. Then we tidied and polished our nails and plaited our hair so that it would curl neatly when it dried. In all that time we hardly opened our mouths, except to sigh with pleasure, as if we were sisters, or had known each other all our lives. Later, as we sat by the window in her bedroom on large Turkish cushions, we fell into conversation. She told me she had read a few pages of the Girona text.

'The words seem to shine with a light of their own,' she said. 'Your book would dazzle a friend of mine, a man who collects all kinds of books and parchments.'

'And who is that?'

'His name is Pico della Mirandola, and although he isn't Jewish, his vision of the world is very similar to that held by the kabbalists, whom he has studied in depth. His knowledge of Jewish mysticism has, in fact, led him to serious confrontations with the Church. He, too, agrees that every part of the visible world has some correspondence with the spiritual matter issuing forth from the Creator. His library is far larger and more important than mine, but every time he comes to Venice he wants to know what new books I've acquired. Besides Latin and Greek he knows Hebrew, Chaldean and Arabic. I haven't seen him lately, but next time he comes to visit me I'll show him *The Chain of Lilies*. May I?'

'Astruc is obsessed with the idea that this text should not be allowed to circulate. He says *The Chain of Lilies* holds thoughts of such a divine nature that only people who are learned enough and well instructed in such matters can truly understand them. According to him, it could be very dangerous to show it to people whose minds are not prepared, especially to a Gentile. Still, I'm sure that if you explain who this Miranbola is—'

'His name is Mirandola! Count Giovanni Pico della Mirandola.'

'Anyhow, I don't agree with Astruc. I myself am incapable of understanding the full meaning of these thoughts, and it would never occur to me to try to reach the state of divine speculation for which its symbols and hieroglyphics were intended, but I have to say that after studying the text many times I have managed to grasp at least one part of its meaning and this has helped me to see things differently, to distance myself from my immediate circumstances and see them in a wider context. In fact, I believe that this is one of the reasons why it is called *The Chain of Lilies*, because every reader can progress through its meaning from one level to the next, according to the possibilities of his mind, like someone moving the beads of an abacus.'

'Or someone climbing up a long ladder.'

'Precisely. As to its circulation, the more copies there are, the less likely it is to get lost. Printing with movable letters must, I am sure, be a very advantageous invention. A lot of people who could not even dream of having a book in their hands can now afford to buy one. I think books have been printed in Barcelona and Valencia for some years now, but, to tell you the truth, I've never seen a printed work.'

Anna got up and took a book from her bedside table. It was kept inside an embossed leather cover, with metal clasps.

'Look, Petrarca's *Canzoniere*,' she said, opening it.

'It looks just like handwriting! Who is this Petrarca?'

'Ah, Petrarca!' said Anna. 'Petrarca is the best poet in the world!'

The afternoon sun and a breeze that moved the blue gauze curtains warmed our skins and our hearts alike. Anna began to recite:

S'amor non è, che dunque è quel ch'io sento?...

If it's not love, then what is this I feel?
But if it is, by God, what is this thing?
If good, then why so deadly is the sting?
If bad, then why is every torment sweet?

It reminded me of the troubadour poems I had sometimes heard in the market square in Girona. But Petrarca's words were more agile, light as feathers and soft as music, and their meaning pierced my heart like an arrow. *S'amor non è, che dunque è quel ch'io sento?* A flock of swallows darkened the sky and I looked out of the window. Suddenly I felt the need to tell Anna my story, everything that had happened to me since the day of the edict, and in particular I wanted to tell her about my confused feelings for Astruc. How could I love him truly when, that very morning, while I dictated the text, I had felt so close to Vidal?

Anna listened in silence, with a grave expression. When I finished speaking, she said:

'Vidal was your first fire, and a part of you will always be in love with him, partly because your union happened at the moment of rupture between your old existence and this new exile, a moment that changed your life and has changed you. But that does not mean you must close your heart to Astruc. He has become your lantern, your star, as his name implies, and you must let his light guide you. You need not forget Vidal, either, but don't think of him as a reality, because if you do, you will become a prisoner of your own feelings, and you will lose your personal freedom. Your reality is Astruc.'

And while I promised myself that I would follow her advice, she began to tell her own story.

She was the daughter of a rabbi from Socino. Her father, who in his youth had written various treatises on grammar and copied many books, had slowly lost his sight, and since both her brothers were merchants and were often away from home and her mother could not read, Anna had become her father's reader. By the age of seventeen she had read all the books and parchments in his library, and had become one of the most knowledgeable members of the Socino community. When her father died she married Giacomo Léon, a rich Jewish merchant from the Venetian island of Corfu, who had acquired a special right of residence in Venice and who shared Anna's love for books. Although they had been married for six years, they had no children.

'But Giacomo doesn't reject me for being barren. "Who knows?" he says, "look how long Sarah took to have children." '

'You have the books.'

'Yes, it's true, we have the books. When I came to live in Venice and discovered Giacomo's library, I was amazed. Until then I had only read the holy books, including some kabbalistic writings, which I loved. I had also read some books on the sciences of the skies and on mathematics. But here, in our library, I discovered the poetry of Dante, the tales of Boccaccio, and all the Greek and Latin authors, some in their original language, others in good Italian translations. And I discovered Petrarca.'

I had heard of the Greeks Plato and Aristotle, but knew nothing of Petrarca nor of the other Italian authors she mentioned; nor of the painters whose pictures hung on the walls of her palace. In a word, I knew nothing of all the things that seemed to matter so much to the inhabitants of that dazzling city.

Anna laughed and said that neither did she know anything about the poets of my country, or of its painters. She explained some of the peculiarities of the Venetians, and told me about their form of government and institutions, all of which reminded me greatly of the manner of government enjoyed in Catalonia which, according to Senyor Muntaner, was now in danger of being lost under the rule of King Ferran; and I remembered my conversation with Muntaner that spring afternoon, with Girona in the distance, looking as snug as a bird in its nest, but mortally wounded.

Anna also told me about the feasts and processions that took place in Venice, about the fashions and customs, and about the artists and scholars who came to her house to use her library; and when I asked her whether these people did not belittle her for being Jewish, she answered that although the Jewish religion was officially discriminated against in public, even insulted, privately and individually being a Jew was not an obstacle in society.

'In Venice, men and women are admired much more for their integrity than for their birth,' she said, 'more for daring to follow their own beliefs than for blindly following those they have inherited; so long as, in doing so, they continue to observe the laws of citizenship and respect for others. We have all been born equal, as Pico della Mirandola says, and it is for us to decide how to live our lives. Within us we are all free, we all have the universe at hand.'

She paused and looked at me. Then she added: 'I know what you're thinking, Alba: that it's not always easy to do what one wants. But in our hearts, at least, we must be loyal to ourselves.'

Everything Anna said seemed as beautiful as the room we were sitting in. The blue gauze curtain continued to move in the breeze and the sun was setting behind Saint Mark's, covering its domes with a fiery hue. I let myself be carried away by her voice and her enthusiasm, answering only with nods and smiles.

'And, you know, Alba? Your contribution will soon be the talk of every Venetian. Our young scribe has already spread the word round the town, and aroused enormous expectations. And tonight, when you walk into my banquet hall and they see that you are as beautiful as you are intelligent and brave, all the men will fall at your feet.'

She suddenly got up, crossed the room and opened a cupboard that was full of clothes. There were tight-fitting dresses and loose tunics, as well as sleeveless over-gowns, skirts, bodices, petticoats, capes, hats, toques, ribbons and all kinds of ornaments—all in a great variety of materials, colours and shapes. I had never seen anything like it and told her so.

'Come,' she said, as if wishing to make little of it, 'let's look for the dress that will suit you best. What do you think of this one?'

* * *

I doubt whether all the men who turned to look at me that night were ready to fall at my feet, though, to be frank, I did feel pleased with my appearance. We had chosen a long, bright-green silk dress with silver embroidery of flowers and birds, very tight round the waist and with a low neckline; its sleeves were wide at the top and tight along the forearm. I wore my hair half gathered at the top with a tiara of white flowers and pearls, half loose over my shoulders. In that attire I looked like a real Venetian lady, and under that liberating disguise I felt, for the first time in my life, that I could be my own person. Until then I had always considered myself, above all, Jewish, for that is how others saw me. The fact that I was Catalan had only become significant once I had left Sepharad, and then only to differentiate me from other Jews: Provençal Jews, Genoese Jews, Tuscan Jews. Until that moment I had always been seen as the weaver's daughter, or the daughter of Regina the baker, or the granddaughter of Rabbi Ismael, but now I was only Alba Levanah de Porta, and with the enthusiasm that youth confers on us, I felt that the whole world was within my reach. My dress moved airily, it danced with me to the music in the hall. A few months longer in this city, I thought, and I will know all Petrarca's verses, and all the different painters of Venice, without turning my back on my Jewishness. My Jewishness will become fused with everything else, but it will no longer mean restrictions, exile or scorn. As I say, I do not know how I was perceived by the gallant young men who were looking at me during the feast given by our hostess, but, in truth, I did not care, for the only presence I was aware of that evening was that of Astruc, who did not take his eyes off me. That night, when we retired to our bedroom in the *palazzo* of Anna d'Arco, I knew that the time to consummate our marriage had come at last, for we were both inflamed by desire and love, and Astruc's promise of a house was his way of saying that he could now possess me as his wife. I felt a mixture of shyness and pleasure when at last we lay together under the bedclothes, and he covered my whole body with passionate kisses.

But later, in the small hours of the night, I was awoken by Astruc, who was talking incoherently in his sleep in a mixture of Hebrew, Aramaic and Catalan. I drew close to him, and the heat from his body was fierce. I tried to rouse him by saying his name slowly and softly, again and again, and by cooling his head with the palm of my hand. But he remained in the same feverish state. So I got up, lit a candle and went quietly down to the kitchen in search of a bowl of water and vinegar. Out of the kitchen window I saw black clouds racing across the moon, and a shiver went down my spine. The words of the old hag came back to my mind, filled with a new doleful meaning: "Wandering Jew, your wanderings will soon come to an end." I closed the window, which was beginning to rattle in the sudden wind and hurried back through the unfamiliar house to Astruc's side, seized with such irrational fear that the long dark corridor separating the kitchen from the dining room turned in my imagination into a dark cavern in which fierce wild beasts were waiting to pounce on me.

Back in the bedroom, I applied wet rags to Astruc's forehead and wrists, wringing them out as soon as they had absorbed the heat, and wetting them again with fresh water and vinegar, as I had seen my mother do on countless occasions. After an hour or so the fever had abated and Astruc was breathing normally. By then the wind had also dropped and I could hear the murmur of rain gently falling on the canal. I went over to the window and looked out at the small canal, bubbling under the rain. Water upon water. *If it's not love, then what is this I feel?* A grey day was slowly emerging from the night, and I stood there for some time, clinging to the light of day for protection, hoping it would melt away the icy fear that had taken possession of me.

The silence was broken by a low wailing sound reverberating through the bedroom. I turned to look at Astruc and saw him sitting up in bed, his eyes fixed on the sheets.

'You're not the woman I thought you were. You're evil,' he said, his voice trembling with anger. 'You are an evil woman, just like Gabriela.'

'Astruc, my dearest, don't say things like that,' I said, running back to his side and wondering why he spoke in that way about me, and about his first wife. 'You're not well,' I added, sitting on the edge of the bed and putting my arm reassuringly round him.

I could feel him stiffen at my touch. 'What's the matter?' I asked.

'What is the matter, you ask? What is the matter?' he muttered, turning to face me. 'You were not a virgin, Alba, you were not pure when you came to me to be my wedded wife. A woman has betrayed me again.'

His voice was stern and shrill, reminding me of the preachers' voices we sometimes heard coming out of Girona

Cathedral. Astruc was a complete stranger to me now.

He looked at me fiercely, his eyes were bloodshot, and I grew very frightened. I could not think clearly. 'Astruc, you're unwell, I must go and ask Anna to bring a physician to you,' I said.

'First let me see your beautiful white night-gown, now that the light is brighter,' he said. The angrier he got, the shriller his voice became. He pushed me back brusquely and I fell off the bed, onto the floorboards.

'Yes, an exquisite garment,' he said, tugging at the skirt of my night-gown, while I tried to get back on my feet. 'No doubt another gift from our rich hostess, like the green dress you wore at the party, which revealed half your breasts. But look, there is not a trace of blood on it, and nothing on the sheet. Where is the token of your virginity? I thought you were chaste, Alba, but the Lord only knows how many men you have given your body to before me! I thought your soul was transparent and truthful, but perhaps it hides a mountain of lies.

'No, Astruc!'

'Don't you understand,' he went on, throwing his hands up in despair and pulling his hair, 'that the Messiah will only come when we can all walk in the light of righteousness? Only then shall we be ready for Redemption. What of all the prophecies? Has it not been said that our exile from Sepharad is the first of the Messiah's birth pangs? Is this how you behave, you, the descendant of our devout Nahmanides, you, the granddaughter of my teacher Ismael? No, do not speak, I have banished you from my heart already, as I banished Gabriela, my first wife, who abandoned me for a Christian, and was later burnt at the stake by the Inquisition.'

His voice broke off and he began to sob. I stood in front of him, and although I was hurt by his accusations, I also felt his pain as my own. It was enough to see him to understand how he must have suffered from Gabriela's betrayal, and her horrible death.

'It happened about five years ago,' he said between sobs. 'I can't remember the exact date, but when I heard of her sentence I travelled to Valencia, where she had been living, to try to help her in some way. Perhaps she was not so evil, since she had remained secretly in the faith, I thought. However, I soon discovered there was nothing I could do to alter the course of events. I watched her from afar on the day of the *auto de fe*. She walked with her head high. Then she was tied to the pyre. The smell of the burning flesh is still with me. Oh Gabriela, why did you betray me? I loved you, Gabriela,' he sobbed, 'I also loved you, Alba.'

'I still love you, Astruc,' was all I could say. No other truth seemed to matter at that moment. I sat down next to him again and held him in my arms like a child; and he offered no resistance. I cried with him and tried to soothe him with gentle, heartfelt words. Soon exhaustion sent him to sleep, and I placed his head on the pillow and tucked the sheet around him. Then I dressed hurriedly and ran to Anna's room for help.

* * *

When the doctor arrived, Astruc was still asleep. The doctor roused him and spent a long time with him, looking grave and saying nothing. He took his pulse, observed some red spots that had appeared on his chest, examined his urine, consulted calendars and charts, and made notes in a book. Although Astruc had opened his eyes, he lay listless and silent, and the fever had returned. At last the doctor prescribed some remedies which he said would be brought to me by the apothecary, since I should not leave my husband alone. But he warned me that he had caught a fever of the worst kind, and he feared that his constitution would not be strong enough to withstand it.

After he had gone, and Anna had returned to her rooms, I went back to the little window and fixed my gaze on the persistent rain, praying with all my heart for Astruc's health to be restored.

'Bless those in need of healing with *r'fua sh'leima*, the renewal of the body, the renewal of the spirit, and let us say, Amen.'

The thought of losing him became terrible to me. I felt I would be sucked into a void if he died, a second exile. Poor Astruc! He was not alone in his conviction that our exile was the beginning of the end, the first sign of the coming of the Messiah and of the return of the Chosen People to the Promised Land, but he had imposed on himself more desire for perfection than was reasonable. And yet, his integrity gave me strength; it made me love and admire him. I could understand his anger at discovering that I was not a virgin, his terrible disappointment. In his eyes I was a sinful woman, and I knew how much this had hurt him, but now all I could think of was the immediate threat to Astruc's life, and how precious his life was to me. The revelation of his truth had joined me to him forever. Above all things, I wanted him to live. From a clothes hook by the window, the green silk dress, sad and lifeless in that sickroom, seemed to be reminding me of how different I was from Astruc. And yet, I knew that if he lived I could be Rabbi Astruc's wife without having to give up being myself, as Anna said.

During the next few days I gave him the prescribed remedies and nursed him with the greatest care. But he could not hold anything down, and grew weaker by the hour, not speaking, not smiling, showing no signs of wanting to live, moaning only when he felt the scourge of his illness. To break the stifled silence I sometimes sang to him, or told him tales I had heard from my grandfather when I was a child, about wise men who understand the speech of birds and beasts, or read him psalms from his psalm-book. I also talked to him about our house in Mestre, about the life we would lead there and the children we would have together, to whom we would teach our Catalan language. And yet I knew, even as I spoke, that none of that would really happen, because nothing stirred him from his slumber. I began to see that he had fallen into death's trap. Only once did he speak to me, and that was with great difficulty, for his breath came in fits and starts and he seemed unable to find the strength with which to voice his words.

'Don't... forget... the *men... orah...*' he said.

I had, indeed, forgotten all about the illuminations of the text. So, later that day, when Anna came in to visit us, I asked her to bring the finished book for Astruc to see, which she did at once. My heart was beating fast when I held the book in my hands and opened the first page to see the lily pattern, and then the other illuminations. But Astruc could not see the beautiful coloured illustrations that adorned the title of every chapter, not even the candelabrum he had so particularly wanted. I found it: paragraph 4, chapter 3, part 2. I read the text beside it out loud, for him to hear:

In the middle of the night, the absence of light enables us more easily to turn the eyes of our soul to the Creator and see the light that shines without fuel, being itself its own fuel. For it is said in the Book of Samuel: 'He made darkness pavilions

157

round about him, dark waters, and thick clouds of the skies. Through the brightness before him were coals of fire kindled.' The dark waters symbolise magnanimity and mercy, the divine attribute through which judgement and punishment are mitigated.

'The Lord be praised,' said Anna.

Astruc looked at me for a moment, and I could see he was trying to speak. But he only sighed, then groaned and went into another stupor.

Anna came twice a day to visit us, because I refused to leave Astruc's bedside. She brought tasty broths, fresh fruits and other delicacies with which to tempt his appetite, but all to no avail. Rabbi Giuseppe also came once from Mestre and he shook his head unhappily as he left the room.

The days passed, slowly and painfully, like the creaking wheel of an old mill that can hardly sustain the effort of being pushed forward. I knew it was a time of waiting for an end, but nonetheless my whole being became a prayer for Astruc's health. I kept praying that at least he might recover sufficiently before his death to be able to see how much I wished him to live, how close I felt to him. The disclosure of his hidden anger against women, whom he seemed to blame for all the misfortunes of our people, and the love he still felt for his first wife, Gabriela, had suddenly made him more understandable to me, more human. I felt sure that if only we had been given enough time, I would somehow have succeeded in chasing away his anger and his disappointment with me. But he never once recovered consciousness.

As Astruc lay dying we came to the feast of Rosh Ha-Shanah, and since we could not go to the synagogue,

Anna asked a *shofar* blower to come to her palace. The wail of the ram's horn, announcing the New Year and preparing us for the ten days of repentance and the Yom Kippur, was like the echo of Astruc's own wailing that filled our bedchamber day and night. Although he did not even open his eyes, I hoped that perhaps, in some part of his consciousness, he would be hearing the call of Elijah, and in his delirium would believe that the moment he had been predicting had finally arrived: the resurrection and the blessed age of the Messiah, when the Jews of all generations, persecuted and scattered over the world, would at last see the holy city of Jerusalem and the Temple miraculously restored, and all men would live in a reign of peace and justice.

Outside, the weather remained unsettled, with sudden storms followed by bright sunshine, and windy spells that ruffled the surface of the canal waters. When I was not sitting next to Astruc, I stood by the window, looking at the grey stones of the buildings opposite, which reminded me of the stones of Girona, and occasionally catching sight of the tall mast of a merchant ship making its way up the Canal Grande, three or four streets away. One morning I heard a neighbour complaining to another, as they both hung out their washing on a line above the canal, that on the mainland figs were rotting on the trees and grapes were turning to wine before they got to the press. Their words brought back a longing for the simple things in life, for a settled home with children and a crowded dinner table on the eve of the Sabbath, with the candles lit, and all our voices joining in song and prayer.

Exactly three weeks after the start of his illness, the Angel of Death flew in through the bedroom window to take Astruc's life. I was sitting next to him, holding his hand in mine, when all of a sudden he opened his eyes and looked at me. He was trying to speak, but the effort was too great for him. The next moment he was gone. Only his body remained, horribly swollen on account of his illness. But Astruc was no more.

For a moment I closed my eyes and my mind filled with images of him: Astruc in my grandfather's study, helping me memorise the book; or later, riding on his mule beside me, on our way to Marseilles; or walking hand in hand with me through the streets of Genoa, looking for the rabbi's house. I saw that worried look he often had, and the goodness in his eyes, and the way he smiled at me sometimes, and I could not bear to think that I would never again see that smile. But when I opened my eyes all I could feel was relief for him, for at last he rested in peace. I covered his body with a clean sheet, then opened the door and called Anna's name. It echoed through the house, like a church bell announcing death. She came running to my side.

'He's dead,' I said.

From that moment until the end of the week of *shiva* rites that followed the burial, Anna took charge of all the proceedings, as if Astruc had been a member of her own family. I just followed her instructions: put on this black tunic, sit on this chair, eat this food, follow me. Despite small differences in the rituals and in the wording of hymns and prayers, I did not feel an outsider. The ceremonial of death returned me to my people. Anna's husband, Giacomo, had come back from his travels and took part in all the prayers and funeral rites. I was grateful for his presence and that of Rabbi Giuseppe, brotherly and paternal figures who comforted me. At one point, Anna asked me whether I wished to attend the burial. 'Here, women usually stay behind,' she said, 'but if you feel a strong desire to go, the rabbi says it will be all right.' I nodded vigorously. Poor Astruc, away from home, in this city which he did not like, how could I let him go alone? How could I abandon him now?

Walking through those narrow alleyways behind the men who carried Astruc's coffin was like reliving my grandfather's funeral. It was then that I finally wept, disconsolate, grieving for both men. But I have only vague recollections of those days. I remember small things like a moth-hole in a corner of the black cloth covering the coffin, and a crack on the bench of the funeral boat that ferried us over to the Jewish graveyard on the Lido. And the insults and whistling of a few coarse young men who were waiting for us as we passed under the bridge of San Pietro di Castello. And the moment when Astruc's body was buried in his shroud, and the sack of earth that was placed under his head. And the way Rabbi Giuseppe's voice trembled as he chanted: "Mourn for those who are left; mourn not for the one taken by God from earth. He has entered into the eternal rest, while we are bowed with sorrow."

When we returned from the burial it was raining hard. I remember a larger boat overtaking us, leaving high waves in its wake that rocked our boat. And back in the city, its streets deserted because of the rain, I saw some children looking at us from a window, silent and surprised at our black clothes, and I remember in particular a little round face that looked over his mother's shoulder and smiled at us.

During those days Anna and I had not spoken of the future; it was too soon. But at night, alone in my widow's bed, I thought every now and then of Venice, of a life among books, of the freedom that had touched me lightly during the banquet, like the silk of the green dress touching my skin. Those thoughts were almost unarticulated, clouded by the death of Astruc, but as the days went by they became clearer, until they took the form of a decision. I would stay here. I would send for my mother. Anna would help me materially and, in exchange, I would help her in some way, cataloguing books and parchments, perhaps...

On the last day of the week of mourning, a letter arrived from my mother, addressed to me at the synagogue in Mestre, which pulled me out of my musings. Its content filled me with dismay:

> *Alba, my only child, my beloved daughter, peace be with you.*
>
> *Since you left things have gone from bad to worse, and I beg you, Alba, to return to Perpignan with your husband as soon as you can, for we are in great need of help. I myself am sick and frail, as are the majority of those who came with us from Sepharad, having caught a sickness that spreads from one to the other, due to the great weakness of our bodies and the lack of wholesome food. All I know is that I cannot move, and need you back by my side.*
>
> > *Your ever loving mother,*
> > *Regina.*

Suddenly I felt so dizzy I had to sit down. I handed the letter to Anna and she read it.

'How can I travel alone?' I asked her. 'But I must get back to my people, to my family.' I felt anxious and saddened about my mother, but at the same time I realised that this would be the end of my Venetian dream, that if I returned to Perpignan I would become trapped again in the responsibilities and demands of that life of poverty and exile. My wishes would count very little; all decisions would be taken by Isaac. My mission was now over and done; I would be what I had always been, one more person in our community. I could almost hear my mother: "What do you want to go to Venice for? Look what happened to Astruc. And all on account of those wretched books..." I felt like a child who has been offered a sweetmeat but then has it snatched away when he is about to eat it, and I could not stop thinking of the green silk dress, as if my spirit had remained fixed to that beautiful garment. No, I did not want to go. I would ask Anna to send a messenger to my mother, with money and medicines, and a letter saying that I would be waiting for her in Venice. But suddenly, the very thought of doing such a thing filled me with shame. At the same time I felt a terrible fear of the future. What could I do?

Anna sat down beside me and put her arm around me. As if she could guess my thoughts, she said: 'She's your mother.'

Coming from Anna, those words did not seem like an order that I must obey blindly, but an open road which I must follow if I wished to remain at peace with myself. It was something I could understand now better than ever, for I was beginning to feel a new life growing inside me. I too was going to be a mother.

XI

RETURN TO PERPIGNAN

By then it was already the month of Heshvan, when trees start shedding their leaves and humans wrap up against the fresh northern winds. With great sadness I said goodbye to Anna on the quay of St. Mark's and boarded the ferry to the mainland with the group of merchants under whose protection I was to travel as far as Genoa. Giacomo had seen to all the details of the journey, and Anna had given me money, a bag full of remedies, and some warm clothes. The green silk party dress would be left hanging in her cupboard, said Anna, in case I should return one day.

'Come back' Anna insisted from the quay. 'Come back with your mother as soon as she has recovered; and may the good Lord bless you.'

'I'll try,' I answered, above the shouts of the sailors. I had not told her that I was with child. Had she known, she would have realised how difficult it would be for me to return.

A thin mist hung over Venice that morning and we had not moved away half a mile before the whole of the island was engulfed by it. The ferrymen clanged their bells and blew their conches to avoid collisions in the busy waters.

I was thinking about Anna, about the happy afternoon we had spent together before Astruc's illness, and the visits she had paid me when Astruc became ill. When she came through the door, the room seemed to light up with her presence. In Anna nothing seemed borrowed from the books she had read; everything about her was natural. In this respect she reminded me of my grandfather Ismael. But whereas my grandfather dedicated his whole life to the study of the Kabbalah and saw the creation with the eyes of the spirit, as a dim reflection of its Creator, Anna, with no less awe for the Divine Being and His creation, observed the world from below, with sensory eyes, admiring those artists who could capture and express light, colour, movement and mood in order to stir the heart of the listener or the beholder. Above all she believed in the importance of the individual.

'What use is the individual,' I asked her one day, 'if we can do nothing to avoid the events fate has laid down for us? I left Girona because I was dragged away by a force stronger than my individuality, stronger even than my love for Vidal. And this same force has brought me here.'

'You left Girona because you were true to yourself. No other decision would have been in accordance with your true self.'

I was indebted to Anna. At a moment when I felt completely lost, uprooted, disconnected from my natural surroundings and from my people, she taught me to look for a strength which lay hidden within me, a strength placed in the innermost chamber of my soul when the Lord created all souls at the beginning of time. And so it was that I learnt to lean solely upon myself. Hitherto, in moments of loneliness and grief I had searched for Vidal's image in my mind, but my pregnancy had displaced that image; he was absent from my heart, which now only had room for Astruc. And as I moved away from Venice in the mist, I understood that as Astruc lay dying, so had I, in a sense, been reborn. That open society had opened my soul; it had shown me a world transformed by freedom. The memorised book, which was now held effortlessly in my mind, continued to make me see the spiritual side of the world, the stamp of the Creator, the mysterious union of all His aspects. But Venice gave a new meaning to many of those concepts.

Arrangements had been made for me with great care, so I had little to fear from the journey itself; nonetheless my heart was heavy, due to the uncertainty that lay beyond the journey, and to the sadness of having lost Astruc. Later, as I retraced my steps through the lands of Italy with Astruc's child growing inside me, a sense of purpose slowly began to cheer me. I looked at the silver boughs of the olive trees, listened to the singing birds, breathed in the fresh mountain air and played imaginary games with my unborn baby on the gentle slopes of the valleys. I was not alone.

We were taking the same route as I had taken with Astruc on our outward journey, and as I passed certain landmarks—a house, a tree, a bend in the road—fragments of our conversation returned to my mind, as if they had been engraved there for me to read on my return.

"How I long to unburden my mind, Astruc!"

"I'm sure you do. But it won't be long now. And I will unburden mine too."

"What do you mean?"

"In due course you'll understand, Alba."

I now wondered again what he had meant. Perhaps he was referring to the death of Gabriela. But I knew that his feverish account of that episode had not been prepared beforehand. What could it be? Then my thoughts went further back to our first meeting in Girona, and I remembered how then too he had seemed to keep something to himself, something he had not told Rabbi Leví or me. What did he know that he had not told anyone else, not even me? And yet in Venice he had said nothing, unless he had confided in Rabbi Guiseppe Caravita. I thought again of those numbers—4, 3, 2—which pointed to a precise place in *The Chain of Lilies*. What did they mean? Were they perhaps connected to some Messianic prophecy? How would I ever know?

But I did not spend too long over such matters, for no secret seemed as important as the infant I now carried in my womb. I crossed the same bridges I had crossed with Astruc and journeyed through the same long mountain passes where eagles circled slowly, as if they owned the air. At last, after two weeks, we arrived in Genoa. There, after parting company with the Venetian merchants, who were heading for Sicily by sea, I returned to the backstreets of the city. I found the rabbi still in his house by the synagogue building, still wondering how long it would be before he would be forced to leave.

'Your Spanish brothers are dying out there in the port,' he said, 'and there is nothing I can do to help them. Take my advice, Alba: if you have enough money for the journey, leave this place as soon as you can, do not tarry here a minute more than you have to. But mind the port authorities; don't let them see you until you have paid your fare.'

Then he said a prayer for Astruc and blessed the child I bore.

I walked apprehensively out to the port and the scene that met my eyes was even worse than I had feared. A much larger number of Sephardim now filled the quayside, and a wooden fence had been built around them, to prevent any possible escapes. They were thin and pale, their eyes deeply sunk in their sockets; they looked more like ghosts than human beings, so famished they could hardly move. Some women held babies in their arms, motionless infants, slumbering from hunger, too weak to cry. But the most shocking spectacle was on the outside of the fence: five or six sturdy young friars, each holding a crucifix in one hand and a loaf of bread in the other, were crying out: 'Convert, brethren, convert! You have only to embrace this crucifix and you will receive food and be welcomed among our people! Come to the sweet bosom of Jesus Christ!' And my Jewish brothers, having resisted so long, having left their homes and their country to avoid conversion, stood there listlessly, turning their heads away from the tempting bread.

From my hiding place under the dark arches, I scanned the port in search of the old hag but could not see her among the piles of nets and crates, or huddled up in any corner, or behind any of the columns. She must have died of the same illness as Astruc, I thought.

As I stood there by the waterfront, I felt the guilt that goes with survival. The still waters of the port seemed to accuse me silently. I was well nourished, and in all the time since I had left Sepharad I had not suffered real hunger. But what could I do to help? The food in my bag was not enough to make any difference to those starving people, and I needed all the money I had left to buy my fare by sea to Marseilles and from there by land to Perpignan. I had to get back to my people with the remedies.

Yet the scene I beheld was too appalling to bear. I could not go on looking and do nothing. Choosing the quietest streets, I went back to the rabbi's house.

'What are you doing here?' asked Salomone Canetti. 'I thought you were looking for a ship to take you back to Marseilles.'

'We must do something. Between us, we must help these people. They are our brothers.'

'We can do nothing, Alba de Porta,' he answered, shaking his head as he spoke. 'Even if I could take them in, even if I could feed them all—and that would be impossible—they cannot leave the port without a permit. You don't seem to realise the danger you're in by roaming around the city. I've tried, time and time again, to obtain permits, but the Church exerts too much influence over the government. What has happened in the kingdoms of Spain is spreading like a disease to these parts. And now, please take my advice; go straight to find the captain of a galley, show him your money, and you will obtain a passage. Go back to your family, Alba. Don't make things more painful than they are. Do you think I'm not tormented too? I have to live with this every day.'

'Where is the bakery?' I asked.

'You turn right at the end of the street. Then left. But don't go, Alba. You have your own people to think about. There must be over a hundred Spanish exiles in the port by now. Two days' bread is all you could get for them with the money you have, and I doubt the baker would comply with your request. Besides, how could we get it to them?'

But I was already half way up the street.

I ordered the bread. In my Venetian cloak and without the badge, the baker did not take me for a Sephardi. 'Is there a wedding?' was all she asked.

Once night had fallen and the friars had gone back to their vespers, the old rabbi and I took the sacks of bread to the port. The guard in charge of them was sitting on a stool, half asleep, and he shrugged his shoulders when we asked for permission to hand out the bread. The exiles took their rations quietly, with cold bony fingers.

I like to think that my action did more than ease my conscience and their hunger, that it might have helped to save at least one life; but I will never know how that episode of our Jewish history ended. As for me, on the following day, among the many ships anchored in the port I found a galley bound for Marseilles. After some arguing, I managed to buy myself a seat on the ship by offering the captain the leather medicine case Anna d'Arco had given me. The remedies I tied up in a bundle.

* * *

As we sailed across the Italian gulf towards Toulon, the Mediterranean waters smelt of Catalonia, and the Provençal language of the sailors reminded me of my mother tongue. I looked ahead. The sea was calm all the way and dolphins jumped about as if to greet my child-to-be. The sky unrolled like a soft wool blanket towards the horizon behind which lay the Pyrenees and my lost home. I thought of the times before Vidal, of my childhood, when my world consisted of the alleyways of the *call*, where I played hide-and-seek with my friends, of the patio behind our house, with its rows of flower pots and the dovecote up high, and of my grandfather's study, always smelling of parchment and ink. And of my mother's wide skirts, on which I nestled when she sat by the fire.

In Marseilles I went to the stables where our horses had been left, and inquired after *Falaguera*. My mare had been sold to a lady of the highest rank, I was told, who had set her heart on her the moment she saw her. She lived in a castle outside Marseilles and rode her to town on market days. Well, I thought, at least my mare will have a comfortable home, even if I don't. The stablemen told me there was a merchant cart setting off for Narbonne. I paid for my journey with a cloak of fine wool Anna had given me: it enabled me to have a seat all the way, for which comfort I was grateful, as I felt very weak at times and in much need of rest. The familiar landscapes kept passing by, each one a separate picture, like the images in a pack of cards, until at last the walls of Narbonne came into sight.

For the last lap, from Narbonne to Perpignan, I travelled by foot with a shoemaker and his wife whom I knew from our journey out of Sepharad, and who were returning to Perpignan after a fruitless attempt to settle in Narbonne. They had a mule and allowed me to put my baggage in its saddlebags, and when I told them I was with child they insisted that I ride the mule from time to time, whenever I felt too tired to walk. The days were getting very short and we had to spend two long cold nights in the open. On the third day, as we journeyed through a landscape of low bushy hills, we sighted the walls of Perpignan and remembered how different and how promising the town had looked to us when we had first arrived from the other side of the mountains.

'There's only one answer to our situation,' said the shoemaker. 'Emigration to the Ottoman Empire. Turks welcome Jews. The only problem is how to make such a long, expensive journey, when none of us has any money left or any means of making more.'

'The Lord will help us,' I said, without much conviction, for the Lord was obviously testing us and wanted us to find ways of helping ourselves, of becoming stronger and more resourceful without waiting for manna to fall from Heaven.

We entered the town after sunset and made our way up the steep slope towards the streets of the Jewish quarter. The mule struggled desperately under its load, but at last we came to the door of the shabby house where my mother and Isaac's family lived. The shoemaker unloaded my bags and I thanked them both for their kindness. Then they went their way.

I knocked on the door and waited, leaning against the doorframe. Soon I heard Rosa running down the passage crying: 'Who's there?'

Then she stopped running and waited by the door until I replied: 'Open the door and you'll see!'

'Cousin Alba! Cousin Alba! Father, come, look who's here!' she cried, opening the door and throwing her arms around me. Then she peered over my shoulder and looked up and down the street with a puzzled expression.

'I have come alone, Rosa. Here, help me take the cases in, they're so heavy!'

By then Isaac had come to the door. He dragged his feet and stooped slightly as he walked; he had black circles round his eyes and had grown very thin. He made me think of the faces on the quay of Genoa.

'How is my mother?' I asked.

'Not very well, but she'll be all the better for seeing you. Where's Astruc?' he added, almost in a whisper.

I just shook my head. 'A fever,' I said.

He put his arms around me. But there was no strength in them.

The house was, if anything, more derelict than when I left it. I walked up the uneven steps, past windows with dangling, unhinged shutters, and patches of damp plaster on the walls. The whole house reeked of poverty and ill health, increasing the nausea that was already plaguing me due to my condition. Isaac's wife, Coloma, came out to the landing and her eyes filled with tears when she saw me. She covered her face with her apron and wailed: 'Would to God we were back in Girona, Alba, this is no life for anyone.' I embraced her, then went on up to the top floor where my mother had her room.

I knocked gently on the door and opened it slowly. She was lying in her bed, her veil only half in place, revealing her thick grey hair that was unkempt and in disorder, the only sign of vitality in her whole body. She looked at me for a few moments without speaking, as if wanting to tell me everything with her eyes. I ran to her side and put my arms around her.

'Mother, Mama, I have come to make you better. I have brought remedies that will cure you and all the others.'

'Where's Astruc?' she asked.

'He died, Mother,' I said. 'He was very ill and then he died. I looked after him day and night. I wanted him to live. But now he lives in me. I am going to have his child.'

'Oh, Alba, my poor daughter, my poor lass,' she cried. 'First you lose your first suitor, then you lose your lawful husband, and now you are left a pregnant widow. Even if there had been a bachelor brother in Astruc's family you would not have been entitled to marry him, because you are with child. What are we to do now? A curse seems to have been laid upon us all.'

She broke into sobs and I drew closer to her and stroked her matted hair. Poor Mother, she had seen too many calamities and now, in her weak state, she could take no more. After a while she looked at me again and suddenly her expression changed from misery to anger.

'Do you know what I say? That with the help of the Lord, blessed be His Name, I will see that you marry a good Catalan or Aragonese Jew, and that you get the wedding you deserve, with song and dance and food and merriment. Nobody is going to hurt my beautiful Alba ever again. I will make quite sure of that.'

* * *

I lay down by her side and after a while we both fell asleep. But during the night I was woken by intermittent sounds that I was not used to: the clang of church bells from the convent at the bottom of the road, the crying of a

173

child in the house opposite ours. As soon as it was light enough I crept out of bed, wrapped myself in my travel cloak and made my way down to the kitchen on the ground floor of the house.

Isaac was already up, blowing on a small pile of coal over which he was heating up some bread and garlic soup. We sat by the tiny fire and he told me all that had happened since I had gone away.

Two whole families of Aragonese relatives from my mother's side of the family had arrived about a week after my departure, some from the town of Saragossa, others from Alba, my mother's birthplace. (That is the origin of our name, Alba Simha; my father insisted on giving it to me, knowing how much my mother missed her childhood home.) They had all rejoiced and thanked the Lord for bringing them together so unexpectedly and had taken this as a sign that they must stay together from then on. They had brought plenty of food with them and shared it out generously among the whole community.

But as a result of a series of edicts and laws that were approved in Roussillon, it had soon become clear that all Jews arrived from Spanish lands would have to abandon the French county. The first of these decrees was made public towards the end of August, when a judge of Perpignan ordered the five members of the council of Girona to hand in all the scrolls and any other objects which they had brought with them from our synagogue, and forbade them to leave the town. The second came directly from King Charles of France, when he authorised two of his representatives in Roussillon to take any action required to control the groups of Jewish exiles.

After that life had become intolerable. A few of our young men had found work with the grape harvest, but local vintagers were complaining that they were stealing their work from them. And if any locals had at first viewed us with pity or curiosity, they changed their minds now, for they saw us only as a threat to their own livelihoods. Soon the Christians of Perpignan managed to have a law enforced by the local government whereby all Jews, not just the exiles, were forbidden to set up as tailors, shoemakers or furriers.

Isaac, who had been telling me all this in a matter-of-fact way as he ate his soup, now put down his spoon and looked earnestly at me. 'Not only are we Jews here, Alba,' he said, 'we are also considered foreigners. And we are falling ill, out of weakness and worry. Poor Benavist has died, he who had been so convinced he would return to Sepharad; and we have also buried five or six others from Girona. Bonadona's husband died; Raquel died two weeks after giving birth to her dead child; and old Simon, the *shohet* at the Girona butcher's; and Josep, you know, the one who lived in Carrer de la Ruca.'

I put my hands over my mouth to stifle a gasp.

'We all want to leave,' he continued, 'but we're trapped here because of illness and also because we cannot go until all our debts have been paid. I see no solution, do you? Your mother has the letter of exchange, but I can't take it to the banker. Others, who also had promissory notes for various amounts, took them to him and haven't seen them again—the notes or the money. We must try to get out of here and reach Naples, where your letter is registered and where it will be much easier to present it.'

I did not answer. All I could see was that the garlic soup was grey and watery. In Girona it would have been thick, with golden crusts of bread. I did not even want to think of the soups Anna prepared in Venice. Isaac swallowed another spoonful and went on, his voice becoming agitated and angry: 'Those commissaries of King Charles,

Spanyol de Camon and Pierre Irraxeta, are two tyrants, Alba. They enjoy so many privileges and collect so many taxes that they live better than the King himself. And now, with the King's order at hand they can exercise their power as they please. They investigate each and every one of us, making inventories of all our goods for the use of our creditors, and we live in constant fear with their threats of confiscation and prison. I don't dare mention the bill of exchange to anyone; your mother has hidden it, but if the word got round and the commissaries found out, they'd be capable of beating her to death to obtain it. And to make matters worse, even the Jews of Perpignan have turned against us. The secretaries of the Perpignan Council called a meeting of all Jews at the synagogue a few days ago, and there our Roussillon brothers forbade any of us exiles to leave without first satisfying all our debts. We were told that our debts would be bound to fall on the permanent Jewish community if we went away and left them unpaid. There were some harsh words spoken, and my heart cried out for shame. Is this what we have left our country for, I thought, to quarrel with our Jewish brothers? Sometimes I feel so discouraged I wonder why we did not remain in Girona, like Vidal.'

'Vidal didn't intend to stay forever. He was going to find me—'

'No, Cousin. Vidal should have married you and come with us. I should have spoken to him before his conversion, I should have forced him to come. He was almost betrothed to you.'

'He said he would join me as soon as he could.'

'But did he, eh?'

'And did I wait for him? Oh Isaac, we just have to accept the designs of the Lord,' I said. 'And do not despair, we're still alive, and the Lord will help us if we first help ourselves.'

176

I sat there for a while longer, by the warm coal fire, but could think of nothing else to say to Isaac. I, therefore, decided to go out that very morning and see what I could do to help the sick.

Taking Rosa as my helper I did the rounds of the Perpignan quarter like a veritable doctor, carrying my bundle of remedies and giving as much sound advice as I could piece together from what Anna and the Venetian doctor had taught me and from what I had heard Grandfather Ismael say when we went gathering herbs in the hills of Girona. Some were suffering from fevers, with swollen throats and pains in different parts of the body; others had a more general ailment, a weakness of the whole body and cramps in their arms and legs. But although the mixtures, infusions, ointments and poultices provided some relief, I knew that there was no substitute for a good hot meal of mutton and vegetables, or some fresh, tasty fruit.

XII

THE SECRET OF GIRONA

One of the sick I visited was our Girona rabbi. He and his wife had a squalid room next to a stable. I found him sitting on a wooden bench, wrapped in an old blanket, looking very pale and thin. He was only a shadow of the man he had once been and seemed to have lost all the enthusiasm with which he had led us during our journey into exile. His wife, Violant, sat next to him mending a torn sheet. She pointed to a small chair by the door and indicated with a nod that I was to sit there. When I told them that Astruc had died, Rabbi Leví hung his head down and was silent for a while; Violant gave me a brief, commiserating look and sighed loudly before resuming her sewing. Then Rabbi Leví looked at me and asked:

'Was the text delivered?'

'The book is secure, rabbi,' I reassured him. 'And copies are being made to guarantee its survival.'

'The Lord be praised! The Lord be praised!' he cried. 'Thank you, Alba, in the name of our community, for all you have done. Had we taken the book with us and not asked you to memorise it, it would now be lost forever. It would have been taken from us at the border, or else here, in Perpignan.'

'Yes,' I answered, 'Isaac told me about the confiscation of all the synagogue effects. I wonder what they were hoping to gain by it?'

'I ask myself the same question,' said Rabbi Leví.

'Why were they so eager when none of these items was of any material value to them and yet meant so much to us? What also puzzles me,' he went on slowly, breathing heavily, 'is that on the very same day as that order was made public, August 27th, a diplomatic protocol was being signed between the representatives of Ferran and those of King Charles VIII of France, to determine the fate of the two counties on this side of the Pyrenees. Perhaps there is a link between the two things.'

His words hung in the air like smoke.

'Are you saying, rabbi, that the confiscation of the synagogue objects here in Perpignan was in fact requested by King Ferran?'

'That is what I'm beginning to realise, Alba. Contrary to what some people think, and despite the title of Prince of Girona which is given to the heir of the Crown of Aragon, Ferran has a grudge against Girona, against the citizens who opposed his father during the civil war, and in particular against the Jews of the *call*. Even after we have left his kingdom he seeks to plague us, and he knows very well how he can hurt us most. You see, he cannot forget the days he spent in Girona during the siege of 1462, when he was only a child of ten and had to hide with his mother in La Força. He was a very fearful child.'

His voice broke off, and he looked mesmerised. 'Tell me more about the siege, rabbi,' I said. 'Why do you say Ferran has a grudge against us? I've always heard that all the inhabitants of La Força helped him on that occasion: Old Christians, New Christians and Jews alike. And that he rewarded many of those families who sided with him and his mother. Yes, I know the Inquisition later punished the *conversos* who had helped him most during the siege, but I thought that was just the Inquisition showing its teeth and that Ferran was in fact committed to us.'

Violant looked up at her husband, then patted his knee and said: 'Why must you stir up the past, Daniel?' And turning to me she added: 'Don't tire him with questions.'

I stood up to go. But Rabbi Leví raised a shaky hand. 'No, no!' he said. 'There is something I must tell you, Alba. And you too, Violant. I might die soon and then no one would ever know this story, which has probably more to do with our fate than the very edict of expulsion. It has weighed heavily upon my soul for years.'

I sat down again and wrapped my cloak around me against the damp cold air, while our rabbi, with his watery eyes fixed on the wall, travelled to the distant regions of his memory.

* * *

I was thirteen at the time. It was the spring of 1462 of the Christian era. King Joan was away in Aragon, and his wife, Joana Enríquez, had arrived hurriedly in Girona with her son, her mind set on controlling the peasant revolt that had started in the countryside around Girona and in the mountainous regions of the north. She hoped to get the peasants on the side of the monarchy by warning them that an army, raised by the Catalan Government, had already left Barcelona against them. If she was successful, she would strengthen her position and that of her husband among the Catalans, who were becoming divided between those who accepted and those who did not accept the King and his heir, Prince Ferran. Girona received the Queen courteously—after all, she was still their legitimate sovereign—but without enthusiasm, and Joana Enríquez only secured the support of a handful of the more distinguished citizens.

In the meantime, the Catalan army, aware of these events, had changed its direction. Instead of marching against the peasants, it was marching openly against Girona and against the Queen. Terrified, Joana Enríquez took refuge in La Força, together with her supporters. When the army from Barcelona arrived at the gates of our town, the people of Girona offered no resistance; but La Força, with its fortified walls and its situation at the top of the hill, was impregnable.

The siege began, and we Jews were trapped inside. We were her subjects and offered her all our respect and assistance. We gave her everything we could: food and also money to acquire more provisions and defensive arms through the enemy lines; but it was the conversos of the call who gave the Queen the greatest monetary support during the siege, and probably saved her life. Although they called themselves New Christians, they still had the Torah engraved in their hearts, and with it the sense of loyalty due to their monarchs.

Despite our help, and the courage of the men who went out in search of provisions, food soon became so scarce that we were reduced to eating almonds and broad beans, rationed to only ten beans a day per person, and we were even forced to eat horse-flesh; yes, I know, the very thought of eating forbidden food is repulsive, but in those circumstances it was a religious duty to eat it, in order to preserve life. What little fresh fruit was available was reserved for Prince Ferran.

Besieged by the army and with her husband outside Catalonia, the Queen was beside herself with fear, and could see no way out of her situation. Ferran was a very nervous child, and was terrified by his mother's constant outbursts of emotion.

One day a squadron of the enemy managed to break

into the call *through an underground passage. It was, in fact, the son of one of the* conversos *who had given money to the Queen who discovered the open mine in the patio of his house, but by the time he had rushed to warn his father, a few soldiers had already managed to get through, and were heading for the house of Bishop Margarit, where the Queen was living. Those who saw the soldiers thought the siege had come to an end, and when Joana Enríquez found out what was happening, she rushed around the streets of the* call, *looking for her son, screaming and pulling her hair. However, the squadron was soon captured and the irruption came to nothing.*

A few minutes before the alarm was sounded, I happened to be sitting by the cathedral porch when the Prince came up to me.

'What's your name?' he asked in his rudimentary Catalan.

'Daniel Leví,' I answered.

'Are you Catalan?'

'I'm a Catalan Jew,' I answered.

'My mother says Jews are evil.'

'Nobody is born evil, but everyone can do good or evil in his lifetime,' I said.

'Do you go to church?'

'I go to the synagogue.'

'Synagogues are small and ugly, as small and ugly as the Jews themselves. Your miserable little synagogue can't be compared to this magnificent cathedral.'

'Perhaps not in size. But it has some astonishing treasures,' I said, tired of being trodden on. 'Our ancient candlestick is more valuable than anything in your father's court. And besides, it has magical powers.'

'I don't believe you,' he said.

'I'll show it to you, if you like,' I answered. 'My fa-

ther is the synagogue keeper, and I could use his key.'

'All right. I'll meet you there at midnight.'

I was about to say that I could not do such a thing, when we heard the clash of swords and the screams of women coming from the streets below. Then we saw the Queen running towards the cathedral, calling Ferran's name. She called him 'Fernando,' of course, because she spoke Castilian to her son. 'Fernando, Fernando, where are you?' she cried. When she found him she grabbed him by the arm and hurried off to the bishop's palace. I heard her shout: 'And don't ever talk to a Jew again!'

Just before disappearing round the corner, Ferran turned his head to give me a last look and a nod. I knew I would have to keep my word, and wished with all my might I had not bragged in that manner.

That night, just before midnight, I managed to creep out of my home and run to the synagogue, hoping Ferran would not be there. But he was waiting by the front door.

'Show me the treasures,' he whispered.

I had taken the keys from my father's writing desk, may the good Lord forgive me, and decided it would be safer to use the side door. Our footsteps echoed as we walked down the covered alleyway, and when I opened the door it creaked so loudly that I was sure the noise would rouse the whole neighbourhood. But we did not even hear the bark of a dog, so we stepped in. I took the small oil lamp that hung on the wall by the door and told the Prince to follow me into the main room, where I lit its wick from the perpetual lamp in front of the Ark. Ferran looked at the thick embroidered curtain covering the Holy Ark, but I shook my head.

'They're not in there,' I said.

Holding the oil lamp as far up as I could, I led the way back into the room by which we had entered the build-

ing and down the corridor that lead to the archive. There, hidden behind piles of dusty books and rolls of parchment, was the door to an alcove where the synagogue's treasures were kept. Soon the light from the oil lamp was shining on gilt-edged books, silver boxes, cups and breastplates, a Torah case decorated with a flower-design, and other valuable objects; but the gold menorah, *which was the most precious possession of the Girona Jewry, seemed to shine with a light of its own. It was about three spans high and equally wide, with a stepped base surrounded by two circles of precious stones, one of rubies and one of emeralds, while the candlestick itself stood like a tree with three branches on either side. Each of its seven arms was finely fluted, decorated with carvings of petals and other motifs, and crowned with an almond-shaped cup. Ferran stared at it with his mouth open.*

'It comes from the Temple in Jerusalem,' I said. 'It's very, very old and very holy. Sometimes it rises and is left suspended in the air, as if it were flying, because it contains all the magical powers of the Kabbalah in its arms.'

'Of the what? Oh, never mind, I don't believe that, anyhow,' answered Ferran.

Suddenly we heard a loud bang. Someone had come in through the side door and was advancing down the corridor. Although the door of the archive was wide open I could not see who it was, because he was wrapped in a dark cloak, but I guessed it must be my father. The figure came into the room, and the Prince froze.

'Who is that?' he gasped, holding his breath and clutching me so hard I almost dropped the lamp.

'Where?' I asked, pretending I could see no one.

'There!' hissed the Prince, backing away.

'I see no one, Your Highness,' I said calmly. The trick had worked. Prince Ferran was white and trembling.

*'Let's get away! It's a ghost; it's an evil Jewish ghost!
It's the Kabbalah!'*

*Not daring to look at my father, I left the lamp on the
floor and ran out of the archive with the Prince, down the
corridor and finally through the side door into the deserted
street. Ferran scurried off and disappeared.*

*The next time I saw him he was walking around the
call with his nurse and he ignored my presence. I knew he
could not have told his mother about his escapade, any
more than my father could scold me publicly for my action, though he did make me polish all the synagogue
benches until they shone like the gold* menorah. *And one
day I heard my mother and a neighbour talking about how
the Prince was heard screaming every night in his sleep.
'He must be dreaming about the soldiers who got into the
call,' said my mother.*

*The siege ended a few weeks later, after King Joan
signed a treaty with the King of France by which he handed
him the counties of Roussillon and Cerdagne in exchange
for an army of twenty thousand men. With the arrival of
the fearsome French troops, the Catalan army fled and the
French entered our town without difficulty, liberating Joana
Enríquez and Ferran.*

* * *

Rabbi Leví turned to his wife. 'I fear I have brought
great harm to our people by not telling them what happened. Will the Lord ever forgive me?'

'Don't speak like that, Daniel,' answered Violant,
without raising her head from her needlework, as if by not
looking at him she was minimising the importance of a
confession she would have preferred not to have heard.
'You were only a child.'

'What made you say it came from the Temple in Jerusalem?' I asked.

'My father had told me so, and he would have been incapable of inventing such a tale. He said this candelabrum was almost an exact replica, though on a much smaller scale, of the large *menorah* of the Temple. According to a parchment which explained its history, it was kept in one of the Temple's chambers and was used for training priests in the very complex and elaborate ritual of lighting the main *menorah*. The Girona *menorah* was a seven-branched candlestick, you see, not an eight-branched one, and, as you know, the Babylonian Talmud forbids the making of seven-branched *menorahs*. That, in itself, was proof of its authenticity, and showed that it came from the Temple. My father went on to explain that when the Romans sacked and burnt the Temple in the year 70 of the Christian era, they took this smaller *menorah* along with the large one stolen from the Holy of Holies, as part of their booty. Some three centuries later the Visigoths had in turn plundered Rome and taken some of these treasures to their new domains in the Southern regions of France, among them the small *menorah*. And some time after that the *menorah* had been discovered by a group of pious Jews who had smuggled it over the Pyrenees and handed it for safekeeping to the Girona synagogue. The bit about the Kabbalah was pure invention, may the Adonai forgive me.'

'Where is the candelabrum now?'

'It disappeared a few years later, during another of the sieges Girona suffered in the civil war. Who knows where it ended up? After my adventure, my father had hidden it underground, in a metal box. But the synagogue was plundered and when my poor father was able to enter it again, the metal box lay open and empty. All that was left were the few ritual objects we brought with us to Perpignan.

'And you believe King Ferran could still be looking for it?'

'The more I ponder over this, the more certain I am,' he answered. 'The gold *menorah* would have been a substantial addition to his treasury. I am convinced he must have ordered a search of the synagogue as soon as we all departed last summer and is now trying to find some clue among the documents we brought with us that might lead to its discovery. How wise of your late husband to ask you to memorise that unique text. He managed to preserve the only treasure we had left.'

This was true. But now I suddenly saw what Astruc's secret burden had been. He must have known where the *menorah* was, but he had not wished to tell me, so that I would not have to share his fears. Of course! I did not tell the rabbi what I was thinking, but I realised that I ran the risk of being questioned, if only because I had been married to Astruc, the archivist of Girona. I would have to leave Perpignan as soon as possible.

Rabbi Daniel Leví died in his sleep a few days later. The memory of a righteous person be blessed.

XIII

NAPLES

The months that followed were dismal. We wanted to leave Perpignan but were unable to do so for want of money or means. The day after I spoke to Rabbi Leví I began to feel ill. It might have been the fear for my own safety that caused my sudden weakness, or perhaps it was just due to the general exhaustion of my body: all my strength seemed to be sapped by the little being growing in my womb, and I lost my customary vigour. Soon I was unable to nurse the sick, for I had to nurse myself, and I kept to my home, praying that we would be able to leave Roussillon soon, so that I could deliver my child in a safer land.

That was not to be, however, for about four weeks after my return, half-way through the month of Kislev, when the days were at their shortest phase and I was in my third moon of gestation, I miscarried. But despite the numbing fear that governed my actions during those dark winter months, my spirit did not hibernate: I travelled endlessly through the most desolate landscapes of the mind, through barren fields of loss and of death, with no other purpose than to reach the truth of my feelings. I let the pain left in me by Astruc's death and the loss of our child sweep over me like a bitter wind, until at last it subsided and I was able to face my daily trials more peacefully.

The whole family shared the work of the bakery, which my mother had set up in the house. Coloma and I kneaded, Isaac put the loaves in and out of the oven and took care of the fire, and my mother, who had no strength left for working, would sometimes leave her bed and sit by the oven to feel its warmth and give us instructions. We sold bread to Jews and to some Christians too, and in this way we managed to scratch a living; but since many of our Jewish neighbours would run up accounts which they were unable to pay, at times we could not even afford wood or flour. I went to see merchants and traders and offered to do sums for them or write letters. I also asked a few ladies of Perpignan whether they would employ me to clean their homes and do their sewing. But nobody wanted to give me work. On two or three occasions I begged at the city gates, but all I received were insults. The days passed by, and the miller, who was not a bad person, would sometimes give us flour on trust, and others would order large quantities of bread for a banquet at the court, so we were able to re-pay the flour with our work. And some mornings, Cousin Isaac would go out into the woods with Rosa and collect as much timber as they could carry on their backs.

Spanyol and Irraxeta continued to plague us with their sudden intrusions, banging on the door and announcing that we owed them such and such in dues and taxes—which they made up as it suited them—and threatening us with a thorough search of our homes if we did not pay up quickly. My mother and I lived in constant fear lest they should discover the bill of exchange, which she had sewn into her petticoat hem as soon as Isaac told her it would be impos-sible to negotiate it in Perpignan.

There were times when, sitting near the oven for warmth, I would close my eyes and think about Venice. In my heart I longed to go back to that city of marvels, to resume my friendship with Anna d'Arco and begin a new life in that society, which seemed so well suited to my na-ture. My thoughts would dance like coloured butterflies, stopping now on this memory, now on that, and when I opened my eyes I would look in dismay at the mouldy walls and ramshackle furniture all around me. But I did not so much as mention these yearnings to my mother, knowing she would not listen to me. What I had feared, happened: I fell into the dense net of family and communal responsibilities, as if my will had been left in Venice, imprisoned in the green silk dress, among its silver birds and flowers. Besides, one part of me was beginning to feel the way animals do when they are in danger and form packs for their greater protection, and I instinctively resolved to follow my people wherever they decided to go. Stories abounded of the peace and prosperity in the faraway lands of the Turks. Soon our desire to escape from our predicament became coupled with the hope of sailing to Salonika and establishing a communal life there.

And so those months went by, cold and sad. Despite the proximity of Girona, we had no news at all from what we still called 'home.' Only occasionally I would hear some market vendor cry out, 'Apples from Girona! Get your juicy apples from Girona!'—but I never saw anyone I recognised, and I believe that if I had, I would have been ignored, as I had been by the Girona merchants in Marseilles. At times the thought of Vidal being so close— only a few days' walk away—raised small whirls of hope in me, but so small that they soon vanished. For although I was now a widow and I could have reconsidered the possibility of meeting him again, by sending him a message, perhaps, the loss of my baby had made me give up any dreams I may have once had. Besides, after what Rabbi Leví had told me, it would have been very foolish to send a message to Girona, even if such a thing had been possible, because of the risk it involved.

Shortly after the start of the year 1493 of the Christian era, the two commissaries of King Charles announced our immediate expulsion from the two counties and the confiscation of all our goods. 'What goods?' you may well ask, for we had almost nothing left to call our own and what few possessions we still managed to keep we had hoped to sell in order to pay for our journey. Moreover, the weather was very cold, with snow all about, and icy winds from the north raged day and night, making the sea unnavigable. How could we leave? In view of our desperate situation a group made up of thirty-two men of the exile community had the courage to stand up against the order, and named two mediators to parley with the Perpignan judges. As a result, a new sentence was proclaimed at the beginning of February saying that in view of the bad weather and the sickness of many of the Jews newly arrived from Spain, these Jews were allowed to postpone their departure until the end of March, by which date they must have paid the sum of 500 francs to the Princess Madame de Foix and twelve gold *escuts* to the judges who signed the new order. 'And what do we owe this Princess of Foix?' said my mother from her bed, 'I don't even know who she is! They're sucking our blood! That's what they're doing!'

In order to meet this sum, some of our men travelled all the way to Marseilles with a cart full of our remaining assets, to sell them there at a better price than they would fetch in Perpignan, where everyone took advantage of our situation. Pots, pans, utensils for our trades—all my mother's baking tins—household linen, combs and ribbons, belts, buttons, buckles and anything of any value whatsoever. I was also forced to part with my pretty ceremonial ring, the only material token left to me by Astruc, and a little book of Petrarca's sonnets which I had already learned by heart; but the key-box, which I had never shown to anyone, I kept, may the good Lord forgive me; and my mother also refused to give up her patchwork cloth. 'You'd have to kill me first!' she cried, clinging to it with all her might.

Around the middle of March, as soon as debts were cleared with the representatives of the French Crown, and we had managed to pay our passage as far as Naples (at the exorbitant price of two gold ducats each, which we had struggled to collect), all the exiled Jews from Catalonia and Aragon who had taken shelter in Perpignan began to leave. Every few days a boat would be hired to take a group of Sephardim out of Roussillon. They left from the ports of Colliure and Port-Vendres and headed for Naples, which was considered the most welcoming port for us this side of Italy. It suited our family, moreover, for that was where our bill of exchange was registered. The Kingdom of Naples had belonged to the Crown of Aragon during the reign of Alfons V—the Magnanimous, as he was known. When he died, about forty years before these events, he left Naples to his natural son Ferran, and Naples became detached from the Crown of Aragon. Ferran, or Ferrante, as he was called in Naples, was still king when we passed through that city in 1493, and although he belonged to the same family as our own King Ferran, he did not persecute Jews. Indeed, people said that there was a flourishing Jewish community there, who worked for the most part in finance houses or as small moneylenders, and many Sephardim settled in the busy town. A year later however, at the death of Ferrante, all Jews were thrown out of the kingdom. Fortunately, by then we had already left.

Our group, which consisted of what remained of the exiled Girona community and of the Aragonese relatives of my mother, left Perpignan on one of the last days of March. By the time we filed out of the town, in the early hours of a grey, gusty day, we were all truly destitute, with nothing left to eat and only rags to keep us warm. I wore my red tunic—I had no other garment to my name. It was old and torn now, a symbol of my past life. Even my mother's wall-hanging was beginning to fray, from having been used as a blanket during those cold winter months. We must have made a pitiful sight as we proceeded to the port of Colliure; but nobody came out to comfort us or to offer us any food. We had two carts for the children and the weakest people, and the rest of us travelled on foot. But without Rabbi Leví to lead us, no one had the strength or the desire to sing as we had done when we left Girona, and the procession travelled in silence. The only sounds were our sighs, and the cracking of the whips over the backs of the mules.

It was a long journey to make, especially in our condition, and we did not reach the port until late that night. There we huddled together on the quay, under the castle walls, unable to light a fire because of the wind. At dawn the captain came up to us. He took our money and put us all on board, ordering his sailors to prepare for departure.

The ship moved slowly out of the narrow harbour, and on either side we saw the fishing boats coming in with their catch. Tomorrow this fish will be in the stalls of Perpignan market, I thought, and life will continue in the capital of Roussillon as if we had never been there. Nobody will miss us. As soon as we were out in the open sea the waves began to rock the boat, and with every movement came a loud groan from the sick. I remembered the words of Juda Ha-Leví's poem:

> *Let your heart remain firm in the midst of the seas*
> *When you see the mountains heaving and bending...*

Wrapped in my tattered cloak, with my mother, frail and weak, lying on a stretcher by my side, I watched the coast receding, the low hills of the Pyrenees becoming bluer and hazier in the distance, and I knew I would never set eyes on those lands again. The dark pine trees overhanging the Colliure headland swayed in the wind; they looked like arms waving a silent farewell, and I remembered how, a few months earlier, the flags of Perpignan castle had also seemed like arms to me, welcoming us to their land. Above the pine trees the sky had lost the crimson tones of early morning and was a pale shade of blue, almost white, the colour of oblivion.

A year had elapsed since the edict of expulsion was proclaimed in Girona, and in that year I had seen the whole spectrum of the rainbow colours, from the soft pink of first love to the sombre purple of grief and death. Now the white sky marked the end of an epoch: I turned my head away from Sepharad and looked out to sea.

The sails were unfurled and soon they puffed out with a favourable westerly breeze, but on the second day the dreaded north wind blew again, pushing the vessel off course. All day long the sailors cursed their lot as they struggled with the waves in the rough sea, and I felt just as frightened as on my first sea voyage. When the storm was at its worst my mother called Isaac to her side.

'I am very ill, Nephew,' she said; her voice was almost a whisper. 'And in case I die before we reach Naples, I want you to know that the money from our bill of exchange is to pay for a ship that will take you all to Salonika; as many Sephardim as it will cover, even if they don't belong to our community, for we're all brothers.'

Isaac was lost for words. Although his face was wet from the foam that cascaded over the deck, I knew that he was weeping.

Mercifully, by the morning of the fourth day my mother seemed somewhat restored. The wind had changed again and was driving us speedily towards land. Soon we sighted the huge bay of Naples, with the Castel Nuovo standing in the middle of the harbour and the city spreading from the shore to the slopes of the hills behind it, like an amphitheatre of the ancient Greeks.

As soon as we disembarked a representative of the Jewish community, alerted by the Neapolitan authorities, came up to welcome us. From that moment on we were treated with the utmost kindness, and the despair that had been on everyone's countenance for so long vanished. I thanked the Lord for his mercy and remembered the words of the Psalm:

> He maketh the storm a calm,
> So that the waves thereof are still.
> Then are they glad because they be quiet;
> So he bringeth them unto their desired haven.

We were given fresh water and bread and then taken to a large room by the custom's office where a scribe took down our names, professions, town of origin, and other details. Temporary residence permits were handed to each of us when Isaac, who acted as spokesman for us all, expressed our intention of travelling on to Salonika at the earliest possible opportunity. After that we had to be inspected by the port physician, but always with civility and respect. The sick—about two dozen, including my mother—were taken to the Jewish hospital with strict orders not to leave until they had recovered. We were told that hundreds of Sephardic Jews had arrived in Naples the previous summer and that this measure had been established because so many of them had carried infectious diseases. I went with my mother to the hospital. She was so weak after the sea journey that she could not even speak, but as I helped her off with her cloak and dress, she pointed at the hem of her petticoat. I unpicked the small, tight stitches and took out the bill of exchange.

* * *

The notary's office was easy to find. It was in the high street, not far from the Castel Nuovo. Its front door led into a large open courtyard of the sort that is very common in noble Catalan houses, with a stone well in the middle surrounded by a profusion of potted plants. There were various doors leading off this Neapolitan patio, each one decorated with plants and stone statues, and two wide flights of stairs, one on either side of the central well, came together on the first floor, forming a circular balcony that gave access to the doors on that level. I went up the wide staircase and found the placard I was looking for: "Ambrosio Panocchi. Notary". I knocked on the door and a melodious voice called out: '*Avanti,*' so I went in.

'Signor Panocchi?'

'*Si?*' answered an extremely corpulent man with bluish-red cheeks. He was looking up at me from his desk, which was literally covered with documents.

I handed him the letter of exchange, but even before reading it he must have understood the reason for my visit. It was enough to see my ragged clothes and my Sephardic features to guess what I was doing in his office. Many other Jews from Spain must have done the same before me.

'This is from Senyor Bernat Muntaner of Girona,' I said in my poor Italian.

'From Bernat Muntaner, you say? But what a coincidence!' said the notary. 'He was here this very morning asking me whether this letter had been brought in. Well, well,' he continued, as he unfolded and straightened out the document. 'It's had a rough time, this letter, eh? Been through a bit of stormy weather!'

'Did you say Senyor Muntaner is here in Naples?' I asked, trying hard to suppress my astonishment, and without revealing how accurate his joke had been. How I would like to see him, I thought, and ask him about Girona, the house—

'Yes,' he answered, but offered no more information. I did not insist, not wishing to expose my benefactor by showing any eagerness to see him, however tolerant the Neapolitans might be towards our people. Besides, perhaps it was better this way, better to leave the past alone, distant and forgotten, white as the sky in Roussillon.

Signor Panocchi handed me a note, which was an order of payment, something I had never seen before, and was told I could turn it into coins the next morning in the bank. I slipped the piece of paper carefully into my pocket and left.

As I was walking down the steps I saw Bernat Muntaner coming up on the other side.

'Senyor Muntaner!' I cried.

Bernat Muntaner stopped and looked at me. It took him a few seconds to realise who I was. Then we both ran down and met on the ground floor.

'Alba! I've been so concerned about you!' he said, taking both my hands in his and looking at me from head to foot. 'It's been hard for you, eh?' he said.

I nodded. 'But with the help of the Lord I have survived, and so has your letter of exchange.'

'When I came here this morning and was told you hadn't claimed it yet, I couldn't think what had happened to you. Why didn't you take it to a notary in Perpignan as soon as you got there? But come, let us go to the *palazzo* where I am staying and there you can take some refreshment and give me all your news. And I will give you mine: I have a lot to tell you.'

'But you were on your way to the notary.'

'That can wait,' he said, putting put his arm round my shoulder, as if I were his daughter. We left the building and walked together through the streets of Naples, I in my frayed cloak and bare feet, he in his flounced velvet cape. Two or three times he raised his hand or touched his plumed cap to some acquaintance, without the slightest embarrassment at his ragged companion. He might have been walking with a queen. When we reached a wide street and passed the Castel Nuovo, Muntaner pointed at the Triumphal Arch, all in white marble, on whose front was sculpted the entrance of our King Alfons the Magnanimous to Naples.

'In those days Catalonia was still the greatest maritime power in the Mediterranean,' he said, ' and the benefit of that power spread to all spheres of our confederation. Now our empire is a thing of the past; nor has the union with Castile favoured us in the least. We are doomed to decline; and without your Jewish presence to enrich the texture of our society, even more so.'

'There are many Jews left among you, even if they call themselves New Christians.'

'Yes, but now their way of life has merged with ours. There is no more competition, and it was the constant tug in one direction or another that kept us alert and aware of our own identity. Now the same rivalry continues, but in an ugly and destructive way, under the encouragement of the Inquisition, and the Old Christians worry to an absurd degree about the purity of their blood. Commerce and business are greatly affected.'

Presently we reached the *palazzo* and Bernat Muntaner showed me into a spacious room where we sat in comfort on large cushioned chairs, something I had not done since leaving Venice; there was an open fire, bowls full of dried fruits and almonds, which he placed near my chair, flowers in vases, beautiful hangings and paintings. Muntaner wanted to know my story, which I told him, omitting only two things: what little I knew about the candelabrum, for I thought it more prudent to keep that to myself, and the truth about my love for Vidal, which seemed to me irrelevant. When I had finished my tale he commiserated with me for the loss of my husband and for all the hardships I had suffered, and praised me for undertaking the task of memorising the text.

It was now my turn to ask questions. How was our house? Was anyone living there? Had the pigeons left the dovecote? What about the cat, was he still lying in the sun, as usual?

'The pigeons and the cat are still there,' he answered, 'and the house is as well looked after as ever. My daughter Clara lives in it. I gave it to her as a wedding present when she married at the end of last year.'

I was pleased to hear that the house was being lived in, even though I had always disliked Clara. Empty houses soon fall to ruin. I asked him who she had married, and was at the same time trying to work out how I could enquire about Vidal without sounding too interested, for it suddenly became clear to me that this might be the only chance I would ever have of knowing how he fared, and whether his mother was still alive. Depending on what he answered, I thought, I might be able to deduce whether he was still intending to be reunited with me. Despite my previous resolution to let things be, to look only ahead, I found myself entertaining new hopes. But the answer came before I had even asked my question.

'Well, the truth is that I had some trouble convincing my wife of the suitability of the match,' said Senyor

Muntaner. 'She's a very devout woman and the man on whom my daughter Clara set her heart is a *convers*. A young merchant from Barcelona who has worked for me occasionally.'

'Might I know him?' I asked, my heart beating madly.

'Yes, you must, for he lived not far from your house. His name is Pau Barceloní. His Jewish name was Vidal Rubèn.'

I can't remember what I said. I was horrified at the thought of Vidal in my house with his wife, the proud, calculating Clara Muntaner. 'I don't think I'm feeling very well,' I blurted out at last.

'Oh, my poor Alba, how selfish of me. You are still so weak. And you must be anxious to get back to your family. Let me walk with you as far as your lodgings.'

I accepted his company but said goodbye before we reached the inn where my family was staying.

* * *

I wanted to be alone, but Isaac was sitting on a stone bench outside the inn. 'Did you get the money?' he asked.

I showed him the document. 'Praised be the Lord!' he cried. 'Praised be the Lord!'

I wanted to be alone, but the innkeeper, a jolly buxom lady with a voice as thick as a fishwife's, insisted on leading me up a narrow wooden staircase and showing me our room, where Coloma and the children were lying on mattresses.

'One ducat a week,' she sang as she left. 'And if you pay me one more, there'll be hot fish soup at night for everyone.'

'I'm going to visit my mother,' I said to Coloma and ran downstairs again. I left the inn and wandered out, not quite knowing where to go in search of solitude. Soon I abandoned the crowded streets and ended up walking along the harbour until I found a small sheltered cove. And there I sat, on the edge of the sea, alone at last.

Vidal was married. And living in my old home. Just as I had feared, he must have heard about my marriage from the Girona merchants who saw me with Astruc in Marseilles and given up the idea of following me. He would never know the truth, that circumstances had forced me to marry Astruc, that I could do nothing to prevent it. He must have thought that I had given up waiting for him. We were both victims of these times, these upside-down times, as my mother called them. And of all people, he had married Clara. How I hated her! Jealousy flared up in me and I cried miserably. I gazed at the sea stretching far out into the distance towards Sepharad. The sunlight twinkled mockingly on its surface. Then I thought: when his father-in-law returns he will hear my news from him, and I wept again, this time for Vidal and the pain he would feel when he knew my side of the story, when he realised that he could have married me after all, had he only waited a while longer. I felt I had lost all the people and all the things I most cared for in this world, and no amount of reasoning could make me think otherwise. The sun was setting.

XIV

SALONIKA

We did not spend long in Naples. After about a fortnight's rest and good nourishment—the innkeeper's fish soups were well worth the ducat she charged us—my mother and all those who had been taken into hospital on arrival had recovered sufficiently to be able to embark on the long sea journey to the Ottoman Empire. I was pleased to be going to the other extreme of the Mediterranean, as far as possible from Vidal and Sepharad, and all thanks to the money Senyor Muntaner had paid for the house in the *call* of Girona.

They say that this journey, even with favourable winds, takes an average of three weeks, but we thought we could better that estimate by five days. Our ship was a large and sturdy caravel, one hundred feet long, with three masts, and when a strong wind propelled us we seemed to fly, so smooth and quick was our movement. Moreover, we had good supplies of food and water, as well as blankets to cover ourselves against the cold nights on deck, and we met with none of the difficulties and dangers that are so often encountered by ships travelling to the East. Indeed, I felt sure that once again the good Lord was protecting us, for during our stay in Naples we had heard stories of recent shipwrecks due to violent storms, and of vessels being attacked by terrifying pirates who threw all the passengers into the sea to drown.

We had left behind fifteen of our community buried

in Perpignan, on them all be peace, and seven had decided to remain in Naples. I counted all together thirty-two Girona Jews on board. With our relatives from Alba and Saragossa and three families from Navarre, we made a total of fifty-seven. Such a large number of passengers meant that we were very cramped, but nobody seemed to mind.

Old Abraham the cobbler was still with us. He sat in a corner of the deck, holding forth in conversations, and though he had no needles or any other tools, his crooked, bony fingers seemed to hold an invisible thread that joined our past to our future. There was much singing and chatter during the voyage and hope weaved its way through our words and through the stirring melodies of our Catalan and Hebrew songs. The men played card games to while away the hours and spoke of their new life ahead, making plans for setting up work-shops together; the women sat and mended clothes; and the younger travellers, like myself, watched over the small children. During prayers I remembered all the people who had helped me during the past few months.

Being at sea for days on end and disconnected from the chain of circumstances that govern one's life on land, gave me room for meditation. Many days I would wake up before dawn, when all was quiet, and listen to the sound of the wind in the sails and the murmur of the sea whispering its dark secrets as we went by. Sometimes it would seem to me that I could hear my grandfather Ismael's voice within that whisper. 'Don't forget us, don't forget us,' it said, as if I could possibly forget my dead. 'I carry you in my heart,' I answered. I spent long spells of time in this way, lost in thought, looking at the sea, remembering what my grandfather used to say to me when he saw that I was sad or irritated. 'Knock on the door of your soul and go in,' he would say. 'Only there will you find the peace you need.'

And then I would recall passages from the memorised book that spoke of the soul, and in particular this one, which quoted my ancestor Bonastruc de Porta, the famous Nahmanides:

The soul has three aspects or spheres: the vital, the spiritual and the hidden soul, which is a spark of the divine light of the Creator, in whose image man was created. Together they form a whole, which in turn corresponds to the Tree of God with its ten sephiroth. *Man's soul emerged from the radiant light, came down to the material world, which is the garden of the King, and will return to His divine light. This is how Nahmanides of Girona expressed these thoughts*:

> *From the very origins of the world*
> *I was among God's hidden treasures.*
> *He made me emerge from Nothing;*
> *And at the end of time*
> *I will be called back by the King.*

Looking at the calm sea I thought: like me, my ancestor had to go into exile, and only because the Church, aware of his high standing as a Talmudist and a scholar, had forced him to take part in a theological disputation with a Dominican friar, and he had defended our religion in public with intelligence and fervour. Our King, who was on my ancestor's side, wanted him to remain in Catalonia, but he was pressed by the Church to order his exile. One day, Grandfather Ismael showed me a letter Nahmanides had sent to his family in Girona. It was written in Jerusalem, where he settled after his travels, and where he died. The letter said: 'I left my family, I abandoned my home; there, with my sons and daughters, those beautiful, well-loved children raised at my side, I also left my soul. My heart and my eyes will always be with them.'

Looking at the calm sea I also thought of myself, and I studied the different aspects of my soul. Slowly I began to accept that we are all responsible, to a certain degree, for our lives, and that I could not blame the world and its turmoil for all my losses, least of all for my loss of Vidal. I moved resolutely away from the dejection that had taken hold of me in Naples and entered a new region of thought, in which a soft light smoothed the sharp edges of pain and nostalgia.

At the end of the month of Iyyar, in the middle of spring, we sailed into the Aegean Sea, past dozens of islands that are like gems, with their luminous sandy beaches and their brilliant green forests, and we entered the gulf of Salonika, guarded on its left by Mount Olympus. When the city came into view we all broke into song, praising the Adonai, for we knew, even before landing, that this was to be the end of our long journey. And when we had disembarked in the busy harbour and saw the good spirit with which we were being greeted, we were filled with a deep sense of gratitude to the Ottomans for offering us the possibility of beginning our lives afresh. We were soon to learn from our brothers in Salonika that Sultan Bayazid II had ordered the governors of each and every province of his empire to welcome us warmly, and had even imposed the death penalty on anyone who dared ill-treat or cause any damage to an immigrant Jew. He needed to repopulate his lands and cities, weakened by long years of wars, and in particular Salonika, where twenty thousand men, women and children had been massacred by his predecessor Murad some seventy years before our arrival, during the Turkish invasion. Above all, Bayazid needed our knowledge and our skills to bring prosperity to his young empire, and to make gunpowder for his wars. There were many Ashkenazim in Salonika, as well as native Jews, but soon, as is common knowledge, we Sephardim would outnumber them all. It was as if a new Sepharad was being created at the other end of the Mediterranean lake. It is said that Bayazid II, upon hearing praise of King Ferran, once told his courtiers: 'You call Ferran of Aragon a wise king, when he has impoverished his country and enriched ours?'

In that atmosphere of material optimism it was difficult to imagine that we were getting close to the coming of the Messiah and the redemption of His people, though there was no lack of preachers in the synagogue and in family gatherings who, like my poor Astruc, were still hopeful that the prophecies which had circulated in Sepharad before our departure would be borne out at any moment.

Certainly, for our small community of Catalans, the arrival here felt like a true deliverance from our sins, or the prize for our endurance, depending on how one looked at it, for we were immediately caught up in a fever of work and settlement and nothing seemed to go amiss for anyone.

Each group of exiles joined the community to which they belonged by birth. My mother and I went to live with Isaac's family in the Catalan quarter with the rest of the Girona Jews, one of the smallest groups in Salonika. My mother's relatives joined the Aragonese community, which was by far the largest. And the families from Navarre went to their quarter. My mother set herself up as a baker, and her skill was such that soon she received commissions from other communities. Even with Coloma's help, she had almost more work than she could handle. I had never enjoyed baking, and now it reminded me too much of the sad days of Perpignan. Instead, I was allowed to become a teacher at the Catalan school where I taught small children to read and to count and to sing the songs from my own childhood.

But there was little here to remind us of Girona. The hills and the sea, the colour of the earth and sky, the vegetation and the food, the languages we could not understand, all were new and unfamiliar. The costumes also impressed us, especially those of the Ottomans. There were men in multicoloured turbans and wide trousers. Veiled women with jet black eyes reminded me of the Arabian tales my grandfather used to tell me and of the miniatures I had seen in his books. And then, of course, the architecture: the low, whitewashed houses, the mosques with their coloured mosaics and their huge gilded domes, the palaces. All those fanciful buildings, many of which were later lost in the great fire, were novelties to us and contrasted greatly with the dark, austere houses of Girona.

Needless to say, my mother's main concern, after we arrived, was to find a good husband for her daughter. Though a widow, I was only eighteen. 'You have a pretty face and a strong body,' she said. 'And you have a good head for letters and numbers. You might appeal to a young trader who needs a wife to help him with his accounts.'

I had no fortune, but all the people who had travelled on our ship from Naples promised to return their share of what the journey had cost as soon as they had some money in their pockets, and thus provide me with a substantial dowry. So during the first few months, when we were living with my cousin Isaac, Regina Sara Benjamí, widow of Elies de Porta, went around visiting all her neighbours and relatives, and managed to find out who were the most desirable young men in Salonika.

Salomó ben Haví was the first of these suitors to come up to me, but I did not have to go through the torment of being examined by different men, like an apple that is taken and put down again in a market—something that tends to happen when marriage-makers do not choose couples well. Salomó had much to recommend him, especially in my mother's view. Not only was he a successful merchant, but his family was of Catalan origin. Although he had been born in Salonika, his paternal grandparents were from Barcelona and those on his mother's side were from Reus. He, therefore, spoke enough Catalan to hold a simple conversation, though his Castilian, which had already become the language of all the traders in the town, including the Ashkenazim, was much more fluent. He seemed a good-natured and judicious man who did not boast about his wealth as I had feared he might; it did not take me long to feel that with him I would have a good life.

I came to that conclusion on our first encounter, partly because there was something strangely familiar about his appearance, which invited me to trust him. He had bold features and a muscular body, but his robustness was tempered by the pale skin of his clean-shaven face, and the pale brown hair that he wore cut short just below the ears. This combination of vitality and gentleness I found very pleasing. What also drew me to him on that first visit was the way in which he glanced occasionally at my mother and at me while he talked with Cousin Isaac, as if wishing to include us in their deliberations on the price of grain and other matters. In my long life I have known few men who have shown such deference to women, and this courteous acknowledgement of my intelligence was neither short-lived nor false. It grew in time and strengthened my natural respect for his abilities and virtues. That first day, as we sat on brightly coloured cushions round a low copper table, sipping lemon juice and eating grapes and sweetmeats, I felt that beneath the talk that took place between the men, there was another wordless interchange going on between Salomó and me, during which we both explored our inner natures and discovered a strong affinity.

The next time I saw him was one Sabbath after prayers, outside the Catalan synagogue. I was standing there with my mother and a small crowd of neighbours when he came up to us.

'Madona Regina,' he said to my mother. 'May I walk you and your daughter home? Would you mind, Alba?' he asked, looking hopefully at me.

My mother answered for me. 'Alba, you walk ahead with Salomó. I have things to talk about with Valentina here.' She looked at Salomó and smiled.

Under the gaze of my mother and our gossiping neighbours, who followed at a distance, we began to talk, awkwardly and tentatively at first, but soon as openly as if we had been old friends. After that day Salomó often met me at the school when I had finished my teaching, and walked home with me. He showed an interest in all I had to say, and was moved when I told him about the turbulence of my exile. I told him everything, just as I am recounting it to you now. His own conversation was so enjoyable that soon we were taking the longest route home to prolong our time together, and about a month later we were officially engaged. That day he gave me a copy of Petrarca's sonnets, which he had found in Istanbul: 'Here,' he said, 'I'm not much of a reader—my only reading is in the synagogue—but I would like you to start a library for our home.' The wedding was fixed for the following year. First, Salomó wanted to build a house on a plot of land he had recently inherited, on a small hill above the town. Once it was finished, we would get married and live there. I did not mind waiting; on the contrary, I thought, this way I would have time to get to know him better.

Though still a young man of twenty-three, Salomó

was also widowed. His wife had died during her first child-birth, as had their baby girl, and this had left a great emp-tiness in his heart. But we both had a strong desire to for-get past sorrows, and that desire was coupled with a need for comfort and affection. What also drew us together was Salomó's love for Catalonia. He would question me inces-santly about details of our life in Girona. What were the streets and the houses like? How did we celebrate our feasts? What did we eat, how did we cook? And when I showed him Vidal's box with the key of our home, he looked at the smooth piece of iron as though it was some rare treasure. He took it out of the box, and then remained pensive for a long while, while he stroked it with his fin-gers. He had delicate hands for a man.

'I know!' he shouted suddenly, throwing the key in the air and catching it again with both hands. 'Why didn't I think of this before?'

He seemed very happy, but I could never have imag-ined what he was thinking. 'What?'

'Do you think you could make a detailed drawing of your house in the *call* of Girona?' he asked me.

'Of course!'

'We could build an exact replica. That way you would live in the house of your ancestors again. Everything would be the same, from the kitchen to the dovecote, from the patio to the stones in the entrance hall.'

'From the chimneys on the rooftop to the well in the kitchen. Salomó, what a good idea!'

It proved very easy for me to do what he was sug-gesting, and soon I found myself drawing the plans of the house. Now *The Chain of Lilies* had become the instru-ment with which to memorise my old home. The process had been reversed, and as I sat at a table reciting the holy words, I drew the lines of each room and then a picture of the whole building from each of the four cardinal points. As I worked, I felt closer and closer to understanding the concept of interaction between creation and Creator, symbolised by the continuous embrace of the circle, by the fish biting its tail, by the closed chain which is its own beginning and its own end. From the outer shell of the building I made my way through its principal structures, to its beams and crossbeams, its arches, vaults and windows, its four levels and the spiral staircase that connected them. The words of the holy text gave meaning to the geometry of my home, revealing hidden proportions, symmetries and points of balance of which I had hitherto been unaware. I then understood that those lines created the kind of spatial harmony that confers peace on the soul. The numerical and geometrical symbols of the Kabbalah—the 4 of the four worlds in creation or of the four consonants that form the unspeakable name of God, the 3 of the triads, the 8 of the octaves, the 10 of the ten *sephiroth*, the 12 of the signs of the Zodiac, the 22 of the Hebrew consonants, and other significant numbers—were present in the shape of every room, and in the distribution of the house as a whole. Perhaps, I thought, it was Nahmanides himself who had made the plans for our house in the *call* of Girona. The house was the book, and the book was the house, and nothing seemed to have beginning or end.

And in Salonika, my city of refuge, Salomó began the work on the new house, measuring and building with precision and skill, like the other Solomon when he built the Temple:

> *And the house which King Solomon built for the Lord, the length thereof was threescore cubits, and the breadth thereof twenty cubits, and the height thereof thirty cubits.... And for the house he made windows of narrow lights...*

For thirteen months we both supervised the building, he the quality of the material and the work, I the faithfulness to its original. I watched the workers place stone over stone and join them with mortar, then insert the beams and cross-beams, lay down the floors, shape the arches and vaults and windows. Ladders and pulleys were used as the building grew in height, and people would stop to gaze in wonder at this strange new house. After the great fire that raged through Salonika, which by good fortune did not destroy it, there have been many others built in a similar fashion to ours, but at the time it was the only one in its style. I insisted on precision, and would even make the men pull down what they had already built if it was not quite right. With the exception of some of the building materials and the outer coat of whitewash, the house in the Catalan quarter of Salonika was identical to the house in the *call* of Girona. Even the patchwork cloth, delicately mended by my mother, was once again hanging on the dining room wall.

One summer's day, in the year 5254 since the creation—the year 1494 of the Christian era—I was at last able to walk up the spiral staircase to behold my new world from the open loft on the top of the house. I leaned over the parapet, as I had done that spring morning in Girona, and looked at the view: the bay of Salonika, the whole city with its mosques, synagogues and churches, the hills behind me, all could be encompassed by the eye.

Finally, when all the work was done, Salomó had the smith make a lock to fit the old key of our house in Girona, and over the door he fixed a coloured tile which said: 'The Memory House of the Call of Girona.'

* * *

And so came my wedding, one of the greatest celebrations of the year. All the neighbours joined in the festivities and wore their finest clothes, decking the streets with flowers and coloured ribbons. I remember the look of satisfaction on Isaac's face when he led me to the synagogue, and the tenuous smile of Coloma, pregnant again after her arrival in Salonika. The celebrations lasted three days and there was all the song and dance and food which my mother had promised me. Her dream had come true, and she was happy for the first time since we had left Girona. I too felt happy looking at Salomó and watching how my mother laughed among the crowd of well-wishers, but I felt an even deeper joy within, for I had found something that I thought was lost forever; and my mind kept going back to the bright green silk dress I had made for myself, an exact replica of the one I had worn in Venice, which I kept jealously in a cupboard to wear on some future occasion. Salonika was not Venice, but Salomó was a man with an open spirit and I felt free in his company.

My mother came to live with us and occupied the same bedroom, the one right above the kitchen, that had been hers in our old home. Then came my first child, Moisès, ten months after the wedding, and a year after that Aaró was born. I nursed them and cherished them with all my heart. Those tiny beings, with their little hands reaching out to me, with smiles that held unbounded love, filled me with wonder.

Shortly after Aaró was born, my mother died, surrounded by all her most immediate family. A smile of satisfaction lingered on her face even after her death, and everyone who came to pay their respects made the same comment: 'It seems she has died happy.'

'The Lord has changed our fortunes,' she had said to me the night before, 'be grateful, be grateful, Alba.'

For weeks after she had passed away I felt empty and lost and could not even find comfort in my children. I missed her vigorous presence, her earthiness, her good management of life's difficulties and her silent love for me. Then, slowly, I learned to listen to her even though she was no longer there, and I realised how much of her spirit she had left behind, in every corner of the house that she had loved so much.

Three months after her death, at the end of the mourning period, something happened that was to change my life again quite unexpectedly.

XV

THE PRINCESS IN THE TOWER

It was a windy day, at the beginning of spring. Salomó was away in Istanbul, where he had gone to supervise the arrival of a shipment of precious stones from the East. More than one fortune had been known to disappear mysteriously, said Salomó, after goods changed hands in the port. At home, the children were restless so I decided to take them with me to the market place, despite the bad weather. We set off, and on our way the wind was blowing so strongly from the port that Moisès had to hold on to my skirts to avoid falling, and Aaró, who was in my arms, blinked and looked at me as if to say: 'What is this force I can feel but cannot see?' On our way back home, after I had finished my shopping, I chose a more sheltered, though less direct route, zigzagging through the streets that run parallel to the port, and passing by our synagogue.

In those days, the Chief Rabbi of Istanbul, Moïssis Kapsali, had travelled all around the country, from community to community, imposing a special tax on the wealthier Jews. This collection was used to pay for the ransom of Spanish Jews who, in their attempt to reach the Ottoman Empire, were captured by pirates near our coasts; and every so often, a notice would be placed on the walls of our synagogue, saying that the authorities were dealing with the release of such and such a person. That morning, as I walked past our house of worship with the children, I saw a white piece of paper on the notice board, held down by a single pin and flapping in the wind like a banner. Aaró pointed at it with his finger and laughed with enthusiasm. I left my shopping basket on the ground, held the paper down with my free hand, and read: 'Jewish captives ransomed and freed thanks to the generous contributions of our brothers.' I skimmed curiously down the list of about twenty souls, but none of the names meant anything to me. Until I came to the last one, Vidal Rubèn! My heart seemed to stop. I looked again. Of course, the name was not uncommon, I told myself. It was bound to be a coincidence. I started to walk away. Suddenly, a strong gust of wind ripped the paper off the board. Moisès ran after it excitedly, but every time he got close to it, the paper blew further away.

'Leave it, Moisès!' I shouted after him. 'Let it fly away.'

He turned his mischievous face to me, and tried once more to catch it. Then he thought better of it, and watched it dance away down the street. Aaró clapped his hands with delight. I too began to laugh. My heart was dancing like the piece of paper, flying away, dancing with unsuppressed joy. But another voice inside me was saying: 'Forget the piece of paper, forget you ever saw that name. It is most probably not Vidal at all, and besides, what would be the good of seeing him now? It is too late, much too late.'

'Mama, let's find another piece of paper to fly up, up in the sky,' said Moisès.

'No, Moisès,' I answered. 'Let's go home now. The wind is too cold for little children. It will swallow us like a big, big dragon and churn us into little pieces. Come, when we get home I'll tell you a story.'

'About a dragon?' Moisès loved frightening stories.

'About a dragon and a princess who was locked up in a tower.' It was the first thing that came into my head.

He took my hand and we walked quickly back to the

house. I remember that I was shaking all over and unable to make sense of my feelings. And then, as I opened the door and stepped across the ten river stones of our entrance hall, a sense of detachment possessed me. I looked at my children and they seemed like little strangers. I tried to think about Salomó, and drive away the old passion for Vidal that, despite myself, was growing in me again. But Salomó also seemed remote from me. I was back in Girona again, I was Levanah, I was the girl inside the woman, sitting on Grandfather Ismael's knee; I was the girl awakening to womanhood, and the memory of Vidal was tender and sweet and devoid of sorrow.

'Tell us the story, Mama' said Moisès. 'The story about the princess who was locked up.'

'Later.'

'No, Mama, you promised.'

I sighed. Then these words suddenly came to me from nowhere. 'Once upon a time there was a princess who was locked up in a tower. For years she had been there, and there was no escaping. A moat surrounded the tower, and on the other side of the moat was a dark forest in which a fierce dragon was said to live. She had never known freedom, nor did she know why she was being punished in this way. An eagle brought food to her every evening, but she never saw another human being.

'One afternoon, as she sat waiting for the eagle to arrive, she saw an old man walking along the edge of the forest. He was carrying three lanterns, one in each hand and the third hanging round his neck. The old man saw her and cried out: "I've come to save you, princess!" Then he climbed into a boat and rowed over to the foot of the tower. "Come down, princess," he said, "and take one of these lanterns, so that you may light your way through the forest once the sun has set. The dragon is afraid of light and will not attack you. But I must warn you: only one of these three lanterns will serve you, and you will only have one chance to guess. If you take the wrong one you will be doomed." The princess was in a quandary, but after a while she decided to take the risk. She knotted her sheets together to form a long cord, tied one end to her bedpost and lowered herself slowly into the boat.

'When the princess and the old man were both ashore on the edge of the forest, it was already getting dark. The princess looked at his three shining lanterns and said: "I'll take the middle one." And, lo and behold, as he handed it to her, the other two grew dim, for their light had been but a reflection of the middle one.'

'But how did she guess?' asked Moisès.

'Because being locked up in the tower, and gazing at the trees in the forest day after day, she had had time to reflect on the nature of the universe, and she had realised that just as a branch grows on the left of the tree, and a branch grows on the right, neither branch could exist without the trunk, which draws the sap from the earth and holds the balance.'

'So the dragon didn't catch her?'

'Certainly not! When the dragon saw the light it ran away and was never seen again in that part of the world.'

All at once, the house in Salonika, my memory house, seemed to me no more than a comfortable tower, like the tower of the princess, where I lived in isolation. Should I escape into the dark forest if I was given the chance? Would I choose the right lantern? I felt incapable of putting any order in my mind, and it was not until the evening, when both children were in bed and I sat down by the warm glowing fire, that I could begin to think at all.

Might it be him? And if so, where was he, I wondered. Would he come to our synagogue and join our community? Why was he here? Questions and more questions. I tried to settle into my sewing, but was too restless. The windows and doors kept banging in the wind. Salomó was away. And my heart was pounding.

And then the key rasped in the lock.

'Salomó!' I cried, relieved that he was back. His presence would help me recover my calm.

But it was not Salomó.

A dark figure filled the doorway. Then the wind slammed the door behind him. 'Vidal?' I said.

'Alba!' His voice was hoarse and thick; he could hardly speak. He stretched out his hand and showed me the key. The key to the house in Girona.

'I thought I was dreaming—the house—it's exactly the same. And it's the same inside too.'

I turned around to face the mantelpiece over the hearth, picked up the box he had thrown up to our open loft that morning, five years before, and placed it on his open palm. He looked at the box and it seemed as if a cloud were drifting across his face. The sudden touch of our hands opened the memory of our senses, but still we stood there, at arm's length, looking at each other.

Vidal looked haggard, exhausted. His face was unshaven, his cheeks hollow and emaciated. He gently took my hand off the box, which I was still holding, and let it rest on his wrist. Then slowly and solemnly, like someone performing a ritual, he opened the lid and placed his own key over mine. Key over key, the smooth, worn, well-loved metal objects were reunited. My hand could feel his pulse beating fast. Then he closed the box again. I took the box and returned it to its place on the mantelpiece. Neither of us could speak. Vidal took a step forward and then, as he came into the sphere of light from the oil lamp, I saw his features so clearly that my heart melted with love.

Suddenly we were holding each other tight, and we stood like that for a long while, without speaking or moving. Then his face searched mine and our lips met and nothing could stop the huge wave of love that was engulfing us. Once more we were beyond all earthly laws, and beyond the laws of the Torah. We were finding each other again, one soul finding its other half, joined in the light of the central lantern. Nothing was said, no questions were asked. I lay down with him in front of the fire and we made love as we had done in Girona all that time ago. It was as if we had never been apart, as if we had made love countless times before, and not just once, as if nothing and nobody had ever come between us. And later, only much later, we began to talk.

I spoke first, giving him a full account of my days since we left Girona, omitting nothing, not even the rush of understanding which had drawn me so close to Astruc at his death, or the warmth and harmony I had found with Salomó. I bared my soul to Vidal, showing myself as I was, because he was to me the mirror of my truth, and the love I had always felt for him was behind every word I uttered.

Vidal did not answer. The wind had stopped and a strange silence filled the room. We were sitting on the floor by the fireplace, our clothes in disarray, our backs against the stone bench that formed a semicircle round the hearth. The dancing flames seemed to be receiving the impact of our thoughts, and I wished I could read in them what he was thinking.

Two big tears rolled down his hollow cheeks, catching the glimmer of the flames. He brushed them away roughly and sighed. When at last he spoke, his voice was heavy with pain.

'So you don't know where it is hidden, do you?' he said. He was still looking at the fire.

'Where what is hidden?'

'The treasure, Alba, the treasure. The shining gold *menorah* Rabbi Leví told you about. The greatest Jewish treasure in all the kingdoms of Spain.' He had turned to look at me now and his words were charged with urgency. His eyes were wild.

'No. I suppose Astruc knew, but he did not tell me. Why are you so interested? What does that Jewish treasure mean to you?'

'What does it mean, you ask? It has meant three years in prison and a lot of suffering,' said Vidal. 'It has altered the course of my life. Now I need to find its hiding place. I need to *know*.'

He lifted his hands in a gesture of despair.

'I'm sorry, Vidal. I'm very sorry you have endured such pain. But now you're safe. Don't think about all that. You're with me.'

Vidal did not reply.

The wind was blowing again. I could hear it making its way up from the port. I looked at Vidal and realised he had changed. It was as if his soul had been shattered; or perhaps he was never as I had imagined him to be. He seemed like a broken, obsessed man. A *meshummad*.

'Oh Alba, don't look at me like that,' he said suddenly. 'How often must I take the wrong path? It's you I need, not the lamp. It's you I cannot live without. And yet the lamp has become a symbol of my oppression and ill fortune, and I need to recover it, I need to see it and touch it and ensure that it is returned to our people. Only then will I feel even with my oppressors.'

'Why think of revenge?' I insisted. 'We are together now, that's all that matters.'

I knew he was not listening, that my words ran over his soul like water. At the same time I wanted to help him, give him back the peace he needed so much. Then suddenly I knew. How had I been so blind! I knew how to discover the hiding place of the *menorah*. It was only a question of remembering the words that contained the revelation. If I concentrated, it would only take me a few minutes.

But Vidal had already begun to tell his story.

'Do you remember how it was?' he said.

XVI

LUNA

'You looked so beautiful as we walked down the mount of the Jews and were returning to the city. The breeze ruffled your long wavy hair and in your green eyes I could see the power of your love. I felt very close to you, to your body and your soul, and never, not for a moment, did I imagine I would be unable to join you in exile. It all seemed so simple, so easy, and the only problem was that we would have to be separated for a time. But as we had our whole life ahead of us, what would a few months matter? I remember how I congratulated myself on the way I had dealt with the situation, and on my plan of action. I would follow my brothers' example and convert to Catholicism with my mother. That way we could all stay together. It would make her happy and help her get stronger. You know I'm not religious, at least not the same way as you are. In Girona there was a special atmosphere, with all those stories of the Kabbalah of your ancestors, but in Barcelona Judaism was different, more traditional, I don't know. Anyway, for me the Christening ritual was not that important, and once I was baptised, my two older brothers would introduce me to the more influential tradesmen, the ones who do their business with Naples, Genoa and other foreign ports. I would soon find a way of securing a post in one of them. Then, having reassured my mother that I would come back to visit her once a year at least, I would leave. I would know where to find you, I would make quite sure of that.

My hunch was that you would take the route over the mountains to Perpignan and settle there with your family. It was the obvious place to go. I would find you easily, and then I'd marry you.

'You looked beautiful, more beautiful than ever, but sadness clouded your eyes, because you knew, you foresaw. Unlike me, who felt sure that everything would be all right.

'After saying farewell to you in the *call*, I went home and began to put my plan into action. Two days later, my mother and I, together with the other Jews who had decided to stay, were baptised in the convent of Santa Clara. My mother cried so much that the priest who was officiating at the ceremony exclaimed: "Nobody is forcing you to convert, madona. If you cannot feel the Roman Catholic Church calling you, then remain an infidel, and depart with the rest of them, for you are not ready to be received into the sweet bosom of our Lord Jesus Christ."

'To which I had to reply: "No, no, my mother is overwhelmed by emotion, that is why she weeps." But I could see that the experience had wounded her soul. I had misjudged her, believing she would be happier to preserve the comforts we had secured in Girona than to suffer the hardship of an exile. After the christening she seemed to be losing her mind, and went about the streets with her hair dishevelled, chanting Hebrew songs and praying out loud at dawn and sundown, and she refused to eat. I feared that the men of the Inquisition would take her away one day and that she would end up making her way to the pyre in an *auto de fe*. But before the Inquisition had a chance to knock on our door, she died. We buried her in the Christian cemetery, far from her people, and only my two brothers and I attended the funeral.'

Vidal's mother had died while I was still in Girona!

Had I known at the time perhaps I would have tried to speak to him, despite the risk involved. But would that have made any difference? As I listened to Vidal I was also trying to work out where, exactly, the candelabrum was. First I would have to go back once more to the text, an easy enough task when I was sitting in the replica of the memory house, and look for the place that corresponded to paragraph four, chapter three of part two. The numbers 4, 3, 2 had nothing to do with Messianic prophecies, but with the hiding place of the Girona *menorah*. Part two corresponded to the left hand side of the house, which was divided from the right by the spiral staircase, and every chapter of the book was situated in my memory on one of the four floors: the top, the middle, the ground floor and the basement. The first part of *The Chain of Lilies* dealt with the creation of the world, with planetary attractions, and, generally speaking, with the network of divine light that encompasses all aspects of the material world; the second part was more concerned with commentaries on the Psalms, through which it sought to guide the kabbalist to a deeper understanding of the mysteries concealed in the word of the Lord.

Vidal continued his account: 'It was only three weeks after the edict had been proclaimed. My poor mother, whose health had interfered with my natural desire to follow you, was dead. I'm glad that you didn't find out at the time. It would have made you think that I was free to go with you into exile. Not at all. Now I was a Catholic, and my new mother, the Church, was keeping me away from you much more forcefully than my natural mother ever had. I still had hopes that you would change your mind about leaving, but how could I speak to you? All the most influential people in Girona, tradesmen, landowners, and above all, the clergymen, had their eyes on me because of my mother. Some watched me because they hoped to score a few points with the Church if they managed to denounce me, accusing me of following my old religion; others because they envied my skill with numbers and my talent for trading and wanted to get me and my brothers out of the way. After my mother's burial, as I was walking out of the cemetery with them, Jordi the gravedigger grabbed me by the arm and took me aside. "I've been appointed official of the Holy Inquisition, Pau Barceloní," he said in a fierce whisper. "You heard me. And of all the New Christians in Girona, it's you I'm most interested in. I'm going to make sure you do not stray one inch away from our Holy Roman Church. You come here with your worldly Barcelona ways and think you are cleverer than we are. Ha! I have only to say one word against you and you're finished!" And he spat on the ground as if to seal his promise.

'After that incident I couldn't go into the street without being followed by him. And one day, unable to bear it any longer, I went up to him and asked him, as courteously as I could, to leave me alone.

'He just laughed in my face. Then he said: "It so happens that I was coming to hand you this letter from my superior."

'I took the letter, and read it: it was an order of detention within Girona. I was not allowed to leave the town under any pretext. I could not believe what I was reading, and my thoughts went to you, Alba. How would I ever be reunited with you if I wasn't allowed to leave the town? And in the meantime, Jordi the gravedigger was saying: "You're a crafty lot, you Jewish merchants. But don't think we are so stupid that we don't know what your plans are. You have accepted conversion only to hide your true design, which is to take the money of your Jewish brothers out of the country."

'I protested, but it was to no avail.'

The more I heard of Vidal's tale, the more I wanted to give him the answer to the question that continued in my mind: Chapter three, part two, belonged to the left hand side of the ground floor, which was made up of the room we were sitting in now, with the hearth and the round stone seat, the dining room, where we had all our Sabbath meals and family gatherings, the entrance hall with the pattern of the ten river stones, and the kitchen, where the oven was and where most of our daily life took place.

'Every day I felt worse,' said Vidal, 'more frustrated and trapped. All I could do was work and try to build a good position for myself, hoping you would change your mind. I worked more often than not with Bernat Muntaner. My brothers had introduced me to him and I was made very welcome at his home. I even had meals with the family at times, because they knew I had been living on my own since my mother's death. One day, as I was standing in his office looking out at the street below, I thought I was seeing a vision, for there you were, by the garden gate, speaking to Muntaner's wife and daughter. I thought my luck had changed, and that perhaps you were looking for me.

'When I came down you had left; I saw you walking out through El Portal de l'Àngel, but I could not run after you for fear of spies. So I decided to wait for your return, and I stood by a top window in the rear of the house, with my eye on the wooden bridge beyond. When at last I saw you emerging from the Mercadal, I left the house and walked down to the bridge. How I longed to hold you in my arms, and how I wished I could help you when you fell over! And when, once again, you refused to stay in Girona with me I felt as though a spear had run through my heart. As you remember, there were people coming and going and I had to stop speaking to you, though I wanted to ex-

227

plain what had happened to me and why I would be unable to leave the country for the time being. I thought we'd meet again in the streets of Girona. I didn't know it would be the last time I'd see you. After that, until the day you left, while you were memorising the book, I spent my evenings carving this key-box for you.'

'And what did the moons and the stars symbolise, Vidal?' I asked, taking the box again from the mantelpiece.

'I don't know. I copied the pattern from a wooden case that had belonged to my family for generations. As a child I used to love running my fingers through the thirty-two stars and then through the nine moons. I learnt to count that way.'

'One of your ancestors must have been a kabbalist,' I said.

'I don't know of any who wasn't a moneylender or a merchant.'

'Moneylenders and merchants can be spiritual men too. But return to your story. I want to know everything.'

'After the departure of the Jews,' he said, 'my only thought was to escape from my tormentors. I worked day and night to make myself reputable enough to avoid suspicion. I went to church regularly and even sat and said the rosary some afternoons with the Muntaner family. I hoped that sooner or later the Inquisition would stop spying on me and my order of detention would be removed or forgotten: then I would cross the Pyrenees into France. But about two months after you had left, a Girona merchant who had been in Marseilles told me he had seen you there. "Remember that pretty Jewish girl from the de Porta family? You must remember her, she had long dark hair and a body that made one feel lusty just to look at her. Weren't you after her when she lived here? Well, she's married that tall red-bearded rabbi from Besalú, the one who looks as if he's never noticed a woman in his life. An odd couple they made!"

'I was so hurt, Alba, and at first my pride did not allow me to consider that you might have been forced to marry Astruc. The thought that he was enjoying your body made me mad with jealousy. I grew angry with you, then despondent about everything, and I began to lose my appetite and my enthusiasm for work. Only Bernat Muntaner, who noticed the change in me, was able to raise my spirits a little, though I never told him what was wrong. He would talk to me about what he called "the good old days" before the expulsion, and would worry about the bad effect that the absence of the Jews was already having on Catalan commerce. I began to feel more at home with him than with either of my two brothers, whom I secretly blamed for having induced me to stay in Girona in the first place, and soon I spent more time with the Muntaners than in my own home.'

In my memory I found chapter three, paragraph three: *He who seeks knowledge of God must seek His light, and follow the path which that light illuminates. The words of the Torah are comparable to a starry night, and each word is a speck of the Supreme Light of the Lord. Therefore it is written: 'Thy word is a lamp unto my feet, and a light unto my path.'* Those words belonged to the kitchen table. Then came the paragraph next to which Astruc had asked the scribe to draw a *menorah*.

Vidal was silent now. He stared dejectedly at the floor and shook his head, like a soldier defeated in battle. I stood up and went into the kitchen, remembering the words of the book as I touched the table and the chairs, and then walked by the sink with the small window above it and the pots and pans hanging on the wall. I cut a slice of bread and reached up for the oil jug. The words of the text swam around in my head. Vidal came in and, without saying a word, sat down and ate the food I had prepared for him. I felt so strange, watching him eat in my kitchen, where I shared all my daily meals with Salomó and the children, but I felt light and happy too, as in a dream. What was happening to me? Were we now going to join our two lives? I knew Vidal was like the wind that had so intrigued Aaró, an irresistible force, but one that could take no permanent shape; even so, I still needed him. I felt such an intense love for him that every breath and every heartbeat seemed to occur only in response to his presence. My will seemed disconnected from me; it had suddenly taken flight like a bird from its nest.

Between mouthfuls, Vidal went on with his story: 'It was then that Clara began to show an interest in me, or rather, in my soul. She was extremely pious, and I believe she interpreted my melancholy as a longing for the religion I had abandoned. Whatever her thoughts, she undertook my Christian salvation as a personal task.

' "Come, Pau," she would say, "let us pray together to Jesus and let us meditate on the meaning of every word. If you don't learn to love the Lord the way I do, you will burn in Hell forever, forever and *ever*, with no hope of redemption. Imagine the horror of the never-ending pain."

'And after the prayer she would look at me with compassion, like a mother who has had to coax her son into an unwilling task. However stifling those moments were, the warmth in which she enveloped me was comforting, and soon I could not live without it. She was tying a loop round my neck, and I was so lonely, so in need of you, Alba. I did not love Clara, but I married her, much as you married Astruc, because I felt that nothing could change my destiny and that I must allow things to take their course. Clara, as you say, was vain and wilful, and perhaps because she was his only daughter, Muntaner spoilt her and always let her have her own way. When she told her father that she wanted to marry me, Muntaner saw no objection to it; on the contrary, he encouraged the marriage. But his wife felt that marrying her daughter to a New Christian would be like invoking a curse on the family. One day I heard her saying to her husband: "Bernat, don't you see how mistaken you are? Don't you see how much danger lies in this wedding? You have so many enemies, but no one can harm you while all you do is right."

' "There's nothing wrong with my daughter marrying an intelligent, well-mannered young man with whom she is in love," answered Muntaner.

' "There may be nothing wrong in your eyes, because you have always liked the Jews," she replied. "But mark my words: all those who sided with Joana Enríquez during the siege and who now enjoy so many privileges and favours granted them by Ferran, secretly envy your loyalty to the Catalan ideals and would like to see the fall of your lineage and the disappearance of your wealth. The marriage of our daughter to a New Christian is just what they are waiting for. And if you can't see that, you must be blind!"

'As you know, Alba, we did get married. And then, by a cruel irony, we went to live in your old home. Clara changed its appearance, filling it with Italian furniture and coloured silks, but the spirit of your ancestors remained. It was almost as if you had left a part of yourself there for me, and when I sat by the hearth in the evenings and the lights were dim, I could feel your presence next to me. It made it impossible for me to forget you, though I wanted to, I truly did, at that time.

'Life went on in this way for some months, and then one day, when my father-in-law returned from a voyage to

231

Naples, Clara and I were invited to dine at his house. He had brought a coffer full of silks and laces for Clara and was talking about his voyage when he suddenly turned to me and said: "Vidal, did you know the previous owners of your house, the de Porta family?" When I nodded, he said: "I've just seen Regina's daughter in Naples, and she has told me how they've all fared since they left Girona in July last year." He went on to give me all the details that you have recounted to me tonight, and I was filled with an unspeakable sadness. I could hardly believe what I was hearing. Here was I, with my wife Clara, who was by now with child, enjoying a good position and a comfortable life, and there were you, dressed in rags, having suffered so many misfortunes.

'But perhaps the Adonai heard my lamentations and decided to give me a few troubles for complaining about my lot, for only a few nights after this incident, Jordi the gravedigger and two others knocked on my door and marched me off to the offices of the Holy Inquisition to be interrogated. Clara tried to stop them by threatening to call her father, but they paid no attention to her words, which became hysterical screams when she saw me being led away and disappearing down the steps of the *call*.

'The interrogation went on for hours, as usually occurs when the person being questioned truly knows nothing. They began by asking me what did I know of the treasures of the synagogue, and in particular what did I know about a seven-branched gold candelabrum studded with jewels? They were convinced it was being hidden by some *convers* and had searched many New Christian homes in Girona; but now they had reason to suspect that I was the hider.

' "What are you talking about?" was all I could say.

' "Come now, Vidal Rubèn... are you not married to Muntaner's daughter?"

232

' "Yes, but…"

' "And is not Muntaner well-known for his friend-ship with certain Jews?"

' "I believe he is."

' "And did he not see the granddaughter of his old friend Ismael de Porta in Naples? We have proof, you see, so it's no use denying it."

' "Well, and what if he did?"

' "You and your wife Clara Muntaner live in the house that belonged to the de Portas and you have the insolence to ask 'What if he did?' "

'And so on and so forth, hour after hour, with beat-ings and threats. They insisted that there must be a con-nection, that Muntaner had delivered a message from me to you in Naples concerning the hiding-place of the trea-sures. It was all quite clear, they said.

'I, too, began to see clearly. These people had obvi-ously received instructions from the highest ranks of the Inquisition, perhaps from Torquemada himself, to recover the valuable candlestick. But at the same time I was being the victim of certain influential persons who had harboured a grudge against Muntaner since the days following the civil war. My mother-in-law's predictions were coming true: I was the only person near him they could attack.

'I was tortured, but they got nothing out of me be-cause I knew nothing. I had never heard any mention of the confounded *menorah*. However, instead of admitting their mistake, this only infuriated them all the more. Jordi the gravedigger testified against me with a long list of in-stances in which my mother had lapsed into Judaism, and he pinned some of her "sins" on me. "What's bred in the bone will come out in the flesh!" said Jordi, laughing his head off.

'In the meantime, Muntaner tried to exert his influence in court, but the iron hand of the Inquisition stopped each and every attempt he made to free me. I was told that Clara was beside herself with grief and acting like a madwoman. But there was no way out. I was sentenced to life imprisonment and all my possessions were confiscated. I would have been burnt at the stake but for Muntaner's intervention, which, in that respect at least, was successful. It was also thanks to the undeniable weight of his name that I was sent to the monastery of Sant Pere de Rodes for my incarceration, where conditions were less severe than in the town jail.

'There I was told that Clara had been delivered of a son, and that she had handed the baby over to a relative and entered a nunnery. But in the monastery cell my wife's fate and the birth of my son seemed unreal events. I had two thoughts only: you, and the *menorah*. The more I thought about you, Alba, the more I longed for you, and the more I thought about the *menorah*, the more I understood the deep force that had driven you away from me. Our common legacy was at the root of our personal misfortunes: the hiding of a holy object, the preservation of a holy text. There seemed to be nothing we could do to change our fate, nothing on earth we could do to save our love.

'During those long days of solitude I was filled with a mixture of love and hatred for the religion of my birth, and yet the love prevailed, as did a deep respect for my Hebrew people, which my mother had infused in me as a child. Perhaps Jordi the gravedigger was right: "What's bred in the bone will come out in the flesh." But a voice inside me kept repeating: "What of us, of Alba and me, of our love?" Did that not also need preserving? At times I no longer knew what to think.'

'We have both gone a long way since the day of the

edict,' I said. 'Following the road before us from dawn to nightfall.'

'Searching for the right path in moonless nights,' said Vidal.

My mind wandered through chapter three, paragraph four:

> *For it is said in the Book of Samuel: 'He made darkness pavilions round about him, dark waters, and thick clouds of the skies. Through the brightness before him were coals of fire kindled.' The dark waters symbolise magnanimity and mercy, the divine attribute through which judgement and punishment are mitigated. And also we must remember the river that issued forth from Eden, which is the water of life, abundant and never failing, which spreads the spirit of the Lord incessantly throughout creation, that mortal man may quench his thirst for the knowledge of his Creator and behold the radiance of His presence.*

That was the paragraph next to which Astruc had asked the scribe in Venice to depict the *menorah*. Until that moment I had not understood why.

'Vidal,' I said, 'I know where the candelabrum is.'

I recited the paragraph. Vidal looked at me without understanding as I walked round the kitchen to the well and stopped there. 'I suppose Astruc must have found it in the same place as *The Chain of Lilies*, under the synagogue tiles. Rabbi Leví's father must have hidden it there, and not in the buried metal box, as he had told his son. The only way of keeping an important secret is not to share it with anyone. And Astruc, realising the importance of that object, must have thought the same: I'll hide it and not tell anyone.'

'But, where is it hidden now?' said Vidal.

'It's in the well. At the bottom of that large, dark well in the house of the *call*. Astruc must have dropped it in the water one day when we were alone in the house and I was upstairs memorising the book. There is no other explanation. But you need not fear, for it will never be found. Ours was the deepest well in the neighbourhood. In winter, the rain that runs down the roof and along the gutter tiles used to fill it, but it is also supplied with water from an underground stream, and it is never empty, not even in years of drought. And the bucket doesn't reach the bottom.'

Vidal looked bewildered, confused.

'How will we ever recover it? It *must* be recovered. I must go back and find it and take it out of Sepharad.'

I observed the face of my dear love. He looked so tired, and so full of loneliness. And now he seemed to be losing his mind.

'How did you get out of the monastery?' I asked him.

'I escaped.'

'Then how do you think you can ever return to Girona?'

'But the lamp...'

'The lamp will remain hidden for generations, until the Lord signals the right moment for its disclosure. The illustration in the margin of the book is a record of its hiding place, and the sentence Astruc added at the end of the book links it to the house in Girona. All we can do is hope that the right person will one day interpret its meaning.'

'Where is the book now?'

'Anna d'Arco was going to have several copies made of it, but the master copy is in the State Library in Venice.'

'And which copy is only in Jewish hands?'

'The copy that Rabbi Giuseppe has in Mestre, I suppose. But Vidal, who can tell what will happen to that book?

Why not let things be? Circumstances always change un-expectedly, like the wind.'

'No, no. I shall go to Venice and speak to Rabbi Giuseppe. I shall ask him to write this precious secret in his copy of the book. The illustration in the margin is not sufficient. Nobody will be able to guess what it means. It has to be made clearer.'

At that moment Aaró started crying. I ran upstairs to quieten him. Moisès stirred in his cot, next to Aaró's. I picked the baby up, not wanting him to awaken his brother, and took him downstairs.

Vidal looked at me and smiled at the sight. He touched little Aaró's face and Aaró smiled back at him.

'May I hold him?' he asked.

I gave him my child to hold and sat looking at them both, wondering why I had not been able to marry him, why had he returned, why our love could not be.

When Aaró fell asleep I took him back to bed. I put him into his cot gently, carefully. Then I looked at him as if I had forgotten how beautiful he was. I realised I was seeing him through Vidal's eyes; I was so full of Vidal's love that I was seeing everything through his eyes, the cots with the sleeping children, the carpet, the table. I looked around the room. There was a closet near the window, it's door half open, and in it was my green silk dress. I took it out and put it on. Now, to complete our perfect union, I would make Vidal see me the way I wanted him to see me. Through my eyes. The silk fell all about me like a cascade; the silver birds and flowers seemed to have come to life. I looked at myself in the mirror and saw myself as Vidal would see me: free to love him now and forever. Suddenly everything seemed possible. I took the candle hurriedly and went downstairs.

But Vidal was gone.

I felt dazed, frozen. I could not even manage to say his name, to call him uselessly, as I would have wished, to say his name over and over again in order to fill the emptiness of that house surrounded by wind. Once more he was an absence. Then I was filled with an irrepressible anger, and without even understanding what I was doing, I ripped off my Venetian dress, tearing it, treading on it, turning the silk into shreds, turning my love for Vidal into shreds, until I was left naked in the middle of the hall. I put my arm over my belly and held it tight. Outside, the wind was blowing so hard it seemed to be taking the whole world with it. Day was breaking.

Yes... yes, Alba Simha. I had conceived your mother, Luna. But I never could have told her this story. She would not have understood. She was too like her father, who could never quite see what mattered most in life. But enough. I can speak no more. We have been up all night, just as Vidal and I stayed up all night many years ago in this house, this house of memory. Look out of the window. See the old moon? She is lingering on until dawn, because at last Levanah wishes to join Alba. Then, for the first time, she will feel complete.

* * *

Today, the seventeenth of Tishrei of the year 5324 since the creation, the fifth day of October 1563, I have finished writing this account, just as my grandmother Alba Levanah de Porta narrated it to me on her deathbed in Salonika. When the first rays of light touched her face, she passed away peacefully. May her memory be blessed.

Since her death, two years ago, I have dedicated much time and effort to discovering what became of my grandfather, Vidal. I wrote to Anna d'Arco, and to Rabbi Giuseppe

Caravita's daughter. But such a long time has gone by since those events took place! And as I received no answer from either of them, I must assume that they are both dead. However, it is my guess that Vidal went to Venice to make the annotation in the book and then possibly returned to Girona to try to recover the lamp.

One day, to my great pleasure, I saw a copy of The Chain of Lilies *in a printer's shop. There are now a great number of kabbalistic books for sale, not only in Salonika and the neighbouring towns, but also, I am told, in Istanbul, and more and more Sephardim are talking about the importance of these wondrous writings.* The Chain of Lilies *is among the best-loved books, because of the simplicity, lightness and lucidity of the text. I have also been told that it is greatly prized by the kabbalists who have come from all parts of the world to form a community in Safed, in Palestine, where they meditate on the divine purpose of this great new Diaspora that began when my grandmother was a young girl, and has continued with the expulsion of the Jews from Portugal and other lands.*

About ten months after the night I spent with my grandmother Alba I gave birth to my third daughter. I have named her Antonina after the granddaughter of the rabbi in Mestre, because I hope she too will be fearless and free to do as she wishes in her life. And when I go to visit my cousins in Salonika I take to wandering through that beautiful building that was my grandmother's home, reading passages from the text she once memorised, driven by a force that came from the deepest recesses of the earth and the highest spheres of the skies, for the glory of the Lord. In so doing, I am at peace with myself, and my mind is filled with a heavenly music, as delicate as the silver birds and flowers on her Venetian gown.

EPILOGUE

In the year 1492 of the Christian era, following the order of expulsion decreed by the Catholic Monarchs, the Jews of this story were forced to leave their homeland. They found shelter in Salonika, together with many other Spanish Jews, and in that city their beliefs and their work were allowed to flourish once again. Salonika became the capital of Sephardic Judaism, one of the most exotic and dazzling cities in the Ottoman Empire. Five centuries later, the year 1942, the numbers inverted, as in a kabbalistic sign, saw the start of the destruction of this community which still preserved the keys of its Spanish homes as its greatest treasure. On November 9, 1942, several hundred Salonika Jews were arrested in Paris, and deported to Auschwitz. The following year, 45,000 left Salonika, crammed in cattle trains, with the same destination. Many others were executed in their home town. Of the 56,000 Jews who formed the Jewish community of Salonika in 1943, fewer than 2,000 were left at the end of World War Two. A small number managed to escape and, among these, some were able to take temporary refuge in Spain, thanks to the help of Spanish diplomats in the Balkans.

Today, fewer than a thousand Jews remain in the city that was once known as 'The Mother of Israel.' But both there and in the narrow streets of the *call* of Girona, one can still see the shadow of their footsteps and hear the echo of their hopes.

CPSIA information can be obtained
at www.ICGtesting.com
Printed in the USA
FSHW020747101119
63939FS